The Last Circus
Non-Science fiction Stories
and
Exclusive Interviews

Dans la même collection

Lire en anglais

Thirteen Modern English and American Short Stories
Seven American Short Stories
Nine English Short Stories
A Long Spoon and Other Short Stories
Simple Arithmetic and Other American Short Stories
The American Press of Today
English Ghost Stories
English Crime Stories
Roald Dahl : **Someone Like You / The Hitch-Hiker / Mr Botibol**
Somerset Maugham : **The Escape / The Flip of a Coin**
F. Scott Fitzgerald : **Pat Hobby and Orson Welles**
Ray Bradbury : **Kaleidoscope / The Martian Chronicles / A Story of Love**
Saki : **The Seven Cream Jugs**
John Steinbeck : **The Snake**
William Faulkner : **Stories of New Orleans**
Ernest Hemingway : **The Killers / The Old Man and the Sea**
Truman Capote : **Breakfast at Tiffany's**
Patricia Highsmith : **Please Don't Shoot the Trees / Trouble at the Jade Towers**
Fred Uhlman : **Reunion *(L'Ami retrouvé)***
James Joyce : **Dubliners**
Graham Greene : **The Third Man / The Basement Room**
American Detective Stories of Today (Hammett — Chandler)

Lire en allemand

Moderne Erzählungen
Deutsche Kurzgeschichten
Zwanzig Kurzgeschichten des 20. Jahrhunderts
Geschichten von heute
Die deutsche Presse
Heinrich Böll : **Der Lacher / Die verlorene Ehre der Katharina Blum**
Stefan Zweig : **Schachnovelle**
Rainer Maria Rilke : **Briefe an einen jungen Dichter**
Arthur Schnitzler : **Fräulein Else / Spiel im Morgengrauen**
Franz Kafka : **Briefe an den Vater**
Patrick Süskind : **Der Kontrabaß / Die Taube**
Friedrich Dürrenmatt : **Der Richter und sein Henker**

Lire en espagnol

Cuentos del mundo hispánico
Cuentos selectos

(Suite en p. 4)

LIRE EN ANGLAIS
Collection dirigée par Henri Yvinec

Ray Bradbury

The Last Circus
Non-Science fiction Stories
and
Exclusive Interviews

Choix et annotations par Liliane et Marielle Yvinec

Propos recueillis par Henri Yvinec

Le Livre de Poche

Cuentos fantásticos de América
Cuentos de América. Destinos
Los cuentos vagabundos y otros de España
Jorge Luis Borges: La Intrusa y otros cuentos
Camilo José Cela: La Familia de Pascual Duarte

Lire en italien

L'Avventura ed altre storie
Novelle italiane del nostro secolo
Italo Svevo : La novella del buon vecchio e della bella fanciulla

Lire en portugais

Contos contemporâneos (Portugal/Brasil)

Lire en français

Nouvelles françaises contemporaines
Maupassant : Pierrot et autres nouvelles / Madame Baptiste

Lire en russe

A. Tchékhov : Aniouta et autres nouvelles

Lire en arabe

Nouvelles du monde arabe

Dans la collection *Premières Lectures en...*

Los Chicos
La Umiltá
Die Puppe
The Umbrella Man and Other Short Stories

La collection "Les Langues Modernes" n'a pas de lien avec l'A.P.L.V. et les ouvrages qu'elle publie le sont sous sa seule responsabilité.

Sommaire

Abbreviations

adj adjective
adv adverb
Am American English
cf confer (see)
fam familiar
fig figurative (meaning), *figuré (sens)*
n noun
pl plural *(pluriel)*
sb somebody
sing singular *(singulier)*
sl slang *(argot)*
sth something
v verb

ø zero article or zero relative pronoun
= synonym
≠ antonym or different meaning (from expected) or not to be mixed up with

6 means line 6 on the same page
8.12 means page 8 line 12
5.14,19 means page 5 line 14 and line 19

Tout naturellement, après quelques années d'étude d'une langue étrangère, naît l'envie de lire dans le texte. Mais, par ailleurs, le vocabulaire dont on dispose est souvent insuffisant. La perspective de recherches lexicales multipliées chez le lecteur isolé, la présentation fastidieuse du vocabulaire, pour le professeur, sont autant d'obstacles redoutables. C'est pour tenter de les aplanir que nous proposons cette nouvelle collection.

Celle-ci constitue une étape vers la lecture autonome, sans dictionnaire ni traduction, grâce à des notes facilement repérables. S'agissant des élèves de lycée, les ouvrages de cette collection seront un précieux instrument pédagogique pour les enseignants en langues étrangères puisque les recommandations pédagogiques officielles (*Bulletin officiel de l'Éducation nationale* du 9 juillet 1987 et du 9 juin 1988) les invitent à "faire de l'entraînement à la lecture individuelle une activité régulière" qui pourra aller jusqu'à une heure hebdomadaire. Ces recueils de textes devraient ainsi servir de complément à l'étude de la civilisation. Celle-ci sera également abordée dans des volumes consacrés aux presses étrangères.

Le lecteur trouvera donc :

En page de gauche

Des textes contemporains — nouvelles ou courts romans — choisis pour leur intérêt littéraire et la qualité de leur langue.

En page de droite
Des notes juxtalinéaires rédigées dans la langue du texte, qui aident le lecteur à

Comprendre
Tous les mots et expressions difficiles contenus dans la ligne de gauche sont reproduits en caractères gras et expliqués dans le contexte.

Observer
Des notes d'observation de la langue soulignent le caractère idiomatique de certaines tournures ou constructions.

Apprendre
Dans un but d'enrichissement lexical, certaines notes proposent enfin des synonymes, des antonymes, des expressions faisant appel aux mots qui figurent dans le texte.

Grammaire
Le lecteur trouvera, au moins pour les nouvelles courtes et sous des formes diverses selon les volumes, un rappel des structures rebelles les plus courantes — c'est-à-dire des tournures les plus difficilement assimilées par les francophones. Des chiffres de référence renverront au contexte et aux explications données dans les *Grammaires actives* (de l'anglais, de l'allemand, de l'espagnol, du portugais...) publiées au *Livre de Poche*.

Vocabulaire
En fin de volume une liste de plus de 2 500 mots contenus dans les textes, suivis de leur traduction, comporte, entre autres, les verbes irréguliers et les mots qui n'ont pas été annotés faute de place ou parce que leur sens était évident dans le contexte. Grâce à ce lexique on pourra, en dernier recours, procéder à quelques vérifications ou faire un bilan des mots retenus au cours des lectures.

Henri YVINEC

Kervizouarn, the springfuls of larks over meadowlands, the savage sea and the strange stillness of rocks and the rugged folk of childhood memory.

Foreword

None of the stories in the present selection have anything to do with science fiction. The truth of the matter is that, if Ray Bradbury[1] is known all over the world as the author of *The Martian Chronicles* (1950), *Farenheit 451* (1953)..., he has tackled virtually every literary genre including plays and film scenarios such as *Moby Dick* (1956), *Something Wicked This Way Comes* (1983)..., poems, essays and so on and so forth.

Indeed the list in the preface which the author has kindly written for this book (let him be thanked here again very sincerely) is impressive. But here is this preface. Turn the page.

1. Born in 1920 in Waukegan, Illinois, U.S.A. At the age of seventy-three, he is still "a tall impressive figure, with a mane of white hair, an infectious sense of humour, the enthusiasm of a young man and the imagination and freshness of vision of a child — a genial giant!" (W.B. Barrie, introduction to *Kaleidoscope and Other Short Stories* by Ray Bradbury, Collection "Lire en anglais", Le Livre de Poche).

Preface by Ray Bradbury

Then is it possible that Ray Bradbury has written much more than science fiction?

You ask the question, this late in time? The answer is yes.

I have known the dear boy for some few years and, peering over his shoulder, have seen flying up from his typewriter, examples of:

The poem, short form.

The poem, extended.

The cantata.

The madrigal.

The aria for opera.

The lyric for a comedy musical.

The essay.

The short play.

The long drama.

The radio excursion.

The novel about summer in 1928 Illinois.

The mystery novel about Venice, California, in the fogs and mists of 1949.

The architectural blueprint.

The concept for a Walt Disney Jules Verne ride at Euro-Disney outside Paris.

But, there. Breathless, I come full-stop.

Is it possible that I have been working all these forty years and no one has noticed any of the above? By the names of all the firework saints!!! I have published 500 short stories, 400 of which are fantasy, weird, horror, or magic realism moving from attic to pantry to cellar, with hardly a glance at the astrological signs or the astronomical transits.

I have written stories about myself when young with my super-favorite dog, based on my guilty conscience fifty or so years ago, honoring, I hope, my dear lost canine friend properly.

(*Bless Me, Father, For I Have Sinned*, p. 65.)

I have written tales about the young man I was back in the early thirties, not wanting to grow up, like many another boy faced with the harsh realities of a world moving rapidly toward war and destruction, with strong desires to hide out somewhere until all the destruction and chaos moved away.

(*Hail and Farewell*, p. 83.)

I have conjured up pictures of a child growing up with and loving carnivals and circuses —unconscious metaphors for life and the collision of this joyful entertainment with the terrible reality of the atom bomb in the mid-forties.

(*The Last Circus*, p. 110.)

I have written yarns about the Night, in which only darkness and crickets and hidden ravine creeks and the sound of owls and late birds are the secret villains, each speaking of eternity and surprise murders.

(*The Night*, p. 137.)

I have put down my real fears of what I knew was waiting for me in the dark hall leading up to the attic shadows in my old home in Northern Illinois —The Thing that *is still* waiting there.

(*The Thing At The Top of The Stairs*, p. 165.)

I have...

But, ah, I *do* go on, do I not?

The sum-total is this:

Ray Bradbury is not a science fiction writer.

What is he, then?

A pomegranate.

Slice him open and find...?

Seeds.

A whole damned skinful of seedbed notions, fancies, dreams, ideas, from two dozen different library rooms, ways of thinking, ways of dreaming, ways of writing.

Call me then a keeper of Ideas.

An Idea Beast, whose ideas leap at him, to seize and bite his neck, and refuse to let go until he has written the poem, the essay, the play, the novel, or the tale.

I never know where my ideas will run me next, but run me they will; head-on into the present, sinking down in the past or falling upward against gravity into impossible futures made possible by grammar alone.

But *science fiction* writer?

Impossible.

When was *that*?

RAY BRADBURY

All the difficult words in the Preface are to be found in the vocabulary (p. 211). The paragraphs beginning with "I have..." are explained in the introduction to each story concerned.

The whole book is annotated in British English spelling in order to help readers make a difference between British English and American English.

We are deeply thankful to Ray Bradbury for writing a Preface to the two collections of non-science fiction stories "Lire en anglais" and for reading some of them on tape.

If you are interested in the cassettes that go with this book you can contact: STANDPOINTS, a magazine for teachers of English
31, rue de la Vanne — BP 359
Fax: 40 92 05 22
Tel.: 46 57 11 17, extension: 393
92541 Montrouge Cedex.

To learn more about Ray Bradbury

October's Country: A Bibliography of Ray Bradbury, edited by Donn Albright and James Welsh, available from October 1993 at 6302 Valley Road, Bethesda, Maryland (U.S.A.)

— 800 pages, 700 illustrations,

— covers R.B.'s work from 1935 to 1991,

— introduction and several other smaller original pieces by R.B.,

— covers everything by R.B. and about R.B. in English plus listing of nearly 400 *first* printing foreign Bradbury books,

— lists and describes over 165 never printed stories by R.B., every anthology, every high school text book, every interview, speech, letter (printed), article, poem that R.B. has published, plus all his reprinted material.

The Stories of Ray Bradbury (100 of them) with an introduction by the author (Alfred A. Knopf Publisher, New York 1986 and Grafton Books, 8 Grafton Street, London W1X3LA).

Zen in the Art of Writing by Ray Bradbury, the inside story of R.B.'s career as a prolific author of novels, stories, poems, films and plays (Bantam Books, 666 Fifth Avenue, New York 10103).

Talking at large

(Exclusive interview. July 12th 1990 — Summary)

The science fiction label does not fit at all — Childhood — I started writing when I was twelve — The first really good story — A happy child up to the age of twelve... — Pretty much of a loner — My three territories: summer. Mars, October — The boy with the tennis shoes — All of life is the best time — Still a child in many ways — Toy stores — Attics — Family life — Grandparenthood — Advice to parents and grandparents — *Everything* is love — What if you were prevented from writing? — Doing the things you love — Taking chances — Conquering one's fears — I never learned to drive... — Hobbies — Moral values — The eleventh commandment — What about the year 2000? — The new, the real Revolution in Russia — Not optimism but optimal behavior — The U.S.A. today — France — The ideal city of tomorrow — Fathers and sons — My favorite (Swedish) relatives — Death — Immortality — Advice to young people.

at large: freely (about various subjects) □ **does not fit:** is not well adapted, is not right □ **childhood:** the time when you are a child (see grandparenthood) □ **pretty much:** to a large degree **loner:** person who spends a lot of time alone, not in groups of people. □ **way(s):** point, detail □ **toy:** object for children to play with □ **store:** (Am.) shop □ **attic(s):** room at the top of a house just below the roof □ **advice:** suggestion made about the best thing to do □ **prevent** (stop) somebody from doing something **chance(s):** (here) risk □ **fear(s):** apprehension, terror □ **to drive** (a car) □ **behavior:** (Am) behaviour, way of acting, conduct **Swedish:** from Sweden (in Scandinavia)

Henri Yvinec. — As you know, a second volume of *non*-science fiction stories is coming out in the series "Lire en anglais" in Le Livre de Poche. How do you like the idea?

Ray Bradbury. — I think it's fine because that's the way I began my career in high school, writing about the things that frightened me. So, in my twenties I published stories in *Weird Tales* which were stories about being afraid of the dark. So it's a totally different thing than science fiction.

H. Y. And I think too that some of your masterpieces have nothing to do with science fiction. I'm thinking of *The Lake*, for instance, or *A Story of Love* or *The Utterly Perfect Murder*.

R. B. That's right, yes. The thing I learned over the years, which I began to learn when I was sixteen, seventeen years old and lost sight of is that we have all these frights put away, inside ourselves. But we don't know they're there. So you have to test for them and then, slowly, they begin to come out and you begin to write excellent short stories at long last.

H. Y. And I remember that in the preface to the previous volume of non-science fiction stories you finished the preface, talking about yourself, by: "Me, a

is coming out: is going to be published
how do you like...?: what do you think of the idea?

fine: very good
way: manner (in which...) □ **high school:** (Am) secondary school **frightened me:** made me afraid □ **in my twenties:** when I was about twenty years old □ **weird:** strange, mysterious □ **tale(s):** (imaginary) story □ **the dark:** darkness □ **different than** or different *from*
masterpiece(s): best work
have nothing to do with: have no connection with
for instance: for example □ **utterly:** totally, completely

right: correct, true ≠ wrong □ **over:** in the course of
learn, learnt or learned, learnt or learned
lost sight of: forgot; sight, the seeing of sth; eyesight
fright(s): fear, terror □ **put away:** kept, locked up
so: consequently □ **test for:** try to get them out

at long last: in the end, after a long time

the previous (preceding) volume is entitled *A Story of Love and Other Non-Science Fiction Stories.*

science fiction writer? Impossible. When was *that*?"

R. B. That's right. That label has followed me for a long while. It's always been incorrect because I was writing seven or eight different kinds of tales in the last thirty years: twenty-five plays, operas, cantatas, fifteen books of poetry — seventy or eighty essays in various fields... plus murder mysteries. So the S.F. label just doesn't fit at all.

H. Y. Do you find it annoying?

R. B. Oh, at times when people want to label me and forget me, yes.

H. Y. Now, most of the stories in the two books, as a matter of fact, are to do with childhood. How about that for a theme?

R. B. I don't know how many people know that I remember being born. I remember lying in my crib when I was four or five days old, having nightmares about being born. I remember being suckled. Forty years ago when our first baby came along I called my mother and said: "At what point in my first weeks was I circumcised?" She said: "On the fifth day." I said: "It wasn't at the hospital, was it?" She said: "No." I said: "And it wasn't at home?" "No." "Did my father take me somewhere?" And she said: "Yes." I said: "Did he take me downtown to the doctor's office?" She said: "Yes." I said: "I remember being placed on a table. I remember the doctor bending over me with a scalpel, I remember the pain." So that couldn't have been inserted into my subconscious by someone else. It's a very personal memory. So that's how my childhood stories got started.

H. Y. It sounds incredible to us, really.

label (describing sth, sb) □ **...followed me:** (here) been attached to me; follow, come after □ **for a long while:** for a long time
kind(s): sort
cantata(s): choral work oratorio but shorter

field(s): domain □ **murder mysteries:** crime stories
does not fit: is not well adapted, is not right
annoying: irritating
at times: sometimes □ **to label:** fix, tie a label on (2)
forget, forgot, forgotten
now: well □ **most of:** the majority of
as a matter of fact: in fact □ **are to do with childhood** (time when you are a child): deal with □ **how about that for a theme:** what do you think of that as a theme?
(the fact of) **being born** □ **crib:** small bed for child
nightmare(s): bad dream
suckled: given milk from my mother's breast
came along: was born

fifth (from "five": notice the change in spelling)

take me somewhere: they *took* him *to* the town centre

downtown: (Am) town centre □ **doctor's office** or surgery (in British English)
bending: leaning □ **scalpel:** small delicate knife
pain: suffering
someone else: another person; sb else, sth else
memory: sth that is remembered
got started: began, started
sounds: seems (when hearing it) □ **incredible:** unbelievable

R. B. Well, as I have often said to you, the reason I'm a very good writer is I *do* have total recall. The more I write the further back I go. So a story like *The Lake*, for instance, is based on an incident when I was seven years old. I was by the lake with my family and there was a little girl with blond hair playing in the sand. She went into the water and she never came out. What a mystery that is when you're seven years old. You don't understand drowning. You don't understand death. You may have seen dead people. My sister died when I was seven. My grandfather died when I was five, so I saw dead people but... swimming in a lake and a disappearance is something else again. It haunted me until I was twenty-two years old. Seated at my typewriter one day I set my mind back, remembered the lake and wrote furiously. It was the first really good short story that I wrote after ten years of writing. I started when I was twelve and when I was twenty-two,... finally, something really fresh and fine came out.

H. Y. Were you a happy child?

R. B. Oh, I think so until I was around twelve. That's the age when bullies start to beat up on you. They discover you're a freak.

H. Y. Like in *The Playground.*

R. B. Yeah! The bullies discovered I wanted to be a writer. That made me very unusual. I loved things like King Kong and The Lost World, dinosaurs..., Dracula, Frankenstein... It was O.K. up to a point. But when you begin to actually write about that sort of thing then you sound idiotic, a fool. So, they beat up on you.

H. Y. Did you mix with other children easily?

R. B. No. I was pretty much of a loner. In high

the reason (why) **I'm...**
have total recall: remember everything; to recall
the further (farther) **back** (in time, in the past) **I go**
an incident (that took place) **when...**
by: near □ **lake** (Michigan, R.B. being born near Chicago)
blond: fair □ **sand** (by the sea, in deserts...): extremely small fine grain of rock

drowning; drown, die in water, get drowned
you may have seen: perhaps (maybe) you have seen
died; die; be dead (≠ living, alive); death ≠ life
swimming: move through water (like a fish...) □ **disappearance;** to disappear □ **haunted:** obsessed
seated: sitting □ **typewriter;** typewriting ≠ handwriting
set my mind (intellect) **back** (to the past), trying to recall what had happened □ **furiously:** with very great energy
The Lake is to be found in *Kaleidoscope and Other Short Stories* in the series "Lire en anglais"
fresh: original, novel □ **fine:** nice, beautiful

around: about, approximately
bullies: bully, schoolboy tyrant □ **beat,** beat, beaten: hit
freak: sb who is considered unusual, abnormal, a monster
The Playground is another story on childhood
yeah!: (fam) yes
loved: liked very much (talking about things)

up to a point: to a certaint extent (degree), not completely
actually: really, in (actual) fact
sound: seem □ **idiotic:** stupid, foolish: **a fool,** an idiot
mix with: enjoy being in the company of other people ≠ **be a loner** (alone) □ **pretty much:** to a large extent or degree

school even more so. By that time I was writing long short stories about science fiction themes in the future and in an enrolment of four thousand students I was pretty lonely. There were only two or three other boys in the school who cared about the future the way I did. So I stuck with those boys and let the rest go.

H. Y. Can you tell us about that "boy with the tennis shoes"?

R. B. Well, summer always has been very special for me. I have laid claim to two territories or perhaps three: summer is my territory, Mars is my territory and October is my territory. I've written about all of them, and the mail arrives every year from all over the world from people who experience my October and write me about it or experience my summer and say: "I thought of you today when I bought a pair of tennis shoes" or see something about Mars and write to me about *my* red planet. So, that particular story you're referring to is a thing that happened forty years ago. I was on a bus going into Westwood Village and the bus stopped and a young boy jumped on, ran down the aisle, flung himself into a seat with such furious energy that I looked at him with envy and thought: "My God, I wish I had that energy! I would write two short stories a day, a novel a week, and an epic poem every other day!" Then I looked at his feet and saw the brightest new pair of white tennis shoes I'd ever seen, and I thought: "My God, I remember what it was like every spring, when winter was finally over, when my father would take me downtown and buy me a pair of new tennis shoes which gave me strength and power over my enemies, running away from them, running toward my friends waiting on

even more so: I was even more of a loner □ **by that time:** already □ **long short stories** or novellas; a story
enrol(l)ment: number of **students** (pupils) officially listed or enrol(l)ed □ **pretty:** quite □ **lonely:** alone + unhappy
cared about: were interested in □ **the way I did:** as I did
stuck with: stayed with, stayed close to (near)

special: particularly great or fine, exceptional
laid claim to: said that these territories are mine
Mars: see *The Martian Chronicles*, also in "Lire en anglais"
october: *The October Country* published by Grafton Books
mail: (Am) post (letters...) □ **all over the world:** every part of the world □ **experience:** feel, know as an experience
I thought of you: notice the preposition
buy, **bought**, bought ≠ sell, sold, sold
write to me or write me (14)
you are referring to: to which you are referring
happened: took place, occurred

aisle: passage between lines of seats □ **flung:** threw with force
furious: very great (20.16)
I wish I had, I wish I were, I wish I did (subjunctive)
a day: per day, every day
every other day: every second day
feet: (sing) foot □ **bright(est):** shining bright
I'd ever seen (in my life)
what it was like: how I felt, what my feelings were
over: ended □ **would:** was in the habit of... (every spring)
take me downtown: (Am) take me to town centre
strength; strong, vigorous ≠ weak
toward(s): in the direction of □ **waiting** (for me)

the hills of summer and conquering gravity with these shoes, and then after two or three days the shoes got dead and tired and I was back on Earth again." So I went home and wrote the short story, a long prose poem, a pensée about tennis shoes. Ever since, people have sent me tennis shoes from all over the world.

H. Y. You still wear tennis shoes, by the way.

R. B. Absolutely!

H. Y. You're wearing them now.

R. B. I'm wearing them now. They're comfortable and some of the best restaurants in Paris allow me to dress this way. They sneak me in; I go to *Grande Cascade* for lunch and they've got a special table for me in the back and when no one's looking they rush me in, get my legs under the table, so no one can see I'm wearing tennis shoes. We all laugh and I'm *in* for lunch!

H. Y. Oh, good. You don't look upon childhood as the best time of your life, do you?

R. B. Oh, no. All of life is the best time. I mean, if you're doing what you love, that's the great secret. And if you're not doing what you love you'd better quit and do something else. You're only going to be here once, which is banal but true. If you're a teacher and hate teaching, you'd better stop. If you are an artist and hate painting, do something else. There are so *many* things to choose from! I could be a priest, a minister, a rabbi because I'm curious about the universe and our relationship to it. I would be a good advertising man because I'm fascinated by the creativity that goes into advertising. I could be a salesman of a lot of things as long as I believed in what I was selling. There's so much to love. I could be a full-time poet, a full-time painter or

hill(s): small mountain □ **gravity:** attractive force by which bodies tend towards centre of earth □ **got** (+ adj): became
dead: no good □ **tired:** of not much use, worn
I went home: no preposition!
prose poem, pensée: see *Dandelion Wine*, p. 19 (Grafton Books)
ever since: from then until now
by the way: incidentally *(à propos, entre parenthèses)*

wear(ing), wore, worn (clothes, shoes...)

allow me to...: give me permission to dress, let me dress
this way: like this □ **sneak me in:** let me in secretly
back ≠ front
rush me in: let me in quickly □ **get:** (here) put
so: in consequence, consequently, therefore
I'm in (at long last!)
look upon: consider

mean, meant, meant: want to say

quit: stop, give up; quit doing sth
here (on earth) □ **once**, twice, three times, four times...
true: real □ **If you're a teacher** □ **hate** ≠ love
teaching: teach, taught, taught; a self-taught man
painting; a painter
choose, chose, chosen: select □ **priest** (Catholic), minister (Protestant), rabbi (Jewish)
relationship: connection □ **advertising:** publicity; advertise a product; advertising man, advertiser
salesman: sales representative; "House for sale" (to be sold)
as long as: on condition that
full-time ≠ part-time (job...); full, complete

an actor. I love acting. I love lecturing. I have much fun lecturing. When it stops being fun, I'll quit. So, the test is: do you love something so much you want to do it with all your heart? It has nothing to do with money. Most people don't realize that I write all of my short stories free. No one pays me to write them. And my poetry, and my novels, are all written free. When I finish them I send them out into the world and maybe they sell and maybe they don't. So you see, I have no tenure, I'm *not* established and don't *want* to be. I want to take chances and write stories and maybe... *maybe* sell them!...

H. Y. ...Are you not still a child in many ways?

R. B. I think so, child*like* without being chil*dish*. Being open is important, to stay open to everything. I hate people who reject things without trying them. I showed the paintings of David, the French artist, to a friend of mine some months ago. He was a young snob who didn't care for anything from another century. All 19th century painting made him tired. I said "Oh come on! Relax! There's all kinds of painting from the Greeks and the Romans to the Renaissance and the Impressionists, to Picasso and Wyeth. They're all excellent each in their own way. Enjoy! Look! Sense! Feel!" What has saved my life countless times is that I've fallen in love with whole periods of history through art and illustration. I've collected the works of John Martin and Gustave Doré and Goya and Hogarth. And comic strips! My God, I've all the Tarzan comic strips put away from when I was a child, plus Flash Gordon, Buck Rogers, Prince Valiant; all the popular cartoonists in American history, I've collected. My head is full of metaphors! I

lecturing: lecture, give a lecture (talk on a particular subject)
fun: enjoyment, pleasure, amusement
so much (that) **you want...** (Am)
it has nothing to do with: it is not at all connected with
don't realize: don't know, are not aware or conscious
free: for nothing

send, sent, sent (by post...) ☐ **maybe:** perhaps
sell: are sold ☐ **...tenure:** (here) permanent, secure job
established (in a firm good position)
take chances: take (or run) risks

in many ways: from many points of views
childlike: like a child (in a positive way) ☐ **childish:** (pejorative) like a child ☐ **open,** open to; open-minded
without trying: without + v + ing
David, a French painter (1748-1825)
a friend of mine ☐ **a snob;** snobbish; snobbishness, snobbery
care for: like, enjoy ☐ **century:** 100 years
tired (of) ≠ interested (in) ☐ **come on!** (used to persuade sb)
there's: more and more often used for "there are" in conversation
Wyeth: an American painter born in 1917 in Pennsylvania
sense: feel ☐ **saved:** save sb from danger...
countless: very many, too many to be counted, innumerable
whole: entire ☐ **though:** by means of, thanks to
John Martin: an English painter and engraver (1789-1854)
Doré, Goya, Hogarth: famous painters and illustrators ☐ **comic strip(s):** series of drawings that tell a story ☐ **put away:** kept ☐ **from** (the time) **when** ☐ **plus:** and also ☐ **Flash Gordon..:** famous heroes ☐ **cartoonists** draw cartoons or comic strips
collect(ed) (stamps)...; collector; collection

borrow metaphors constantly from illustration history, art history, comic strip history, haïku, the sonnets of Shakespeare or Alexander Pope or the novelist Thomas Love Peacock... I'm willing to search anywhere for excitement.

H. Y. Open-mindedness is the word.

R. B. Absolutely.

H. Y. Not getting "full of tiredness" like so many adults.

R. B. Yes... This reminds me of a thing that happened when I was in Sausalito some years ago. I go into toy stores all the time, I love toy shops. When I came out of this one toy shop a bunch of schoolboys ran by from school. They were all twelve or thirteen years old. One boy stopped at the door of the toy store and stared in at all these wonderful objects where I had just wandered. His friends jeered: "Oh, come on, Tom, that's kids' stuff, come on!" I kept whispering: "Don't *listen* to them, Tom. Go *in*, go *in*! Don't run with them... because they'll be old and ancient by the time they are fourteen." He stood there, I wanted to push him. Finally he ran off with his peers. He was lost. Maybe some other day he came back. I hope so. I've gone in toy stores all my life. I've never listened to people who told me not to go. That's the difference between me and them, the difference between me in my tennis clothes and the businessmen in their pressed suits — their ironed suits with the gold manacles around their necks...

H. Y. ...Can you tell us about attics?

R. B. Attics! Yes! Fascinating! I've always loved them. Luckily I grew up in Waukegan where we had a basement and an attic, for both of them are time

borrow from: (here) take (ideas...); borrow money from sb
haïku (pl haïku): Japanese poem with three lines
Pope: English writer (1688-1744) □ **novelists** write novels
Peacock: English writer (1785-1866) □ **I'm willing to search:** I'm ready (with enthusiasm) to try to find □ **excitement:** enjoyment, great pleasure □ **open-mindedness:** 26.15

"full of tiredness": a quotation from *Hail and Farewell* (94, 27); tired of, uninterested in, bored with
reminds: remind sb. of sth, cause sb to remember sth
Sausalito: a town in California □ **toy** (for child to play with)
stores: (Am) shop □ **love** (sth): be very fond of
this one shop: this particular... □ **bunch:** group □ **ran by:** came by (near), running
stared: looked fixedly in wonder
...wandered: among which I had walked about, here and there
jeered: mocked □ **kids' stuff:** (fam) things for children
kept whispering: murmured (said softly) all the time

ancient: very old (and "tired", 8) □ **by the time:** when
stood: remained unmoving □ **ran off:** ran away
peer(s): equal in age... □ **lost** (fig) (20)
I hope so: I hope he did, I hope he came back
not to go: notice the structure; "To be or not to be"

pressed, ironed (with an electric... iron) □ **suit(s):** jacket and trousers □ **manacle(s):** chains on hands or feet of prisoner
attic(s): room at the top of a house below the roof; about attics, read the story *A Scent of Sarsaparilla* (30.15, 16)
luckily: fortunately □ **grew up** (as a child) □ **Waukegan**, Illinois
basement: lowest room in a house (≠ attic)

machines! You store different things: in the basement you store dandelion wine and grape wine and a lot of other things and dark meteors from outer space, the coal that slides down the chutes and builds itself in mounds. But attics are very special, they have a great smell of incense from India, they smell like dust from far places around the world and when I was a kid I used to climb up there because who knows what you'd find up there, big trunks full of costumes and Civil War letters wrapped in ribbons — love letters from my great-grandfather to my great-grandmother, and toys, chandeliers left like big bunches of tears lying in a corner with the sunlight in the prisms. I wrote a short story...

H. Y. A Scent of Sarsaparilla.

R. B. Yes. *A Scent of Sarsaparilla.*

H. Y. Beautiful!

R. B. You step into an attic, you're surrounded immediately by shadows and dust and the glint of the brass locks on the trunks and the clothing-dummy over in a corner keeps the shape of your grandmother when she was eighteen and slender and beautiful and the love letters and the dolls and the fire-engines, all the toys left over from another Christmas or another Halloween, whatever it was.

H. Y. To come to another subject, what about family life? What do you think of the "nuclear family" of today? Nothing to do with life in Green Town with all the cousins and uncles and grandpas and grandmas...

R. B. I don't know. My life with my children hasn't been any different than it was with my parents. I raised them the same way, to love magicians, I told them magic stories every night about Blackstone the magician

store: keep
dandelion: *pissenlit :* (28) ☐ **grape:** green or purple fruit
<u>out</u>**er:** farther out; <u>in</u>ner, <u>up</u>per...
(black) **coal** (used as fuel) **slides... chute(s):** comes down a vertical passage ☐ **...mound(s):** make up a pile or heap
dust: very small dry particles of earth ☐ **far:** distant
when I was <u>a</u> kid (child) ☐ **used to** (a habit in the past)
climb up (a hill, a mountain...) ☐ **you:** people in general
trunk(s): travelling box ☐ **Civil War** (North versus South)
wrapped (together) ☐ **ribbon(s):** long narrow band of fine material ☐ **great-...:** father's or mother's grandfather
chandelier(s): ornamental hanging light ☐ **bunches of tears:** (here) hanging pieces of crystal; bunch (of flowers, carrots, keys...); tear(s), drop of water coming from the eye
A Scent of Sarsaparilla is to be found in the same series in *A Story of Love and Other Non-Science Fiction Stories* (p. 145)
step: walk ☐ **...surrounded by:** you've... all around you
shadow(s): dark form ☐ **glint:** ray of soft light
brass: bright yellow metal ☐ **lock(s)** (for shutting) ☐ **dummy:** a tailor's dummy (model) [for clothes] ☐ **shape:** form
slender: attractively thin and graceful, slim
doll(s): toy representing a baby ☐ **fire engine(s):** vehicle carrying equipment for fighting fire ☐ **Halloween:** October 31 observed with festivity ☐ **whatever it** (the occasion) **was**

nuclear family: two-generation family (parents, children only)
... to do with: no resemblance with ☐ **Green Town:** imaginary town in many stories by R.B., especially in *Dandelion Wine* (Grafton Books) (Waukegan, in reality: 2)
different <u>than</u>, different <u>from</u> ☐ **raise(d)** children (until they are grown up), bring up, rear ☐ (in) **the same way:** in the same manner

who was one of the great American magicians of the last seventy years and his son, Blackstone Junior, who is now performing all over the world. I raised them to love cartoons, Walt Disney, comic strips, to love movies, old movies. I've raised them on Humphrey Bogart, Bergman, Garbo, Hepburn, all the great films of the past. It's individual with each family but some families have missed out on these joys. What a pity!

H. Y. It *is* a great pity. And with the absence of grandparents, very often, children miss something, don't they? What do you think?

R. B. Well, of course, I can't talk about that because, again, my mother-in-law's been around and my father-in-law was around till a few years ago. My mother-in-law's ninety-two and hits me with her cane every chance she gets, if I get in her way... A terrific lady! We've never had a fight, never. She's helped raise our daughters and they love her. The day she leaves the earth will be a disaster.

H. Y. It will be the "leave-taking" again then. That's a beautiful story.

R. B. Beautiful because I came from a family that was a good family for me. There are good parents and bad parents in the world, good and bad grandparents. No matter what is said today, the family has *not* gone out of fashion. I was lucky to be raised with three Bradbury families on one block in three separate houses and I ricocheted between the houses as my parents gave me the freedom to become just exactly what I wanted to be. I'm sure they worried about me but if they did they never said how much they feared I might vanish from the world. Someone would drown me, I'd fall over my

great: famous
Blackstone Junior or Jr.: (Am) son of (≠ Senior or Sr.)
performing: working, acting □ **raised:** (Am) brought up
movie(s): (Am) film; (Am) movie theater
I've raised on...: notice the way this is put (said)

It's individual with each family; it's a habit with him
missed out on: lost a chance to gain advantage or enjoyment
It's a pity! What a pity!, also: It's a shame! What a shame!
miss: feel sorry or unhappy at the absence or loss of sb or sth; I miss my fiancée (notice the construction)

mother-in-law: my wife's mother □ **around:** in some place near

ninety-five now, in 1993 □ **hits:** beats □ **chance:** opportunity
get in her way: am a nuisance and disturb her □ **terrific:** (fam) wonderful □ **fight:** quarrel □ **she's helped** (to) **raise** □ **the day** (when) **she leaves the earth** (world): the day she dies will be a disaster (disastrous, catastrophic)
"leave-taking": an allusion to *The Leave-Taking*, a story by R.B. relating the life and death of his great-grandmother (see R.B.'s Preface, p. 12, l. 11 to 14, and the story itself, p. 109, in *A Story of Love and Other Non-Science Fiction Stories* in the series "Lire en anglais"
no matter: in spite of, regardless of □ **has not gone out of fashion:** is not outmoded □ **lucky:** favoured by fortune
block: (Am) buildings surrounded by (usually) four streets
ricocheted suggests a boy full of life, like Jiggers-Ray in *The Last Circus*, 112,6 □ **freedom:** liberty □ **become:** be in the future
they worried: felt anxiety; worried, anxious
feared: were afraid; fear (n) □ **vanish:** disappear
drown: kill by holding in water for a long time

shoelaces... but they never expressed that doubt to me, they convinced me I could do anything I wanted to do and they were right. I went out and did it. No opposition. No saying "How are you going to earn a living... because writing is difficult?" They accepted it... They shared in my successes as I began to move up through the magazines and they were there at the premiere of *Moby Dick* with me in 1956. My father was around to enjoy at least five of my books being published. He'd go play golf and maybe one of the foursome would say: "Bradbury, hey? Any relation to the science fiction author?" And my father'd say: "Yep!" So, he got a lot of fun out of my career. I'm glad for that, because fathers deserve to have their sons well spoken of.

H. Y. You dedicated *The Toynbee Convector* to your granddaughters. Can you tell us about grandparenthood, grandfatherhood?

R. B. It's super! It's just like raising daughters. It's easier, of course... I'm one of those people who participate. I roll downhill with my kids. You get out in the autumn, on a good hill and you all lie down and roll! I'm sure I look silly doing it but you're part of the exhilaration, aren't you? In order to raise children or do anything you've got to be as loud as they are, otherwise their loudness makes you tired and you've got to be in the centre and rough and tumble and then you don't get tired. It's one of those secrets that people don't seem to understand. You can't be outside, you must be in the core of the family. I've changed three thousand diapers in my time, I'm a "pro" at it!

H. Y. Can you think of other pieces of advice to

fall over my shoelaces (and get killed!); shoelace (Am), shoestring, thin cord for lacing shoe
right ≠ wrong □ **went out** (into the world)
(fact of) **saying** □ **earn** money, a living; win a game...
writing (4); write, wrote, written; writing table; writer
shared in: took part in □ **move up through the magazines** (becoming more and more popular)
Moby Dick, a screenplay written by R.B. for John Huston's film after Melville's novel □ **was around:** was present □ **at least:** as a minimum □ **he'd** (would) **go** (and) **play golf**
foursome: two pairs of partners □ **relation to:** connexion with
yep: (fam) yes (≠ nope)
fun: pleasure, enjoyment □ **glad:** happy, pleased, delighted
deserve: have a right □ **well spoken of** (favourably, with admiration)
dedicated: ("With love to....") □ *The Toynbee Convector* (Bantam Books 1989, contains 23 short stories)

super!: great! smashing! wonderful!
easier, easy
downhill: down the hill (small mountain, slope)
lie down, lay, lain (flat on the ground)
look: seem □ **silly:** stupid □ **you're part of:** you take part in
exhilaration: excitement and happiness
loud: noisy □ **otherwise:** if not
loudness: noise, exuberance □ **tired** (physically and mentally)
rough and tumble: occasion of being noisy, disorderly, unrestrained
outside: out of it (≠ part of it)
core: centre, heart □ baby's **diaper(s)** (to absorb urine)
in my time: in the days when I was a young father
advice: suggestion(s) made about the best thing to do

parents and grandparents?

R. B. No, just love. Actually, *everything* is love. You shouldn't have children if you're not going to love them. As with friendship. Friendship needs to be tended, you must pay attention and the little things are remembered. I remember a thing that happened with a friend of mine who published his first short story years ago. Another friend, knowing how important it was to him, had New York send out a copy of the magazine special delivery. He found out where my friend was in a theatre that night and at the intermission ran through the crowd yelling: "Extra, extra... first published story by William Nolan!" Well, my friend Bill burst into tears. That was an act of love. That showed that someone cared. So, with friendship, with our families, our children, our grandchildren, you must be there to applaud, love and teach.

H. Y. What if you were prevented from writing?

R. B. I would die. Unless I could move into acting or painting, some other art form. Because if I couldn't write every day, if I didn't have that outlet, I'd go mad. There's just too much in my head that wants out.

H. Y. You couldn't live without it?

R. B. It's too exciting. It's such fun, you've got to have fun every day of your life. You have to have many loves. You must have a family to love; a wife to love or a fiancée or a mistress or a girlfriend to love plus your work. Both must be there. It's no use being a good writer if you don't have someone to show it to. We're all like children who cry: "Look what I did today!" So you applaud each other, with a reciprocal love in two fields. You can't do without either... The most important

just: only ☐ **actually:** in (actual) fact, in reality

friend, **friendship** ☐ **tended:** looked after very carefully, in a loving way
happened: took place ☐ **a friend of mine,** a friend of hers...

had New York send: have sb do sth, cause sb to do sth
special delivery (by a special carrier, not at the usual time)
found out: discovered (by making a deliberate effort)
intermission: (Am) interval ☐ **crowd:** large number of people
yelling: shouting ☐ **extra:** special edition ☐ **William F. Nolan:** a Bradbury authority, author of screenplays and short stories (43.5) ☐ **burst...:** suddenly started crying ☐ **cared:** showed interest and affection

what (would happen) **if** ☐ **prevented from:** kept from
unless: except if ☐ **move into acting** (at the theatre): pass on to, change over to
outlet: means of expressing my feelings ☐ **go** (become) **mad**
that wants (to get) **out**

exciting: simulating ☐ **fun:** pleasure, enjoyment
have fun: enjoy yourself

plus: (fam) as well as
it's no use being: it's useless or senseless to be
to show it to: to whom to show it

field(s): domain
do: succeed, manage ☐ **either:** the two (of them)

moment in your life is every night when you're lying in bed and looking at the ceiling and imagining your future — tomorrow, next week, next year — and you as the actor in that future, doing the things that you love, widly, with no pay — with no pay — as long as a few people love what you're doing. So, look to yourself before you sleep. What do you dream about the future? Are you going to let someone turn you off by saying: "Don't *do* that!"?

All my friends told me *not* to write science fiction. All my wife's friends told her not to marry me; I was a loser... Thank God she didn't listen to them. You must take chances. You jump off a cliff and build your wings on the way down. Don't stand up there trying to imagine how to build those wings, because you're never going to know. You just jump off and hope you get the goddam things built by the time you hit, for a soft landing. That's what life is, taking chances. Sure, people have unnatural fears; I'm a mass of them, but one by one I conquered them by *doing* them. I was lying by the side of a swimming-pool in the desert in California twenty years ago and I suddenly realized I'd never learned to dive! You know what I did? I got up, ran, and jumped in the pool head-first. It was a lousy dive but it was a beginning. Now I'm diving. I'd let my fear of pain stop me. I've learned to fly in jets during the last eight years. I was terrified of flying but when I began to fly I discovered that I was afraid of *me*. I was afraid I'd run up and down the aisles and scream and bother the other passengers. When I discovered I didn't do that I relaxed and now I enjoy flying. There are so many fears we have that we haven't tested. We think we're afraid,

ceiling: surface on the top of a room
next week ≠ last week (no articles!) ☐ **as:** in the state, the job of (being the actor)
wildly: passionately ☐ **pay:** salary, wages ☐ **as long as:** on condition that ☐ **look to...:** turn to (and ask yourself)
dream about: (here) imagine
turn you off: stop you from doing what you want

not to write; "To be or not to be" (position of "not"!)
marry sb; marriage (two r!)
loser: sb who is (or will always be) unsuccessful; to lose
chance(s): risk ☐ **cliff** (overhanging sea) ☐ the two **wings** of a bird (to fly with) ☐ **on the way down:** as you go down
build (a house...), built, built

goddam: *sacré, fichu* ☐ **by the time:** before ☐ **hit:** come against (the sea) ☐ **... soft** (≠ sudden, violent) **landing** (like a plane on land) ☐ **unnatural:** abnormal ☐ **fear(s)** (of danger...) apprehension ☐ **one by one:** one at a time
by the side of: on the edge of ☐ **swimming-pool:** place built for people to swim (like fish) in
dive: jump head-first into water
lousy: (fam) very bad, rotten ☐ **dive** (n)
beginning ≠ end; begin, began, begun ☐ **let:** allow to
pain: suffering ☐ **fly,** flew, flown: travel by plane (jet)
I was terrified of flying

aisle(s) (between lines of seats) ☐ **scream:** cry ☐ **bother:** disturb, cause trouble to
I enjoy flying: I like flying
tested: found out what they were like (by trying)

but we're really *not*...

...About driving. Can you remind us of what you said the other day?

R. B. Well, that's different. A really horrible thing happened to me when I was fifteen. There was an accident across the street from where I was visiting a friend and five people were killed in the accident, decapitated, their jaws torn off. I shouldn't have crossed the street. I didn't know what I was going to see. When I got over there, people were dying all around me. It was like being in the middle of a war. When you see real people die in front of you, you never get over that. You want to help these people who are mutilated but there's nothing you can do. And the ambulances come and the next day you read in the newspaper: five out of six people dead. I could hardly walk home from that scene, that accident. So I never learned to drive.

H. Y. What about your hobbies? How do you spend the weekend?

R. B. Oh, I've collected masks, I'm a Sunday painter on occasion... I do a lot of reading when I can; *that's* a very great vacation for me. But people are always saying "Do you need long weekends and vacations?" and I say "No" because I'm never tired and if people would follow my example and do things that they love every day, they wouldn't need a vacation. I'm travelling in France for the whole summer but my routine is not different than it is at home: I do writing every day and then I go out and fall in love with France again...

H. Y. ...What values would you defend most?

R. B. Friendship and the love of family... The value of doing good work because you have to please yourself,

driving (a car...) □ **remind** sb **of** sth: cause sb to remember sth

I was fifteen or I was fifteen years old
across the street: on the other side of... □ **visiting a friend:** paying a visit to a friend □ **kill(ed):** cause the death of
jaw(s): bone structure containing teeth □ **torn off:** removed by force □ **crossed:** walked across, from one side to the other
got over there (across to the other side) □ **dying**; die
middle: centre □ **war** ≠ peace
get over: recover from a bad experience

next: following □ **five out of six:** out of, from among
hardly: almost not □ **walk home,** got home... (no preposition!)
learned or learnt (form in -ed more often used in American)
hobbies; hobby (such as collecting stamps, bird-watching...)

a Sunday painter: an amateur painter
on occasion: from time to time, occasionally
vacation: (Am) holiday; to vacation, to have a vacation

tired; tiredness; tireless (never or rarely getting tired)
follow or take **my example** ("a", not "e")
need or be in need of
the whole (entire) **summer** (as is often the case with R.B.)
at home (in my own house, in my own country)
fall in love with France (a girl...): notice the expression

value(s) (justice, freedom...) □ **most:** more than anything else
please yourself: make yourself happy

you have to please others, but doing excellent work and giving 55 per cent instead of just 50 per cent in anything that you do. Do more than is expected. I have an artist friend Joe Mugnaini who's illustrated a lot of my books. I asked him for one sketch: he gave me twenty! I would say "Joe, you don't have to give me so many, give me two or three" but he gives me twenty. So do more in life than is expected of you... Honesty... When you tell me you're going to be on time, be on time. When you promise to deliver work, deliver it. Try to be faithful to your family and friends. That's all very trite, I know... And then share exuberance, the exuberance of loving what you do.

H. Y. Would you say yours is a Christian message?

R. B. No. If you go back through the philosophies and religions of the various countries of the world, in one way or another they're saying the same thing: "This, above all: to thine own self be true". Someone once asked me what the eleventh commandment would be. I said: "If you turn away from the genetic gift God gave you, that's a sin". So the eleventh commandment would be: "Thou shalt not sin against yourself by ignoring your God-given talent". So you must not turn away from the God-given gift, whatever you were born with. Maybe you haven't found it yet. You don't even know it's there. That's why we must experiment with our loves. There's a wonderful quote I saw somewhere; the Armenians believe that in the moment of birth God thumbprints your forehead with all your genetic information; everything you're ever going to be is in that thumbprint but it fades in the hour of your birth and you must spend a lifetime looking in the mirror to see

others (pronoun), other people (adjective, no s!)
instead of: in place of ☐ **anything:** everything, no matter what
... expected: ... than people think you will do
Mugnaini has illustrated *The Last Circus* in a superb edition with an introduction by William F. Nolan (36.12) (Lord John Press, Nortbridge, California 1980)
twenty (sketches); sketch, rough, not detailed drawing
expect of (from) **you**
be on time: be at the appointed time, be punctual
deliver: do as promised ☐ **faithful:** firm, constant (in love, affection) ☐ **trite:** not original, banal
share (jointly with others) ☐ **exuberance:** enthusiasm, excitement
yours is a... message: your message in a Christian one
go back through...: return (fig) and examine one by one

in one way (manner) or another
above all: most important of all ☐ **"... thine** (your)**... true"** (faithful) (10): Polonius's advice to his son *(Hamlet)* ☐ **once:** one day ☐ **turn away from:** refuse to exploit ☐ **gift:** present
sin: transgression against divine law; to sin; sinner
Thou shalt: (old English) you shall

whatever (gift, no matter which, music, painting...)

experiment with: test for
quote: sentence quoted (cited) from a book...
believe (in God...) ☐ **birth:** being born
thumbprints: makes a mark; thumb: short thick finger ☐ **forehead:** part of face below hair
fades: disappears gradually ☐ **spend** (time...), spent, spent
lifetime: the time during which you are alive or living

the configuration of who you are and what you are and bring the thumbprint out. Another way of putting it: I heard a Laurence Olivier interview years ago where he said when he was ten or eleven years old he felt a gyroscope turning in his body, his soul turning in his flesh and leaning, toward acting. So he went with the gyroscope. If he'd gone the other way, he'd fallen off. So whatever the genetic gyroscope is in you, feel it and say: "Where do you want to go? You want to go *that* way? O.K., I'm *with* you!" Anyone that doesn't know that about creativity knows nothing. It's this inner thing, this humming, this top, spinning.

H. Y. What about the year 2000? Pessimistic?

R. B. Hell, no! Look what's happened in the last few years! It's everything I said would happen. I've been lecturing about Lithuania and Estonia and Latvia. No one would listen. I said: "My God, Russia is ten times worse than we imagined. A terrible country!" And now suddenly we have the new Revolution arriving, the *real* Revolution. What's happening in Russia today is a continuation of 1917 and 1918, the People's Revolution, which was never realized. Lenin and Stalin destroyed it. Now that old real Revolution is continuing, the one they never had, because communism barred the way for the real people's uprising. The last two years have been fantastic years, jubilant years. And it will continue. Most of Lenin's statues have vanished. His body will disappear from the Kremlin wall sometime in the near future. They will spirit it away in the night, even as Stalin is destroyed along with his dreadful history. So not optimism but optimal behavior is what I preach, for all of us, so we can share in the creativity of rebuilding parts

bring... out: cause it to be seen (and develop your talents) □ **putting it:** saying it; how shall I put it? □ **Laurence Olivier** (1907-1989): one of the greatest English actors ever

gyroscope (to maintain equilibrium, direction) □ **soul** (spirit, mind) as opposed to the **flesh** (body) □ **leaning toward(s):** moving in the direction of □ **the other way:** in the other direction □ **so:** consequently □ **feel it:** be aware (conscious) of it

that way: in that direction

anyone: anybody, whoever he is

about: concerning □ **inner:** internal, interior (deep down in you) ≠ outer □ **humming:** continuous murmuring □ **top:** toy to which **spinning** motion is given by hand... (balancing on its point) □ **hell, no!:** (fam) oh no! certainly not

it's everything...: everything happened as I said it would

lecturing: giving talks □ **Latvia** (bordering on the Baltic)

time(s) indicates multiplication; 3 times 2 is 6

bad, **worse**, the worst

suddenly: all of a sudden

today: at the present time

realized: carried out

continuing: continue

barred the way...: bar, block (movement or action)

uprising: rising against the government..., insurrection

jubilant: filled with great joy □ **most of:** the majority of

vanished: disappeared

sometime: at some uncertain time □ **... near future:** soon

spirit...: take away secretly □ **even as:** just at the same time as

along with: together with □ **dreadful:** horrible

behavio(u)r: conduct, comportment □ **preach:** recommend

share in: take part in □ **rebuilding:** building again

of Europe, the world and ourselves. All of the cities of America have been done over. They are in bad shape. My hometown, Waukegan, is a disaster. That's a challenge. It doesn't depress me. Let's go *do* it.

H. Y. How do you look at the United States today? and tomorrow?

R. B. Well, we're super, dammit! We've done much to change the world, mostly for the good. We made a terrible blunder in Vietnam because of Lyndon B. Johnson, one of our worst presidents ever. I would like to dig him up *(laughter)*, put him on trial and impeach him. Beyond that, our influence has been mostly good. Our shared inventions have helped free the world. The proliferation of the FAX and XEROX machines which are printing presses of one sort or another, telephones and radios... got the information into Russia and to all those other countries so that people sensed that freedom was in the air. And it's a matter of time before the true Revolution hits China too. That's unpredictable. As long as they keep the tanks killing people..., it's very difficult.

H. Y. How is it that you seem to spend more and more time in France?

R. B. The French do almost everything right... The history of cities is embodied here. One of my great heroes, Viollet-le-Duc, rebuilt Carcassonne and Pierrefonds and parts of the Louvre and Notre-Dame and the Palais de Justice..., all examples of ways of restructuring the past and giving it to us as a gift.

H. Y. Can you describe your ideal city of tomorrow?

R. B. Well, the ideal city of tomorrow is right here.

all of the cities (without any exception)
done over: (sl) ruined, spoilt ☐ **in bad shape:** in a bad state
hometown (where I was born)
a challenge: sth difficult but stimulating ☐ **let's go** (and) **do it**
look at: judge, regard
tomorrow: (here) in the future, in the years to come
dammit!: (very informal English) we sure(ly) are (super)
mostly: predominantly ☐ **for the good** (the benefit of all)
blunder: big mistake ☐ **Lyndon B. Johnson** (1964-1969)
... ever: one of the worst presidents we have ever had
dig...: take... out of the ground ☐ **... trial..., impeach...:** have him go through the legal process..., charge him ☐ **beyond that:** apart from that ☐ **free:** make free; freedom, liberty
XEROX machines: photocopier
printing press(es): machine used for printing (we can easily imagine how important this is to the author of *Fahrenheit 451)*
sensed: vaguely felt, more or less realized
it's a matter of time (it's inevitable) ☐ **true:** real
hits: arrives in, reaches ☐ **unpredictable:** that cannot be said in advance ☐ **keep...:** cause... to continue to kill

how is it that you...: why is that you... how come you spend

almost: nearly ☐ **right:** properly, as they should be done
embodied: given concrete form
Viollet-le-Duc: a famous architect born in Paris (1814-1879)
Pierrefonds: famous castle near Compiègne

gift (a word often used by Ray Bradbury): present; give, gave, given

right (here): exactly, precisely; right in the middle

We're living in it. Paris is it... There are something like twenty thousand restaurants in Paris. You turn a corner, you know, and you get twenty restaurants in a row. Eating is part of living that we have to learn more about in America. The leisurely lunch, the long dinner, the delight of conversation, millions of trees, millions of flowers, dozens of fountains, wonderful!... Hundreds and thousands of places to sit all over Paris! You have benches everywhere. The great thing is to cross Paris. You walk for a few miles and then you go into a little restaurant and have some coffee and watch all the people and then you get up and walk three more miles. I often cross Paris at night, you know, back and forth. I start at Notre-Dame and walk all the way to the Tour Eiffel and then maybe walk back later and take two or three hours at it. It's beautiful... So, that is the ideal city. It already exists. There're parts of it in London that work, parts of it in Rome, parts of it in Vienna, I'm sure, but France is the ideal example...

H. Y. ... What about fathers and sons?

R. B. I dreamed of my father about two years ago (he's been dead more than thirty years) but I had such a perfect dream in color and he was so real and I was talking to him, saying: "I love you" and I woke so happy he was back in the world, and then I looked around and of course he wasn't there and I burst into tears but... it's that perfect dream then of a perfect relationship.

H. Y. That was another story, wasn't it?

R. B. Yes, I wrote it as *The Wish* and I brought my father back from the dead so I could tell him again. I can't tell that story when I lecture and get through the

Paris is it: Paris is the ideal city
(a street) **corner;** corner shop
in a row: side by side; row, line (of houses, seats...)
(the fact of) **eating, living** □ **part of...:** no article!
leisurely: taken without haste (hurry) in a relaxed way
delight: very great pleasure □ **millions of..., dozens of...,**
hundreds of, thousands of (≠ six million trees...)
sit, sat, sat □ **all over...:** throughout..., everywhere in Paris
bench(es) (to sit on); a park bench □ **cross:** walk across
mile(s): 5 miles = 8 km (approximately)
watch: look at (usually for a period of time); watch T.V.
get up: stand up □ **three more miles** or another three miles
back and forth: from one place to another and back again
repeatedly □ **all the way to:** as far as; it's a long way
take two or three hours at it: spend... doing it

There's Paris: "there's" for "there are" (often in conversation)
work: (here) are like that (ideal places to live in)

dreamed of: had a vision of... in sleep
he's been dead... thirty years or he died thirty years ago
a dream in colo(u)r: no "u" in American in such words
woke: stopped sleeping
so happy (that) **he was back;** go back, return □ **looked around**
(to try to find him) □ **burst into tears:** suddenly started crying

relationship: way in which (two) people feel towards each other
was: (here) turned into, made up

the dead: or dead people □ **tell him again** (that I loved him)
get through the whole thing: read it from beginning to end

whole thing without crying, you know.

H. Y. I'm not surprised.

R. B. Because my father was special... There used to be more schools with mainly men students, and I wanted to help them through that period of antagonism to the father as quickly as possible. All that nonsense fathers and sons fight about and who gives a damn... I left home to be married when I was twenty-seven! I travelled for the first time at thirty-three, came to France and Ireland. On the day of my leave-taking to sail to Europe my father came to the house with the gold watch of my grandfather. He put it in my hands and hugged and kissed me, then stood back and there were tears in his eyes. I said to myself "My God, he loves me! You fool, you fool!" I knew he loved me, but I *didn't* know he loved me. The realization of it burst tears from my eyes. I embraced him and after that, no more arguments, no more fights. It's in the nature of men and boys to be antagonistic. But I put all that behind me... I lectured at a graduation a few years ago and to all those young men I said: "Look! You already know how much you love your mother. But how about your father, hey? I mean, when's the last time you said: 'I love you, I really love you and I appreciate all the years and all the work and your giving me my education', and I said: "On this special day, now forget about ma, hey. She's already got more love than she needs. But you run over to your father, five minutes from now, and you grab hold of him and lift him off his feet and say: 'Dad, I love you, with all my heart and soul' ". Well, I tell you, pandemonium. I never saw so many people so happy, so much crying, fathers and sons

crying: weeping

there used to be: there were (but it is no longer the case)
mainly: for the most part ☐ **men student(s)** or male student(s)
help them through...: help them solve the problems...
quickly: rapidly ☐ **nonsense:** stupid things, rubbish
fight: quarrel ☐ **who gives a damn:** (fam) who cares (attaches any importance to it)
I left home: no preposition! ☐ **at** (the age of) **thirty-three**
leave-taking: departure; take leave, go away
sail to: go, travel by boat to
gold: precious yellow metal ☐ it's six o'clock by my **watch**
hugged me (in his arms) ☐ **stood back** (a little farther away)
tear(s) (as a result of emotion); tear-gas
fool: silly, stupid person; behave in a foolish way
realization: discovery, understanding ☐ **burst tears from my eyes:** suddenly made me cry ☐ **embraced:** hugged (13)
argument(s): quarrel, disagreement ☐ **fight(s):** (n) quarrel
put all behind me: forgot all about that
graduation: (Am) ceremony at which diplomas are conferred
look!: (used to draw attention) listen!
how about or what about...? (making a suggestion, an offer...)
hey: used to attract attention ☐ **mean:** want to say

your giving me...: the fact that you gave me an education
on this special day, on this special occasion
ma: (fam) mummy, mother
over: across a distance (long or short) towards or away from
grab hold of: seize ☐ **lift him off his feet:** take him up, raise him off the ground
I tell you: I assure you ☐ **pandemonium:** wild and noisy disorder, confusion ☐ (act of) **crying** (gerund)

like that *(gesturing)* in a single moment; and it could have been ten years later before the damned fools discovered how much their fathers loved them. They're inarticulate, not all fathers, but a lot... You get self-conscious, you're embarrassed at your love. So, I had a father come up to me on the street a year ago and he said: "Thank God for you." I said: "What did I do?" He said: "I was at that graduation and my son and I have had a relationship since, you can't believe." So there, here we are back with love again, aren't we, and the inability to break through the wall on occasion...

H. Y. ...Can you tell us about *Uncle Einar*?

R. B. Well, Uncle Einar is my favorite uncle. Half of my family is English and the other half is Swedish. My mother was born in Stockholm in 1888 and came over to America when she was only two years old. But all my Swedish relatives are my favorite relatives, just about, because they're all kind of loud and boisterous and full of wine and good spirits. The happiest memories of my childhood are going to visit my Swedish relatives across town in Waukegan, Illinois. My uncle Einar was the most boisterous of them all. He ran a delivery truck for a laundry company, so he'd come to the house at least once a week and visit my mother and deliver her laundry. We'd talk and she'd give him a glass of wine, you know, and they'd come to the house and play cards. He was a very special, loud, boisterous, loving man. And so I got the idea, back about forty years ago, of putting wings on him and flying him. And so, I would have a memorial to this special uncle, that would be around forever. He's been dead about twenty years now and I miss him terribly. But any time I want to visit him

like that (embracing) □ **single:** one only
... **later:** ten years could have passed...
discovered: found out, realized, knew
inarticulate: unable to express their ideas or feelings
self-conscious: ill-at-ease, **embarrassed** (**at** sth)
on the street: (Am) in the street
thank God for you: an expression of great gratitude
my son and I (not me!)
since, since then; ever since
there is an interjection here; there we are with love again!
inability: incapacity □ **break the wall** (of misunderstanding)
Uncle Einar, a short story to be found in *The Stories of Ray Bradbury* (Alfred A. Knopf, New York 1986) □ **favo(u)rite**
Swedish: from Sweden
came over to: across a long distance here (≠ 50.28)

relative(s) ≠ parents (father and mother) □ **just about:** more or less □ **kind of:** (Am) in a certain way □ **loud, boisterous:** noisy, full of energy and **good spirits,** joie de vivre □ **memory** (memories): sth that is remembered □ **across:** on the other side of
ran: drove □ **delivery;** deliver letters... □ **truck:** (Am) lorry (bigger than a car) □ **laundry:** clothes for washing
once a week: once (twice, three times...) every (per) week
'd, would: indicates repetition of an action

special ≠ ordinary, usual □ **loving:** feeling or showing love to others □ **got:** had □ **back** (in the past)
wings (of bird, plane... to fly with) □ **flying him:** making him fly □ **memorial** (to commemorate the dead); war memorial
around: in existence □ **forever:** always
I miss him: I feel sorry about his absence □ **any time:** every...

I go reread the short story.

H. Y. Do you often think about death?

R. B. Oh, all the time. There is a great thing about writing a new book... I've had a new novel come out during this month. It's taken four years to write, but the great thing is getting it done, number one, and then getting it in galleys, and then waiting for the day when the book arrives and it's going to go into the bookstores. I carry it around with me for days. It's my baby, hey! I show it to everyone. "Here's my baby, here's my baby" and here's my life. It extends my life. So there's that exhilaration, plus the fear that maybe you won't live to see the book published. The day that the jacket arrives is a triumph. Then there's the day when the first copy of the book arrives. That's when you beat death again. It's always a competition. We're doing that all the time, all of us. We just don't think about it. We don't say it. But an artist is doing this and saying: "O.K., death, look what I've done. And this is going to be around on the Sixtine ceiling for four hundred years after my death, five hundred years." That's what it's all about. The same goes for our children. People often say to me: "Do you believe in immortality?" I say: "Yes, I have four daughters and three grandchildren, and seven great-grandchildren. So dying is not dying, when you have a family. As my great-grandmother said to the people that gathered at her bedside: 'Tomorrow I will be alive in the world. I will be falling out of a tree. I'll be baking a pie in the basement. I'll be repairing a car in the front yard... Each part of me that stays beyond, the branches of the tree... This root dies but the branches continue doing all their activities...' "

I go (and) **reread** (read again)

great: wonderful, super
come out: published, released
it's taken four years...; how long does it take you to do it?
number one: to begin with
... in galleys (for the first stage of printing, before the book is made up in pages)
bookstore(s): (Am) bookshop ☐ **around,** about, here and there

extends: prolongs
exhilaration: strong feeling of excitement and happiness

jacket: paper cover used to protect the book
copy: printed specimen; I've four copies of that book
beat, beat, beaten: (here) conquer, overcome ☐ **competition:** fight, contest, struggle; compete with

look (at) **what I've done**
around: 53,31 ☐ **the Sixtine** (chapel) **ceiling** in the Vatican
That's what it's all about: that is the real problem, the heart of the matter ☐ **the same goes for our children:** the same (thing) applies to our children ☐ **believe in** immortality, in God...

my great-grandmother: the heroin of *The Leave-Taking* (32.20)
gathered: came together ☐ **bedside of** sb who is ill (here)
alive: living ☐ **I... tree** (meaning her great-grandchildren)
baking bread, a **pie...** (filled with meat, fruit) ☐ **basement:** room below ground level ☐ **yard:** (Am) garden ☐ **beyond** (me), after (me) ☐ **root:** part of a tree that grows down into the soil

H. Y. ...Can you think of advice you would give to young people launching into life?

R. B. Yes. The advice is: fall in love with something and do it. Don't do things because other people want you to do them. Don't do them because it's the popular political thing or the popular intellectual literary thing. Those are lies. You turn away from yourself. You mustn't do that. You must find out what you really like with all your heart and soul and lungs and body and spirit, and then do it, with no guarantees. You can't guarantee anything — I can't guarantee you that if tomorrow you shifted your profession — let's say you got bored with teaching and you went off to do something else — I can't guarantee you are going to succeed at it. But if you love it, you've got a chance. Doing things that you hate means that you are turning away from all this original stuff in here *(striking his chest)*, all the dreams that you've had, that you haven't fulfilled. But you've got to try, don't you? Because you don't want to lie on your deathbed and say to yourself: "My God, I never even found out if I could succeed, I was afraid of failure, therefore I failed." And so you have to take a chance on doing something. When I began my career, when I was twelve, dreaming of being a writer, dreaming of the future, going off to Mars, there was no guarantee I was going to succeed... Who knows? With a few bad breaks maybe I wouldn't have made it. But, boy, I've had a great life, I've had no regrets, and half my life I had no money, you know. Thirty-five years ago is when it began to..., my income began to grow, but before that, my wife took a vow of poverty to marry me. We had about ten dollars in the bank the day

advice: suggestion made about the best thing to do
launching into...: embarking on; the launching of a ship
advice; a piece of advice; to advise sb to do sth
people want you to do: notice the infinitive clause with "want, expect, like..."; I expect him to come tomorrow

lie(s): false belief □ **turn away from:** refuse to look at yourself (fig) □ **find out:** discover
lung(s): breathing organ (to take in air, to breathe)
guarantee(s); to guarantee

shifted: changed ("left off to do something else")
bored with: fed up with (fam), uninterested in

succeed at it: succeed in doing sth □ **chance** (of succeeding)
hate ≠ love; hate (n), hatred; hateful
original stuff (fam. things): what you really are □ **striking** (with his hand) □ **chest:** upper part of body
fulfilled: realized □ **try**, have a try
deathbed: bed on which you die or are expected to die
succeed; success ≠ failure; successful ≠ unsuccessful
therefore: consequently □ **I failed:** I did not succeed
take a chance on doing something ("you've got to try")
career; a careerist
dream(ing), dreamt or dreamed, dreamt or dreamed

bad break: stroke of bad luck □ **made it:** succeeded
(oh) **boy:** (Am) used to express excitement □ **great:** wonderful

income: money received as royalties, salary...
grow: go up, increase □ **took a vow of poverty:** made a solemn decision (like a nun in a convent) to stay poor

I got married and I put some money in an envelope and gave it to the minister and he said: "What's this?" I said: "That's payment for the marriage ceremony." And he handed it back to me and I said: "What are you doing?" He said: "You're a writer, aren't you?" I said: "Yes." He said: "You're going to need this, then." And I said: "Yes, sir" and I took it. So, years later, when I had some money I sent him a decent check.

envelope: only one p!
minister: member of the clergy, especially in Protestant churches ☐ **payment for;** to pay for sth
handed it back: gave it back; to hand; a hand
you're a writer; he's a musician; she's an engineer...
to need: be in need of; money to help the needy

decent: (fam) rather good ☐ **check** (Am) cheque; a cheque for £80

Talking about the short story
BLESS ME, FATHER, FOR I HAVE SINNED (p. 65)

H. Y. Bless Me, Father, for I Have Sinned is another story we've selected for this series. What about it?

R. B. Oh, that's an absolutely true story about myself. I think we all are cruel to animals but never admit it. When we're young..., if the bullies are beating up on you, if your brother's beating up on you — my brother was four years older — I would take it out on the dog, you know, and when my parents weren't looking I'd give him a hit. Well, that's terrible. Oh, it's an awful confession to make... It still bothers me all these years later that the young person I was did that. Well, there was my favorite dog that I loved madly. After all, who do you have to love when you're twelve? You don't have any romances in your life. You have a few friends, you have parents, but you don't have a mad love. A dog is a mad love, when you are twelve. And during the middle of winter, he ran away, he was gone for three days and three nights and I was in despair. I was crying... "Here's my favorite dog, maybe he's dead." So, this is a couple of nights before Christmas. It was snowing and cold and at one o'clock in the morning I hear a scratching at the door. I open the door and here's my dog, covered with frost, and wet, and whining, and he comes in and he rolls around the floor and he licks me. I grab on to him

bless: ask God's favour for □ **sinned:** committed a sin (against God's law); a sinner
true: real
cruel to animals: notice the preposition □ **admit:** confess
bullies: (sing) bully, schoolboy tyrant □ **beat(ing),** beat, beaten

take it out on the dog: express my resentment by making the dog suffer
give (him) a hit: hit, strike, beat □ **awful:** terrible, horrible
bothers: worries, upsets
(the fact) **that**
favo(u)rite (Am) □ **madly:** (fam) very much; mad, crazy

romance(s): love affair
mad; be mad about sb, love or admire very much (20)
middle: just half way between beginning and end
he was gone: he had disappeared, he had vanished
in despair, desperate □ **crying:** weeping (with eyes full of tears)
maybe: perhaps □ **a couple of:** two (fam), a few
it was snowing: (white) snow fell on the ground
scratching: sound made by the dog's legs against the door
covered with: notice the preposition
(white) **frost** (on grass... in cold early morning) □ **whining:** complaining □ **lick(s):** pass tongue over □ **grab:** seize (62.6)

and say: "Oh, you know, glad you're back" and then I beat up on him. I say: "How dare you? How dare you run away from me? How dare you reject my love?" That's really what I was saying. It's all blind, you don't know what you're doing when you're that age. And then, when I saw what I'd done I grabbed him and cried. I wept and I said: "Forgive me, forgive me for hitting you. I'm sorry. I didn't mean that." And so, that memory stayed with me all these years until I wrote the short story about six years ago... So, you see, these are the things I'm looking for. You can't search to find them. They have to happen out of a blind need, and suddenly you write the story. I couldn't have planned to sit down and write that story. It had to happen. And then, as it happened, I wept, you know, and when I tell the story right now, I'm still very close to the point of tears because I still haven't quite forgiven that boy for that crime he committed to an innocent creature..., to an innocent creature.

H. Y. Do you have dogs and cats?

R. B. We had several up until recently and so many of them got hit by cars we couldn't stand it. It was terrible. We had twenty-two cats at one time! But now we're down to about five, so we're feeling a little bereft now.

(I'm) **glad:** happy
how dare you: used when one is very shocked and angry; how dare you speak to me like that?
it's all blind: you don't realize what you're doing; blind, unable to see (mentally here)
saw: understood, realized □ **grab(bed):** seize suddenly
weep, **wept,** wept: cried □ **forgive,** forgave, forgiven: pardon
I didn't mean that: I didn't intend to do that
memory: sth remembered □ **stayed:** remained (in my memory)

look for (as material for stories) □ **search:** examine carefully
have to... out of... need, you can't help it, "I couldn't have **planned** (decided in advance) to... **write** ...", "it **had to** happen", I'm not in charge, I don't control" (188,9,10)

right now (just now) **I'm still very close** (near) **to the point of tears:** even now, so many years later, I'm about to cry
crime: (here) bad, immoral act, wicked act
to an innocent creature: towards, in relation to, as regards

up until recently: up to now... □ **so many got hit by cars** (that)...
stand: bear; I can't stand that noise
at one time: during a certain period of time in the past
we're down to... five: we only have five □ **bereft:** made unhappy by the loss (death) of parents, relatives...

BLESS ME, FATHER, FOR I HAVE SINNED

I have written stories about myself when young with my superfavorite dog, based on my guilty conscience fifty or so years ago, honoring, I hope, my dear lost canine friend properly.

(Addition to the original Preface by Ray Bradbury, August 1st 1993.)

"... I find it hard to believe that on at least one occasion, when I was thirteen, I treated my dog poorly. I find that I cannot read this story without dissolving in tears"

(Ray Bradbury).

when (I was) young
guilty ≠ innocent, clean
... or so: approximately
lose, lost, lost ≠ find, found, found
properly: satisfactorily (as he should be honoured)
hard: difficult
believe: accept as true (≠ false)
at least: as a minimum
poorly: badly, not well (morally, here)

It was just before midnight, on Christmas Eve when Father Mellon woke, having slept for only a few minutes. He had a most peculiar urge to rise, go, and swing wide the front door of his church to let the snow in and then go sit in the confessional to wait.

Wait for what? Who would say? Who might tell? But the urge was so incredibly strong it was not to be denied.

"What's going on here?" he muttered quietly to himself, as he dressed. "I am going mad, am I not? At this hour, who could possibly want or need, and why in blazes should I—"

But dress he did and down he went and opened wide the front door of the church and stood in awe of the great artwork beyond, better than any painting in history, a tapestry of snow weaving in laces and gentling to roofs and shadowing the lamps and putting shawls on the huddled masses of cars waiting to be blessed at the curb. The snow touched the sidewalks and then his eyelids and then his heart. He found himself holding his breath with the fickle beauties and then, turning, the snow following at his back, he went to hide in the confessional.

Damn fool, he thought. Stupid old man. *Out* of here! Back to your bed!

But then he heard it; a sound at the door, and footsteps scraping on the pavestones of the church, and at last the damp rustle of some invader fresh to the other side of the confessional. Father Mellon waited.

"Bless me," a man's voice whispered, "for I have sinned!"

Stunned at the quickness of this asking, Father

midnight: 12 o'clock at night ☐ **...eve:** day (evening) before Christmas ☐ **woke:** stopped sleeping
peculiar: strange ☐ **urge:** strong wish ☐ **rise:** get up
swing wide: open wide (fully, completely) ☐ **let the snow** (come) **in** ☐ **go** (and) **sit** ☐ **wait** for sb or sth

so incredibly (unbelievably) **strong** (that) **it was not to be denied** (rejected) (there was no question of denying it)
going on: happening ☐ **muttered:** murmured (in disapproval)
going mad: becoming mad (mentally ill)
possibly emphasizes "who could" ☐ **need** (to confess his sins)
why in blazes: (fam) emphatic for "why", "why the hell...?"
dress he did...: he did dress in fact and he did go down
stood in awe of: felt respect (plus fear and reverence) for
artwork or art work ☐ **beyond:** farther on
weaving: weave, *tisser* ☐ **lace(s):** *dentelle* ☐ **gentling;** gentle ≠ rough ☐ **roofs:** cover houses ☐ **shadowing:** darkening ☐ **shawl(s)** (worn over shoulders) ☐ **huddled** (all together) ☐ **blessed:** favoured by God ☐ **curb:** (Am) limit of pavement (Am **sidewalk**) ☐ **eyelid(s):** cover of eye ☐ **holding his breath:** not breathing (taking in air) for a time ☐ **fickle:** often changing
following: coming after ☐ **hide** (so as to be unseen)

damn (fam): expresses disapproval, anger ☐ **fool:** stupid man
back to bed: go back to bed; (go, get) out of here!

footstep(s): sound of foot when walking ☐ **scraping:** rubbing
pavestone(s) (of paved surface) ☐ **damp:** wet ☐ **rustle:** light sound made by friction ☐ **fresh to:** just arrived at
bless: ask God's favour for ☐ **whispered:** murmured ☐ **for:** because ☐ **sinned:** committed a sin (against God's law); sinner
stunned: shocked, astonished ☐ **quickness;** quick, rapid

Mellon could only retort:

"How *could* you know the church would be open and I here?"

"I prayed, Father," was the quiet reply. "God *made* you come open up."

There seemed no answer to this, so the old priest, and what sounded like a hoarse old sinner, sat for a long cold moment as the clock itched on toward midnight, and at last the refugee from darkness repeated:

"*Bless* this sinner, father!"

But in place of the usual unguents and ointments of words, with Christmas hurrying fast through the snow, Father Mellon leaned toward the lattice window and could not help saying:

"It must be a terrible load of sin you carry to have driven you out on such a night on an impossible mission that turned possible only because God heard and pushed me out of bed."

"It *is* a terrible list, Father, as you will find!"

"Then speak, son," said the priest, "before we both freeze—"

"Well, it was this way—" whispered the wintry voice behind the thin paneling. "—Sixty years back—"

"Speak up! Sixty?!" The priest gasped. "That *long* past?"

"Sixty!" And there was a tormented silence.

"Go on," said the priest, ashamed of interrupting.

"Sixty years this week, when I was twelve," said the gray voice. "I Christmas-shopped with my grandmother in a small town back East. We walked both ways. In those days, who had a car? We walked, and coming home with the wrapped gifts, my grandma said

retort: make a retort (quick, rather angry answer)
could: notice the italics to emphasize Father Mellon's surprise
I (would be) **here**
prayed: asked God □ **quiet:** calm □ **reply:** answer; to reply
come (and) **open up** (the church)
there seemed (to be...) □ **priest:** member of the clergy
hoarse with emotion, nearly voiceless
itched on: went on impatiently □ **toward(s):** in the direction of
at (long) **last:** in the end, after a long time

unguents, ointments: (fig) expressing kindness, gentleness
hurrying: moving quickly □ **fast:** rapidly, quickly
leaned: bent forward □ **lattice:** *treillis, claire-voie*
could not help (stop) **saying**
load: (fig.) (large, heavy) quantity (hard to **carry)**
driven you out: made you go out, forced you to go out
that turned possible: that became possible

find: see, discover
son (used in the past by a priest talking to a man)
freeze (like water at the temperature of 0 C)
this way: like this □ **wintry:** characteristic of winter
thin ≠ thick □ (wood) **paneling** (Am), panelling □ **back:** ago
speak up: speak louder □ **gasped** (in surprise): caught breath (air), breathed with open mouth □ **that long past:** as long ago as that
go on: continue □ **ashamed of...:** feeling sorry for + v + ing
sixty years (ago) **this week**
gray: (Am) grey □ **Christmas-shopped:** went shopping, buying presents □ **back East:** away in the East □ **both ways:** going to town and back □ **in those days:** in those times
wrapped (in paper) □ **gift(s):** present

something, I've long since forgotten what, and I got mad and ran ahead, away from her. Far off, I could hear her call and then cry, terribly, for me to come back, come back, but I wouldn't. She wailed so, I knew I had hurt her, which made me feel strong and good, so I ran even more, laughing, and beat her to the house and when she came in she was gasping and weeping as if never to stop. I felt ashamed and ran to hide..."

There was a long silence.

The priest prompted. "Is that *it*?"

"The list is long," mourned the voice beyond the thin panel.

"Continue," said the priest, eyes shut.

"I did much the same to my mother, before New Year's. She angered me. I ran. I heard her cry out behind me. I smiled and ran faster. Why? Why, oh God, why?"

The priest had no answer.

"Is that it, then?" he murmured, at last, feeling strangely moved toward the old man beyond.

"One summer day," said the voice, "some bullies beat me. When they were gone, on a bush I saw two butterflies, embraced, lovely. I hated their happiness. I grabbed them in my fist and pulverized them to dust. Oh, Father, the shame!"

The wind blew in the church door at that moment and both of them glanced up to see a Christmas ghost of snow turned about in the door and falling away in drifts of whiteness to scatter on the pavings.

"There's one last terrible thing," said the old man, hidden away with his grief. And then he said:

"When I was thirteen, again in Christmas week, my

got mad: went mad (get + adj = become)
ahead: in front □ **far off:** a long distance from her
call, cry for me to come back: notice the construction
wailed: made prolonged plaintive cries of pain □ **so** (much)
hurt: caused mental pain to □ **strong** ≠ weak □ **good:** happy
even more: still more □ **beat...:** arrived before her...
gasping: breathing with difficulty □ **weeping:** crying
ashamed: sorry, full of shame □ **hide** (so as not to be seen); hide, hid, hidden (see 1.31)
prompted: encouraged him to go on □ **is that it?** (all?)
mourned: lamented, showing regret □ **beyond:** (here) behind

much the same: practically the same thing □ New **Year's** (day)
angered me: made me angry, enraged me □ **cry out:** shout
smiled: smile (n), happy expression on the face; smile at sb
why (did I do such a terrible thing?)

moved toward(s)...: full of sympathy for; move, cause feelings
bullies: bully (sing), cruel child who **beats** others
bush: small low tree
butterflies: colourful insects that fly □ **hate** ≠ love
grabbed: seized □ **fist:** firmly closed hand □ **pulverized them to dust** (powder): pressed them to death, killed them
wind: moving air □ blow, **blew,** blown
glanced: looked rapidly □ **ghost:** phantom, apparition
turned about (by the wind) □ **falling away:** disappearing
drifts (piled by the wind) □ **scatter** here and there, disperse

hidden away (for shame) □ **grief:** extreme sadness, sorrow

dog Bo ran away and was lost three days and nights. I loved him more than life itself. He was special and loving and fine. And all of a sudden the beast was gone, and all his beauty with him. I waited. I cried. I waited. I prayed. I shouted under my breath. I knew he would never, never come back! And then, oh, then, that Christmas Eve at two in the morning, with sleet on the sidewalks and icicles on roofs and snow falling, I heard a sound in my sleep and woke to hear him scratching the door! I bounded from bed so fast I almost killed myself! I yanked the door open and there was my miserable dog, shivering, excited, covered with dirty slush. I yelled, pulled him in, slammed the door, fell to my knees, grabbed him and wept. What a gift, what a gift! I called his name over and over, and he wept with me, all whines and agonies of joy. And then I stopped. Do you know what I did then? Can you guess the terrible thing? I beat him. Yes, beat him. With my fists, my hands, my palms, and my fists again, crying: how dare you leave, how dare you run off, how dare you do that to me, how dare you, how dare!? And I beat and beat until I was weak and sobbed and had to stop for I saw what I'd done, and he just stood and took it all as if he knew he deserved it, he had failed my love and now I was failing his, and I pulled off and tears streamed from my eyes, my breath strangled, and I grabbed him again and crushed him to me but this time cried: forgive, oh please, Bo, forgive. I didn't mean it. Oh, Bo, forgive...

"But, oh, Father, he couldn't forgive me. Who was he? A beast, an animal, a dog, my love. And he looked at me with such great dark eyes that it locked my heart

ran away: left suddenly, secretly □ **lost:** nowhere to be found
special: more important to me than anything else
loving: affectionate □ **fine:** wonderful □ **was gone:** had disappeared, vanished □ **cried:** wept (in grief)
prayed (God) □ **under my breath:** in a whisper, to myself

sleet: mixture of snow and water
icicle(s): mass of ice hanging from roofs
woke: stopped sleeping □ **scratching:** rubbing, scraping (66, 28)
bounded: jumped, leaped □ **almost:** nearly
yanked... open: open it by pulling quickly and violently
miserable: very unhappy □ **shivering:** trembling
slush: wet, dirty snow □ **yelled:** shouted □ **slammed:** shut violently □ **knee(s):** where the leg bends □ weep, **wept,** wept: cried □ **over and over** (again), again and again, repeatedly
whine(s): long plaintive cry □ **agonies of joy:** intense joy
guess: get to know by imagining
beat, **beat,** beaten
palm(s): the palm of the hand (≠ the back of the hand)
dare: have impudence; how dare you say such things to me!

weak ≠ strong □ **sobbed:** cried convulsively; to sob; a sob
stood (there, without reacting) □ **took:** bore, accepted
deserved: merited □ **failed:** neglected, did not respond to
pulled off: moved back □ **tears** come from the eyes when crying
streamed: ran abundantly □ **... strangled:** unable to breathe
crushed: pressed hard □ **this time:** on this occasion
forgive: pardon □ **mean it:** want, intend to do that

great: large □ **locked:** (fig) shut or closed firmly

and it's been locked forever after with shame. *I* could not then forgive *myself*. All these years, the memory of my love and how I failed him, and every Christmas since, not the rest of the year, but every Christmas Eve, his ghost comes back, I see the dog, I hear the beating, I know my failure. Oh, God!"

The man fell silent, weeping.

And at last the old priest dared a word: "And that is why you are here?"

"Yes, Father. Isn't it awful? Isn't it terrible?"

The priest could not answer, for tears were streaming down his face, too, and he found himself unaccountably short of breath.

"Will God forgive me, Father?" asked the other.

"Yes."

"Will *you* forgive me, Father?"

"Yes. But let me tell you something now, son. When I was ten, the same things happened. My parents, of course, but then—my dog, the love of *my* life, who ran off and I hated him for leaving me, and when he came back I, too, loved and beat him, then went back to love. Until this night, I have told no one. The shame has stayed put all these years. I have confessed all to my priest-confessor. But *never* that. So—"

There was a pause.

"*So*, Father?"

"Lord, Lord, dear man, God will forgive us. At long last, we have brought it out, dared to say. And I, I will forgive you. But finally—"

The old priest could not go on, for new tears were really pouring down his face now.

The stranger on the other side guessed this and very

forever: for all time, eternally
memory: sth that is remembered
him: not "it" (the dog is personified as "he")
since: since that time
ghost: the vision of the dog □ **beating:** act of beating
failure: what I did wrong by failing my dog's love
fell silent, fall silent, become silent (speechless)
dared a word: dared to say a word (took the risk of saying a word) □ the reason **why** you are here
awful: horrible, dreadful

unaccountably: inexplicably; to expl<u>ain</u>; expl<u>a</u>nation
short of breath: hardly able to breathe; short of (money...), without very much or enough of

forgive, forgave, forgiven; forgiveness, pardon
let me tell you: allow me to tell you
happened: took place, occurred
of course: naturally
I hated him <u>for</u> leaving me; hate ≠ love; hate (n), hatred
went back to love: loved him again
no one: nobody
stayed put: remained (unchanged)

pause: temporary silence or stop
so: then, consequently
Lord (Jesus) □ **at long last:** in the end, after a long time
brought it out: said it, revealed it (after much difficulty)

pouring down: running abundantly, streaming
stranger: sb you don't know □ **guessed:** knew by instinct

carefully inquired, "Do you want *my* forgiveness, Father?"

The priest nodded, silently. Perhaps the other felt the shadow of the nod, for he quickly said, "Ah, well. It's *given*."

And they both sat there for a long moment in the dark and another ghost moved to stand in the door, then sank to snow and drifted away.

"Before you go," said the priest. "Come share a glass of wine."

The great clock in the square across from the church struck midnight.

"It's Christmas, Father," said the voice from behind the panel.

"The finest Christmas ever, I think."

"The finest."

The old priest rose and stepped out.

He waited a moment for some stir, some movement from the opposite side of the confessional.

There was no sound.

Frowning, the priest reached out and opened the confessional door and peered into the cubicle.

There was nothing and no one there.

His jaw dropped. Snow moved along the back of his neck.

He put his hand out to feel the darkness.

The place was empty.

Turning, he stared at the entry door, and hurried over to look out.

Snow fell in the last tones of far clocks late-sounding the hour. The streets were deserted.

Turning again, he saw the tall mirror that stood in the

carefully: with great care, tact ☐ **inquired:** asked

nodded: bent his head in agreement (meaning "yes"); a nod
shadow: dark form (of a tree on the ground when the sun shines)
they both sat, both sat, both of them sat (the two of them)
moved: made a movement
sank to: was reduced to ☐ **drifted away:** disappeared, driven by the wind ☐ **come** (and) **share** (have...); share, divide and give out in shares; a share of cake
across from: opposite; across the street (on the other side)
struck midnight: struck 12 notes, 12 o'clock at night

the finest Christmas ever: the most beautiful Christmas I have ever had in my life
rose: got up; rise, rose, risen ☐ **stepped out:** walked out
stir: slight, not great (sound of) movement
opposite: (adj); in the opposite direction

frowning: *fronçant les sourcils* ☐ **reached out:** extended his hand
peered: looked very carefully ☐ **cubicle:** very small enclosed division of confessional...
his jaw dropped: (expression) he suddenly showed disappointment and surprise; jaw, bone structure containing the teeth
put his hand out: reached out

stared: looked fixedly ☐ **entry:** entrance ☐ **hurried:** rushed

tone(s): sound ☐ **far:** distant ☐ **late-sounding...:** the last ones to strike midnight; late ≠ early ☐ **deserted:** empty now
turning: no reflexive pronoun ☐ **tall:** large ≠ small, short

church entry.

There was an old man, himself, reflected in the cold glass.

Almost without thinking, he raised his hand and made the sign of blessing. The reflection in the mirror did likewise.

Then the old priest, wiping his eyes, turned a last time, and went to find the wine.

Outside, Christmas, like the snow, was everywhere.

entry; enter ∅ a room
reflected; reflection (of an image...)
glass: (here) mirror, looking-glass
raised: put up, lifted
blessing (asking God to bless or look kindly upon people)
did likewise: did the same (thing)
wiping (to remove or wipe the tears away)
find: (here) get, go and get, fetch
outside (in the streets) ≠ inside

Grammaire au fil des nouvelles

Voici, dans l'ordre de leur apparition dans le texte, des phrases à compléter (ou non !) selon les indications données. Les numéros de pages renvoient à la Grammaire active de l'anglais *(Le Livre de Poche, 1989).*

It was just before midnight, on Christmas Eve when Father Mellon woke, having slept for only ... minutes (*a little, a few, much, many,* les quantificateurs, p. 80).

"What's going on here?" he muttered quietly to ... (les pronoms refléchis, p. 124. Mettez cette phrase au pluriel).

Father Mellon leaned toward the lattice window and could not help ... *(speak)* (*I can't help* + ?, p. 150).

It ... be a terrible load of sin you carry (expression de la forte probabilité, de la quasi-certitude, p. 22).

"Then speak, son" said the priest, "before we ... freeze". (Complétez puis exprimez différemment la notion de "deux", p. 90.)

She wailed so, I knew I ... *(hurt)* her, ... made me feel strong and good (pluperfect, p. 34 — relatifs *what* et *which*, p. 134).

"Go on", said the priest, ashamed of ... *(interrupt)* him (prépositions suivies de ?, p. 148).

What ... gift! What ... gift! (*what* exclamatif, p. 66).

I have told no one. (Utilisez une autre tournure pour exprimer la même idée, *some, any, no,* p. 76.)

The old priest could not go on. (Utilisez le substitut du modal *can* dans cette phrase. Les auxiliaires modaux, leurs substituts ou équivalents, p. 22.)

The ... *(fine)* Christmas, ever, I think. Formez d'autres superlatifs à partir des adjectifs suivants :
the ... Christmas *(good)* — the ... Christmas *(beautiful)* the ... Christmas *(bad)*.

Almost without ... *(think)* he raised his hand (prépositions suivies de ?, p. 148).

Talking about the short story
HAIL AND FAREWELL
(p. 83)

H. Y. What about *Hail and Farewell*? That's a beautiful story!

R. B. Well again, it's a metaphor for a desire we all have. One of my daughters, when she was twenty years old, spoke the truth and said: "Oh, daddy, I miss being young." Even though she was young at twenty she missed being eight and ten, the innocence, the wonderful thing. She wanted to hold still in the stream of life and be like a rock that time washes around. That's natural for all of us. Many of us dream at night, don't we, about being back at school or in a special childhood place? It's all in color, all beautiful, all perfect... In *Hail and Farewell* you stay young because being ten or eight is an ideal age to be young for ever.

hail: welcoming cry
farewell: goodbye
spoke the truth: said something true (≠ false)
I miss being young: I wish I were young
hold still: stay still, without moving
stream: current, flow (of water...)
dream: see during sleep
childhood: time when one is a child

HAIL AND FAREWELL

I have written tales about the young man I was back in the early thirties, not wanting to grow up, like many another boy faced with the harsh realities of a world moving rapidly toward war and destruction, with strong desires to hide out somewhere until all the destruction and chaos moved away.

(Addition to the original Preface by
Ray Bradbury, August 1st 1993.)

tale(s): story
back (in the past...)
early thirties: 1931, 1932, 1933
grow up: develop, become taller
faced with (a difficulty, a danger...)
harsh: severe, cruel
toward: in the direction of
war ≠ peace
strong: great, powerful
hide : (in secret, so as to be invisible)

But of course he was going away, there was nothing else to do, the time was up, the clock had run out, and he was going very far away indeed. His suitcase was packed, his shoes were shined, his hair was brushed, he had expressly washed behind his ears, and it remained only for him to go down the stairs, out the front door, and up the street to the small-town station where the train would make a stop for him alone. Then Fox Hill, Illinois, would be left far off in his past. And he would go on, perhaps to Iowa, perhaps to Kansas, perhaps even to California; a small boy, twelve years old, with a birth certificate in his valise to show he had been born forty-three years ago.

"Willie!" called a voice belowstairs.

"Yes!" He hoisted his suitcase. In his bureau mirror he saw a face made of June dandelions and July apples and warm summer-morning milk. There, as always, was his look of the angel and the innocent, which might never, in the years of his life, change.

"Almost time," called the woman's voice.

"All right!" And he went down the stairs, grunting and smiling. In the living room sat Anna and Steve, their clothes painfully neat.

"Here I am!" cried Willie in the parlor door.

Anna looked like she was going to cry. "Oh, good Lord, you can't really be leaving us, can you, Willie?"

"People are beginning to talk," said Willie quietly. "I've been here three years now. But when people begin to talk, I know it's time to put on my shoes and buy a railway ticket."

"It's all so strange. I don't understand. It's so sudden," Anna said. "Willie, we'll miss you."

going away: leaving
... was up: it was time to go (= **the clock had run out)**
indeed: really ☐ **suitcase** (for carrying clothes... in)
packed (full) ☐ **shined** with polish (made bright, shining)
it remained... for him: the only thing he had to do now
stairs (to go up and down in house) ☐ **front:** façade ≠ back (railway) **station**
make a stop: stop ☐ **for him alone:** just, only for him
Illinois: state in the U.S. ☐ **left** (behind) **far off:** far away ☐ **go on** (his way), continue (travelling to **Iowa, Kansas:** states in the U.S.)
birth: act or time of coming into the world, of being **born:** Ray Bradbury was born on August 22nd 1920 in Waukegan, Illinois
call(ed): cause to come by speaking loudly
hoisted: took up ☐ **bureau:** (Am) chest of drawers *(commode)*
dandelion(s): small wild bright-yellow flower; see R.B.'s novel, *Dandelion Wine*, about his childhood ☐ **summer** (season)
look: expression (in the eyes) ☐ **angel:** divine messenger, (fig) kind or innocent person
time (to go, to leave)
all right: O.K. ☐ **grunting** (like a pig) with discontent
smiling: with a smile (happy expression) on his face
painfully ≠ joyfully ☐ **neat:** impeccable, in good order
parlo(u)r: sitting-room
looked like...: looked as if she was... ☐ **cry:** let eyes fill with tears, weep ☐ **Lord** (Jesus)! Oh my God!
beginning (starting) **to talk** (about me) ☐ **quietly:** calmly

put on (≠ take off) (shoes, clothes) ☐ **buy,** bought, bought

sudden: unexpected ☐ **miss you:** regret your absence

"I'll write you every Christmas, so help me. Don't you write me."

"It's been a great pleasure and satisfaction," said Steve, sitting there, his words the wrong size in his mouth. "It's a shame it had to stop. It's a shame you had to tell us about yourself. It's an awful shame you can't stay on."

"You're the nicest folks I ever had," said Willie, four feet high, in no need of a shave, the sunlight on his face.

And then Anna *did* cry. "Willie, Willie." And she sat down and looked as if she wanted to hold him but was afraid to hold him now; she looked at him with shock and amazement and her hands empty, not knowing what to do with him now.

"It's not easy to go," said Willie. "You get used to things. You want to stay. But it doesn't work. I tried to stay on once after people began to suspect. 'How horrible!' people said. 'All these years, playing with our innocent children,' they said, 'and us not guessing! Awful!' they said. And finally I had to just leave town one night. It's not easy. You know darned well how much I love both of you. Thanks for three swell years."

They all went to the front door. "Willie, where're you going?"

"I don't know. I just start traveling. When I see a town that looks green and nice, I settle in."

"Will you ever come back?"

"Yes," he said earnestly with his high voice. "In about twenty years it should begin to show in my face. When it does, I'm going to make a grand tour of all the mothers and fathers I've ever had."

They stood on the cool summer porch, reluctant to

I'll write (to) **you** □ **so:** in consequence □ **don't you write me:** please don't write to me
pleasure: joy, delight
the wrong size (dimensions)...: unable to find the right words
it's a shame: it's a pity
awful: terrible; awfully sad (fam), very sad
stay on: continue staying
folk(s): people; parents (94, 29) □ **four feet** (91,44 cm) **high** (tall) □ **... shave** (needing no razor)
did cry (in fact)
hold him (in her arms, embrace him)

amazement: great surprise

get used to: get accustomed to
it doesn't work (in practice), it's impossible
once: on one occasion

guessing: getting to know, conjecturing rightly

darned (damned) **well:** (fam) perfectly well
both of you or you both □ **swell:** (Am, fam) wonderful, great
front door ≠ back door

traveling: (Am) travelling (by train, by car...)
Waukegan is called **Green Town** in *Dandelion Wine* (84, 17) □
settle in: stop and live there □ **ever** (not "never"!)
earnest(ly): serious and determined □ **high** ≠ deep, low
show: be visible
when it does: present after "when"!

porch: (Am) veranda □ **reluctant to** ≠ ready to, willing to

say the last words. Steve was looking steadily at an elm tree. "How many others folks've you stayed with, Willie? How many adoptions?"

Willie figured it, pleasantly enough. "I guess it's about five towns and five couples and over twenty years gone by since I started my tour."

"Well, we can't holler," said Steve. "Better to've had a son thirty-six months than none whatever."

"Well," said Willie, and kissed Anna quickly, seized at his luggage, and was gone up the street in the green noon light, under the trees, a very young boy indeed, not looking back, running steadily.

The boys were playing on the green park diamond when he came by. He stood a little while among the oak-tree shadows, watching them hurl the white, snowy baseball into the warm summer air, saw the baseball shadow fly like a dark bird over the grass, saw their hands open like mouths to catch this swift piece of summer that now seemed most especially important to hold on to. The boys' voices yelled. The ball lit on the grass near Willie.

Carrying the ball forward from under the shade trees, he thought of the last three years now spent to the penny, and the five years before that, and so on down the line to the year when he was really eleven and twelve and fourteen and the voices saying: "What's wrong with Willie, missus?" "Mrs. B., is Willie late a-growin'?" "Willie, you smokin' *cigars* lately?" The echoes died in summer light and color. His mother's voice: "Willie's twenty-one today!" And a thousand voices saying: "Come back, son, when you're fifteen; *then* maybe we'll

steadily: (here) fixedly □ **elm**(tree): *orme*

figured: calculated □ **I guess:** (Am) I think
over: more than □ **gone by:** passed

holler: cry out in pain □ (it's) **better to** (ha)**'ve had...**
(for) **thirty-six months** □ **none whatever:** no son at all

luggage: baggage □ **was gone:** had disappeared, vanished
noon: midday (12 o'clock)
looking back: looking behind □ **steadily:** constantly

diamond: baseball playing field
a while: a time □ **among** (<u>many</u> things), between (<u>two</u> things)
oak: *chêne* □ **shadows:** darkness □ **hurl:** throw with force
snowy (white)
shadow: dark shape (form) □ **fly** (in the air), flew, flown
open: no reflexive pronoun! □ **swift:** quick, rapid, fast

hold on to: keep, retain □ **yelled:** shouted □ **lit:** came down from the air on to the grass; (a)light, alighted, or alit
forward: towards front □ **shade:** darkness, shadow
thought of: notice the preposition
to the penny: completely □ **and so on:** and other years like that
down the line to: as far back in time as
what's wrong with...: what's his problem? is he ill?
missus: (fam) madam □ **late** ≠ early □ **(a-)growing:** getting taller
(have) **you** (been) **smoking** □ **lately:** recently □ **died:** ceased
col<u>o</u>r: (Am) col<u>ou</u>r
a thousand: 1.000, (here) a great number of
son: used here as a form of address □ **maybe:** perhaps

give you a job."

He stared at the baseball in his trembling hand, as if it were his life, an interminable ball of years strung around and around and around, but always leading back to his twelfth birthday. He heard the kids walking toward him; he felt them blot out the sun, and they were older, standing around him.

"Willie! Where you goin'?" They kicked his suitcase.

How tall they stood to the sun. In the last few months it seemed the sun had passed a hand above their heads, beckoned, and they were warm metal drawn melting upward; they were golden taffy pulled by an immense gravity to the sky, thirteen, fourteen years old, looking down upon Willie, smiling, but already beginning to neglect him. It had started four months ago:

"Choose up sides! Who wants Willie?"

"Aw, Willie's too little; we don't play with 'kids.'"

And they raced ahead of him, drawn by the moon and the sun and the turning seasons of leaf and wind, and he was twelve years old and not of them any more. And the other voices beginning again on the old, the dreadfully familiar, the cool refrain: "Better feed that boy vitamins, Steve." "Anna, does shortness *run* in your family?" And the cold fist kneading at your heart again and knowing that the roots would have to be pulled up again after so many good years with the "folks."

"Willie, where you goin'?"

He jerked his head. He was back among the towering, shadowing boys who milled around him like giants at a drinking fountain bending down.

"Goin' a few days visitin' a cousin of mine."

"Oh." There was a day, a year ago, when they would

a job: sth to do, some work
stared at: looked fixedly at
as if it were (subjunctive) □ **strung:** put together (as if making up a ball) □ **leading back to:** going back to
kid(s): child (children)
toward(s) him: in his direction □ **blot out:** hide, obliterate (being so much taller than Willie: 9, 13, 14, 28, 29)
where (are) **you going?** □ **kicked** (with their feet); kick a ball
tall ≠ short (23) □ **to the sun:** standing out against...
it seemed (that) **the sun...** □ **above:** over (≠ under)
beckoned: made signal □ **drawn upward melting:** pulled to the sky, turning into liquid □ **taffy:** (Am) toffee
looking down upon... (being so much taller than Willie); look down upon sb (with disdain)

choose up sides: let us make up the teams (in sports)
aw expresses disdain □ **little:** small
raced: ran □ **ahead of:** in front of □ **drawn:** attracted
leaf (of a tree) (pl. leaves) □ **wind:** movement of air
not of them any more: not one of them any longer, cut off from them, a "loner" (see interview, p. 20, 32)
dreadfully: horribly □ **cool** ≠ warm (feeling) □ **better feed:** you had better give food □ **... run:** is... a characteristic
fist: firmly closed hand □ **kneading at:** pressing on
pull up one's roots: move to a new place from one's home
good years: "swell years" (86.22)
where (are) **you going?**
jerked: suddenly moved □ **towering:** very tall ("giants", 29)
shadowing: blotting out the sun (6) □ **milled:** moved about in a confused way, in large numbers □ **drinking fountain** (in a public place) □ **bending down** ≠ standing erect □ **goin'** (going), **visitin'** (visiting); visit sb, pay a visit to sb

have cared very much indeed. But now there was only curiosity for his luggage, their enchantment with trains and trips and far places.

"How about a coupla fast ones?" said Willie.

They looked doubtful, but, considering the circumstances, nodded. He dropped his bag and ran out; the white baseball was up in the sun, away to their burning white figures in the far meadow, up in the sun again, rushing, life coming and going in a pattern. Here, *there*! Mr. and Mrs. Robert Hanlon, Creek Bend, Wisconsin, 1932, the first couple, the first year! Here, there! Henry and Alice Boltz, Limeville, Iowa, 1935! The baseball flying. The Smiths, the Eatons, the Robinsons! 1939! 1945! Husband and wife, husband and wife, husband and wife, no children, no children, no children! A knock on this door, a knock on that.

"Pardon me. My name is William. I wonder if—"

"A sandwich? Come in, sit down. Where you *from*, son?"

The sandwich, a tall glass of cold milk, the smiling, the nodding, the comfortable, leisurely talking.

"Son, you look like you been traveling. You run *off* from somewhere?"

"No."

"Boy, are you an orphan?"

Another glass of milk.

"We always wanted kids. It never worked out. Never knew why. One of those things. Well, well. It's getting late, son. Don't you think you better hit for home?"

"Got no home."

"A boy like you? Not dry behind the ears? Your mother'll be worried."

have cared (about it) ≠ been indifferent (to it)

trip(s): journey (travelling) ☐ **far:** (adj) distant
how (what) **about...?** (suggestion) ☐ **coupla:** couple of, a few
doubtful: unsure, uncertain; doubt ☐ **considering:** given
nodded (meaning "yes" with head) ☐ **dropped:** let fall ☐ **ran out** to the field ☐ **burning** (hot), as if on fire
figure(s): form (of body) ☐ **meadow:** green grassland
rushing: running very quickly ☐ **pattern:** particular way in which sth is done or organized ☐ **Wisconsin:** a state in the U.S.
the first couple: Willie's first "folks"

the Smiths, the Eatons, the Robinsons (notice the s)
husband and wife: also "man and wife"
a knock; to knock; you knock on the door before entering somebody else's house
pardon me: forgive me, excuse me ☐ **wonder:** ask myself
where (are) **you from?**
son (addressing a boy, showing kindness or affection)
tall: big ☐ (the fact of) **smiling** (happy expression on face)
nodding (in approval) ☐ **comfortable, leisurely:** pleasantly relaxed, unhurried ☐ **like** (as if) **you** (had) **been** ☐ **you run off:** have you run off (away, suddenly and secretly)

(oh) **boy:** interjection expressing excitement ☐ **orphan:** child who has lost one or both of his parents by death
kid(s): child(ren) ☐ **it never worked out:** it was never possible
getting late: get + adj = become; late ≠ early
you (had) **better** ☐ **hit for home:** go home; hit the road (fam): start on a journey ☐ (I have) **got no home**
not dry (with dirt) **behind the ears:** with clean ears
worried: anxious; worry, get worried

"Got no home and no folks anywhere in the world. I wonder if—I wonder—could I sleep here tonight?"

"Well, now, son, I don't just *know*. We never considered taking in—" said the husband.

"We got chicken for supper tonight," said the wife, "enough for extras, enough for company..."

And the years turning and flying away, the voices, and the faces, and the people, and always the same first conversations. The voice of Emily Robinson, in her rocking chair, in summer-night darkness, the last night he stayed with her, the night she discovered his secret, her voice saying:

"I look at all the little children's faces going by. And I sometimes think, What a shame, what a shame, that all these flowers have to be cut, all these bright fires have to be put out. What a shame these, all of these you see in schools or running by, have to get tall and unsightly and wrinkle and turn gray or get bald, and finally, all bone and wheeze, be dead and buried off away. When I hear them laugh I can't believe they'll ever go the road I'm going. Yet here they *come*! I still remember Wordsworth's poem: 'When all at once I saw a crowd, A host of golden daffodils; Beside the lake, beneath the trees, Fluttering and dancing in the breeze.' That's how I think of children, cruel as they sometimes are, mean as I know they can be, but not yet showing the meanness around their eyes or *in* their eyes, not yet full of tiredness. They're so eager for everything! I guess that's what I miss most in older folks, the eagerness gone nine times out of ten, the freshness gone, so much of the drive and life down the drain. I like to watch school let out each day. It's like someone threw a bunch of flowers out the

sleep, slept, slept; get some sleep
now: let me see
considered: thought about □ **taking in:** receiving, lodging
got: (Am) (present) have □ **chicken:** meat of young hen or cock
extra(s): more (people...) than usual or than expected here
turning and flying...: passing by quickly one after the other

rocking chair: rock, move backwards and forwards □ **darkness:** dark (n) ≠ light

going by: passing by, going past
what a shame: what a pity
cut, cut, **cut** □ **bright fires:** with big flames shining bright
put out: extinguished, stopped burning
get tall: grow up □ **unsightly:** unattractive, ugly
wrinkle: get wrinkles (lines on face) □ **bald:** hairless
bone (of skeleton) □ **wheeze:** hissing respiration □ **buried** (in the ground) □ **go the road...:** (fig) become like me
(but) **yet** □ **Wordsworth:** English Romantic poet (1770-1850)
all at once: suddenly □ **crowd, host:** very large number
daffodil(s): jonquil □ **beside:** near □ **beneath:** under
fluttering (from side to side in small quick movements)
mean: unkind to sb by hurting their feelings; mea<u>nn</u>ess

tiredness (fig); tired (of), no longer interested (in)
eager for ≠ tired of □ **I guess:** (Am) I think
miss: regret the absence of □ **eagerness (enthusiasm) gone** (vanished) **nine times** <u>**out of**</u> **ten** (most of the time) □ **drive:** energy □ **... drain:** lost □ **let** (children get) **out,** liberate
like: as if □ **bunch** of flowers, carrots... □ **out** (of)...

school front doors. How does it feel, Willie? How does it feel to be young forever? To look like a silver dime new from the mint? Are you happy? Are you as fine as you *seem*?"

The baseball whizzed from the blue sky, stung his hand like a great pale insect. Nursing it, he heard his memory say:

"I worked with what I had. After my folks died, after I found I couldn't get man's work anywhere, I tried carnivals, but they only laughed. 'Son,' they said, 'you're not a midget, and even if you are, you look like a *boy*! We want midgets with midgets' *faces*! Sorry, son, sorry.' So I left home, started out, thinking: What *was* I? A boy. I looked like a boy, sounded like a boy, so I might as well go on being a boy. No use fighting it. No use screaming. So what could I do? What job was handy? And then one day I saw this man in a restaurant looking at another man's pictures of his children. 'Sure wish I had kids,' he said. 'Sure wish I had kids.' He kept shaking his head. And me sitting a few seats away from him, a hamburger in my hands. I sat there, *frozen*! At that very instant I knew what my job would be for all of the rest of my life. There *was* work for me, after all. Making lonely people happy. Keeping myself busy. Playing forever. I knew I had to play forever. Deliver a few papers, run a few errands, mow a few lawns, maybe. But *hard* work? No. All I had to do was be a mother's son and a father's pride. I turned to the man down the counter from me. 'I beg your pardon,' I said. I *smiled* at him..."

"But, Willie," said Mrs. Emily long ago, "didn't you

how does it feel?: what impression does it give you?
forever: eternally □ **silver dime** (10 cents): coin made of white precious metal (at the **mint**) □ **fine:** well, healthy, okay
seem: look

whizzed: moved very fast with a whiz (sound) □ **stung:** hurt, pricked □ **nursing:** holding carefully, lovingly

died; die (→ be dead); dying; death ≠ life
tried; to try
carnival(s): travelling entreprise offering amusements (a bit like a circus but much smaller) □ **midget:** very short person (≠ giant)
started out (from place to place, travelling)
looked like (in appearance), **sounded** like (had the same voice)
go on: continue □ **use:** advantage; no use **fighting it** (doing anything against it) □ **screaming:** crying □ **handy:** possible for me to do □ **one day:** not "a" in this case!
picture(s): photo(graph) □ **(I) sure:** (Am) surely, certainly
kept shaking... (all the time, expressing his regret)
seat(s) (like a chair, an armchair)
frozen: (fig) unable to move, speak...; freeze, froze, frozen
at that very instant: then, exactly □ **knew:** realized
after all: in spite of everything
lonely: unhappy because of being alone (without children)
deliver: take to sb's house; a postman delivers letters
(news) **paper(s)** □ **run errands:** do jobs for sb □ **mow lawns:** cut grass (in people's gardens) □ **hard:** difficult
pride: feeling of satisfaction; he is proud of his son
counter (at which people are served) □ **I beg your pardon,** pardon me (polite): please excuse me

ever get lonely? Didn't you ever want—*things*—that grownups wanted?"

"I fought that out alone," said Willie. "I'm a boy, I told myself, I'll have to live in a boy's world, read boys' books, play boys' games, cut myself off from everything else. I can't be both. I got to be only one thing—young. And so I played that way. Oh, it wasn't easy. There were times—" He lapsed into silence.

"And the family you lived with, they never knew?"

"No. Telling them would have spoiled everything. I told them I was a runaway; I let them check through official channels, police. Then, when there was no record, let them put in to adopt me. That was best of all; as long as they never guessed. But then, after three years, or five years, they guessed, or a traveling man came through, or a carnival man saw me, and it was over. It always had to end."

"And you're *very* happy and it's *nice* being a child for over forty years?"

"It's a living, as they say. And when you make other people happy, then you're almost happy too. I got my job to do and I do it. And anyway, in a few years now I'll be in my second childhood. All the fevers will be out of me and all the unfulfilled things and most of the dreams. Then I can relax, maybe, and play the role all the way."

He threw the baseball one last time and broke the reverie. Then he was running to seize his luggage. Tom, Bill, Jamie, Bob, Sam—their names moved on his lips. They were embarrassed at his shaking hands.

"After all, Willie, it ain't as if you're going to China or Timbuktu."

get or **grow** + adj = become
grownup(s): adult (n); adulthood (time when you are an...)
I fought that out: solved (by fighting mentally, with much effort)
cut myself off: accept to be isolated from
both (a child and an adult) □ **I got to be:** (Am) I have to be
I played that way: I acted in that manner
time(s): occasion, circumstance □ **lapsed into silence:** became silent
(the fact of) **telling** □ **spoiled** (or spoilt): ruined
runaway: child who has left home □ **check:** verify
channel(s): any course or way along which information travels
record: official document □ **put in:** put their names in a list
as long as: on condition that
traveling man: commercial travel(l)er
came through (the town) □ **carnival man:** see 96.11
over: finished, ended □ **to end:** to come to an end

over: more than
a living: way of life; means of subsistance □ **they:** people in general □ **I got:** (Am., present) I have
anyway: in any case, at any rate
childhood: time when you are a child □ **fever(s):** intense emotion or activity □ **out...:** gone □ **unfulfilled:** unaccomplished
dream(s): sth that you think is wonderful
all the way: completely, fully, from beginning to end
(just) **one** (not two) □ **broke:** interrupted
seize: grab, get hold of
the two red **lips** of the mouth
embarrassed: ill-at-ease, uncomfortable □ **shaking:** trembling
it ain't: (non standard English) it is not
Timbuktu or Timbuctoo (in Mali, formerly French Sudan)

"That's right, isn't it?" Willie did not move.

"So long, Willie. See you next week!"

"So long, so long!"

And he was walking off with his suitcase again, looking at the trees, going away from the boys and the street where he had lived, and as he turned the corner a train whistle screamed, and he began to run.

The last thing he saw and heard was a white ball tossed at a high roof, back and forth, back and forth, and two voices crying out as the ball pitched now up, down, and back through the sky, "Annie, Annie, over! Annie, Annie, over!" like the crying of birds flying off to the far south.

In the early morning, with the smell of the mist and the cold metal, with the iron smell of the train around him and a full night of traveling shaking his bones and his body, and a smell of the sun beyond the horizon, he awoke and looked out upon a small town just arising from sleep. Lights were coming on, soft voices muttered, a red signal bobbed back and forth, back and forth in the cold air. There was that sleeping hush in which echoes are dignified by clarity, in which echoes stand nakedly alone and sharp. A porter moved by, a shadow in shadows.

"Sir," said Willie.

The porter stopped.

"What town's this?" whispered the boy in the dark.

"Valleyville."

"How many people?"

"Ten thousand. Why? This your stop?"

"It looks green." Willie gazed out at the cold morning

that's right (correct, true ≠ wrong) ☐ **move** ≠ stay still
so long: goodbye for now ☐ (I'll) **see you next week** (goodbye till next week)
walking off: going away

(street) **corner**
whistle: high sound made by passing steam (from locomotive)
last ≠ first ☐ see, **saw,** seen ☐ hear, **heard,** heard
tossed: thrown ☐ **back** (backwards) **and forth** (forwards)
pitched: was thrown, sent

flying: fly, flew, flown (birds, planes...)

in the early...: towards the beginning of... ☐ **mist** is less dense than fog ☐ **iron:** the most common metal ☐ **smell:** odour
full: entire, complete ☐ **shaking...:** making... tremble
beyond: farther than (far, farther, the farthest)
awoke: stopped sleeping ☐ **(a)rising:** awaking
coming on: beginning to appear ☐ **soft** ≠ loud ☐ **muttered:** murmured ☐ **bobbed:** moved quickly and repeatedly
hush (≠ noise, excitement): silence, peace
dignified: made impressive by **clarity** (being so clear)
nakedly: (here) completely ☐ **sharp:** very distinct ☐ **porter:** (Am) attendant employed in a sleeping-carriage in a train; person employed to carry travellers' luggage at railway-stations

in the dark(ness) (≠ light)

how many people (inhabitants) (are there in it?)
(is) **this your stop** (where you get off the train)
gazed: looked for a long time (in wonder or admiration)

town for a long time. "It looks nice and quiet," said Willie.

"Son," said the porter, "you know where you *going*?"

"Here," said Willie, and got up quietly in the still, cool, iron-smelling morning, in the train dark, with a rustling and stir.

"I hope you know what you're doing, boy," said the porter.

"Yes, sir," said Willie. "I know what I'm doing." And he was down the dark aisle, luggage lifted after him by the porter, and out in the smoking, steaming-cold, beginning-to-lighten morning. He stood looking up at the porter and the black metal train against the few remaining stars. The train gave a great wailing blast of whistle, the porters cried out all along the line, the cars jolted, and his special porter waved and smiled down at the boy there, the small boy there with the big luggage who shouted up to him, even as the whistle screamed again.

"What?" shouted the porter, hand cupped to ear.

"Wish me luck!" cried Willie.

"Best of luck, son," called the porter, waving, smiling. "Best of luck, boy!"

"Thanks!" said Willie, in the great sound of the train, in the steam and roar.

He watched the black train until it was completely gone away and out of sight. He did not move all the time it was going. He stood quietly, a small boy twelve years old, on the worn wooden platform, and only after three entire minutes did he turn at last to face the empty streets below.

Then, as the sun was rising, he began to walk very fast, so as to keep warm, down into the new town.

looks: seems to be □ **nice:** attractive □ **quiet** ≠ noisy
where you (are) **going**
got up: rose □ **quietly:** calmly □ **still:** quiet, tranquil
cool: neither warm nor cold, pleasantly cold □ **dark**(ness)
rustling: small sound (as of dry leaves) □ **stir:** movement

(walking) **down** □ **aisle:** passage between seats □ **lifted:** picked up (and carried)
(the morning beginning to) **lighten:** become brighter, less dark
the... train (standing out) **against,** silhouetted against
remaining: still visible □ **wailing:** plaintive □ **blast:** explosing; blast (of air, steam, wind) □ (railway) **line** □ **car(s):** (Am) carriage □ **jolted:** moved suddenly, violently □ **waved** (him goodbye with his hand)
even as: exactly at the same time as

hand cupped to ear: with his hand round his ear (in the shape of a cup) □ (good ≠ bad, hard) **luck:** good (≠ ill) fortune

best of luck: I wish you all the very best in life; lucky

roar: loud continuing sound (as of an angry lion)
until: one l!; till (with two l!)
out of sight: no longer visible; love at first sight

worn: damaged (old) □ **wooden:** made of wood □ **platform** (on which passengers wait for trains) □ **entire:** full □ **face** (a difficulty with courage) □ **below:** at a lower level
rise; rise, rose, risen: sunrise (in the morning) ≠ sunset
so as to: in order to, to

Grammaire au fil des nouvelles

Voici, dans l'ordre de leur apparition dans le texte, des phrases à compléter (ou non !) selon les indications données. Les numéros de pages renvoient à la Grammaire active de l'anglais *(Le Livre de Poche, 1989).*

His suitcase ... *(pack)*, his shoes ... *(shine)*, his hair ... *(brush)* (passif, p. 50 + prétérit, p. 32-36).

There, as always, was his look of the angel and the innocent, which ... never, in the years of his life, change (modal exprimant une probabilité réduite, p. 22).

And then Anna ... cry (forme emphatique ou d'insistance, p. 18 ; prétérit, p. 32-36).

And finally I ... leave town one night (substitut de *must*, obligation passée, p. 22).

You know darned well how much I love ... you (différentes manières d'exprimer la notion de "deux", p. 90).

In about twenty years it should begin to show in my face. When it... *(do)*, I'm going to make a grand tour of all the mothers and fathers I ... *(have)* (*when* + ...?, p. 38 — present perfect, p. 32).

The boys ... *(voices)* yelled (génitif, p. 98).

... tall they stood in the sun! (forme exclamative, p. 146).

What ... shame, what ... shame, that all these flowers have to be cut (*what* exclamatif, p. 66).

Boy, are you ... orphan? (emploi ou non de l'article *a*, p. 66).

I look at all the little children... faces (le génitif, p. 98).

Are you ... fine ... you seem? (comparatif d'égalité, p. 114).

I worked with ... I had (les relatifs *what* et *which*, p. 134).

I ... live in a boy's world (substitut de *must* au futur, p. 22).

ST CIRCUS

Talking about the short story *The Last Circus* (p. 110)

H. Y. ...And what about your love of circuses?

R. B. Well, part of it is love and part of it is terror. When I was about four my mother took me on a carousel. It scared the hell out of me. I wanted to get off and I couldn't. So we went around, around with these damned horses and I suppose that marked me, so that, later, when I wrote *Something Wicked this Way Comes* a lot of the evil side of the circus, the terrifying side came out... Clowns have always been terrifying to me. I still don't like them and I think a lot of kids feel the same way, that they're not funny. Some of the things they do are funny but, that face! Behind that face, there's a stranger, something terrible. Your father puts on make up, puts on a red nose and it's not papa any more. Kids are afraid of that. Or... Halloween... Your father puts on a mask and makes a gesture like that *(gesture)*. Forget it, don't ever do that, because it's hard enough to identify with a real person behind the real face without that additional thing. So, circuses... Part of it is the romance of early morning... when Ringling Brothers, Barnum and Bailey Circus used to come to my home-town when I was thirteen years old. I'd get up at five and run with my brother down to the railroad station. They had a hundred cars and they'd have fifty to a

part of it: notice the absence of the article
about four: four or so (approximately, roughly)
carousel: (Am) merry-go-round *(manège)* □ **scared the hell out of me:** (fam) made me terribly afraid
damned (indicates disapproval) □ **marked:** left a mark on
Something Wicked This Way Comes, a novel (Grafton Books)
evil: very bad, wicked (bringing trouble) □ **side:** aspect
still: indicates continuation
kid(s): child □ **feel the same way:** react like me; in the same way (manner) □ **funny:** amusing

stranger: sb who is unfamiliar □ **put on make-up** (on his face) (powder, cream) □ **papa,** pop (Am), dad, daddy
Halloween: Octobre 31 (people wearing false faces...)
makes a gesture: make a gesture (not do!)
don't ever do that: never do that □ **hard:** difficult
identify with...: establish the identity (psychological...) of and feel at home with □ **additional thing** (make-up, mask...)
romance: feeling of excitement and adventure, of wonder
used to come: came every year... (but will not any more)
hometown: where I was born and grew up □ **five** is "early morning" □ **railroad station:** (Am) railway station
car(s): (Am) railway carriage

hundred elephants and forty lions and forty tigers and a hundred zebras. It was the biggest circus in the world. I'd follow the animals. I'd walk with them up to the town at dawn to this big meadow that was empty. And then those big mushroom tents would blossom. I'd help put up the tents, coiling the ropes. I'd carry the soda-pop bottles to earn a ticket to see the show later in the day... That is pure magic. You don't have anything like it today. Very few circuses travel the same way. Most of them arrive by truck. There's no railroad station..., there's no romance... So, that all goes into my short stories later like *The Last Circus, The Veldt*.

the biggest circus in the world: notice the preposition
follow: go, walk after □ **up to:** as far as
dawn: first light of day □ **meadow:** area of grassland
mushroom(s): poisonous or edible plant that **blooms** (grows and develops) very quickly □ **coil(ing) the rope(s)** (strong thick cord): dispose in concentric rings □ **earn:** get by working; earn money, a living □ **magic:** (n) enchantment
travel (from place to place) □ (in) **the same way** (manner) □ **most of:** the majority of □ **truck:** (Am) lorry, large vehicle for transporting things

THE LAST CIRCUS

I have conjured up pictures of a child growing up with and loving carnivals and circuses — unconscious metaphors for life and the collision of this joyful entertainment with the terrible reality of the atom bomb in the mid-forties.

(Addition to the original Preface by Ray Bradbury, August 1st 1993.)

There were moments of fear at that time when scientists admitted that they were not at all certain that once a chain-reaction began at atomic levels. This nightmare lies at the heart of *The Last Circus*. We are all thankful that the scientists' fears were not realized (Ray Bradbury).

"*The Last Circus* is a story by Ray Bradbury that I discovered in his files. I showed it to him. He did some rewriting and it was published in 1980." (Letter dated June 13th 1993, from Donn Albright, R.B.'s bibliographer (see p. 10) to whom a superb edition is dedicated (Lord John Press, Northridge, California, introduction by William F. Nolan (reproduced here), illustration by Joe Mugnaini (42. 3 to 9).

"... *The Last Circus* is an elegiac tale of sad warmth and nostalgia, a celebration of the rite of passage from childhood to adulthood. The boy in this story feels that he has seen the last circus. In actual fact, Bradbury's family moved away from Waukegan in 1934, when he was thirteen, leaving the summer big-tent shows behind forever." (William F. Nolan. Introduction to *The Last Circus and The Electrocution*. Lord John Press, Northridge, California 1980.)

conjure(d) up: cause to appear to mind □ **growing up:** developing, becoming taller □ **carnival(s):** (Am) travelling enterprise offering amusement, sth like a small circus □ **entertainment:** show (for amusement) □ **mid-forties:** 1944-1945-1946 mid(dle)

fear: apprehension
once: from the moment that
began: started □ **level(s):** degree, standard □ **nightmare:** bad dream □ **heart:** centre, core □ **thankful:** full of gratitude

files: papers (kept away)

tale: story □ **warmth; warm:** showing affectionate disposition
childhood: time when one is a child
actual: real
moved away (to go and live in Los Angeles)

Red Tongue Jurgis (we called him that because he ate candy red-hots all the time) stood under my window one cold October morning and yelled at the metal weathercock on top of our house. I put my head out the window and blew steam. "Hi, Red Tongue!"

"Jiggers!" he said. "Come on! The circus!"

Three minutes later I ran out of the house polishing two apples on my knee. Red Tongue was dancing to keep warm. We agreed that the last one to reach the train yard was a damnfool old man.

Eating apples, we ran through the silent town.

We stood by the rails in the dark train yard and listened to them humming. Far away in the cold dark morning country, we knew, the circus was coming. The sound of it was in the rails, trembling. I put my ear down to hear it traveling. "Gosh," I said.

And then, there was the locomotive charging on us with fire and light and a sound like a black storm, clouds following it. Out of boxcars red and green lanterns swung and in the boxcars were snorts and screams and yells. Elephants stepped down and cages rolled and everything mixed around until, in the first light, the animals and men were marching, Red Tongue and I with them, through the town, out to the meadowlands where every grass blade was a white crystal and every bush rained if you touched it.

"Just think, RT," I said. "One minute there's nothing there but land. And *now* look at it."

We looked. The big tent bloomed out like one of those Japanese flowers in cold water. Lights flashed on. In half an hour there were pancakes frying somewhere and people laughing.

tongue: movable organ in the mouth, used in talking...
candy red-hot(s): small red candy; candy (Am), sweet
yelled: cried out, shouted □ a **weather-cock** on a roof (top of a house) turns with the wind, showing its direction □ **out** (of)
blew steam: gave out vapour when speaking
Jiggers suggests a boy who moves with quick movements
polishing...: rubbing, making them shine; shoe polish
knee: articulation between leg and foot
last ≠ first □ **reach:** get to, arrive at
train yard: (Am) goods yard: *dépôt, cour des marchandises* □
damnfool...: very stupid old man
by: near, close to, beside □ **dark:** without light
humming: making a continuous sound (that of the train on the rails)

traveling: (Am) travelling: (fam) moving quickly □ **gosh:** (fam) (an expression of surprise) □ **charging on us** (as if in an attack)
storm: violent weather (thunder and lightning)
following: coming after □ **boxcars** (Am) carry goods not people
swung: moved to and fro □ **snort(s):** noise made by animals taking in air □ **scream(s):** piercing cry □ **stepped down:** walked down; a step □ **mixed around** (in a state of disorder)
light (of day) □ **marching:** (in good order, like soldiers)

meadowland(s): grassland (for animals) □ **blade:** piece of grass
bush: small low tree □ **rained** (as if rain fell from it)
one minute...: just one minute before there was...
but: except
bloomed out: opened like a flower
flashed on: were suddenly on; a flash of lightening
pancake: thin, flat, round cake often eaten hot □ **frying:** cooking in oil or fat; a frying pan

We stood looking at everything. I put my hand on my chest and felt my heart thumping my fingers like those trick shop palpitators you buy for two bits. All I wanted to do was look and smell.

"Home for breakfast!" cried RT and knocked me down so he got a head start running.

"Tuck your tongue in and wash your face," said Mom, looking up from her kitchen stove.

"Pancakes!" I said, amazed at her intuition.

"How was the circus?" Father lowered his newspaper and looked over it at me.

"Swell," I said. "Boy!"

I washed my face in cold tap water and scraped my chair out just as Mom set the pancakes down. She handed me the syrup jug. "Float them," she said.

While I was chewing, Father adjusted the paper in his hands and sighed. "I don't know what it's coming to."

"You shouldn't read the paper in the morning," Mom said. "It ruins your digestion."

"Look at this," cried Father, flicking the paper with his finger. "Germ warfare, atom bomb, hydrogen bomb. That's *all* you read!"

"Personally," said Mother, "I've a big washing this week."

Father frowned. "That's what's wrong with the world; people on a powder keg doing their wash." He sat up and leaned forward. "Why it says here this morning, they've got a new atom bomb that would wipe Chicago clean off the map. And as for our town—nothing left but a smudge. The thing I keep thinking is it's a darn shame."

"What?" I asked.

chest: upper front part of body □ **thumping:** beating heavily
trick: *farce, attrape* □ **palpitator:** *soulève-assiette* □ **for two** (penny) **bits:** for nothing
knocked me down: made me fall (by knocking me)
so (that) □ **got a head** (in advance when we **started running**)
tuck... in ≠ pull out
Mom, Mum(my) □ **kitchen stove:** apparatus used for cooking
amazed at: greatly surprised at, astonished at
lowered: moved or let down; low ≠ high
over (his newspaper)
swell: (Am) fantastic □ (oh) **boy!** (expressing excitement)
a **tap** controls the flow of water □ **scraped... out** (from under the table, making a noise) □ **set... down** (on the table)
handed: passed □ **jug:** pot □ **float:** (here) put much syrup on
chewing: masticating; chewing gum
sighed: (in distress): let out air slowly with a sound □ **what it's coming to:** what is going to happen in the end

flicking: striking, hitting with the tip (end) of his finger
germ warfare: biological warfare; war ≠ peace

a big washing: a lot of clothes to wash

frowned: showed displeasure on his face (knitting his brows)
... keg (barrel): in a dangerous situation □ **sat up** (erect)
leaned (bent) **forward** (≠ backward) □ **why** indicates shock, indignation (≠ why?) □ **wipe... clean** (completely) **off the map:** destroy all of Chicago □ **as for:** concerning □ (there would be) **nothing left** □ **smudge:** small trace □ **keep...** (all the time)
it's a darn (damned) **shame** (sth regrettable): it's really a shame. What a shame! What a pity!

"Here we've taken a million years to get where we are. We build towns and build cities out of nothing. Why, a hundred years ago, this town wasn't nowhere to be seen. Took a lot of time and sweat and trouble, and now we've got it all one brick on another and what happens? BANG!"

"It won't happen to us, I bet," I said.

"No?" Father snorted. "Why not?"

"It just *couldn't*," I said.

"You two leave off," Mom nodded at me. "You're too young to understand." She nodded at Pop. "You're old enough to know better."

We ate in silence. Then I said to Pop, "What was it like before this town was here?"

"Nothing at all. Just the lake and the hills is all."

"Indians?"

"Not many around here. Just empty woods and hills is all."

"Pass the syrup," said Mom.

"Whambo!" cried RT, "I'm an atom bomb! Boom!"

We were waiting in line at the Elite theater. It was the biggest day of the year. We had lugged pop all morning at the circus to earn show tickets. Now, in the afternoon, we were seeing cowboys and Indians on the movie screen, and, this evening, the circus itself! We felt rich and we laughed all the time. RT kept squinting through his atomic ring, yelling, "Whoom! You're disintegrated!"

Cowboys chased Indians across the screen. Half an hour later the Indians chased the cowboys back the other way. After everybody was tired of stomping, the

here: see! □ **taken:** needed □ **to get to...** : (after much effort)
cities are larger than **towns** □ **out of** (starting from) **nothing**
wasn't nowhere...: wasn't... anywhere (did not exist)
sweat: perspiration after great effort □ **trouble:** difficulty, worry
we've got it all one brick...: built it all

I bet: (fam) I'm sure; bet, risk money on result of event
snorted (making a rough noise, expressing impatience, anger...)

leave off: stop it □ **nodded:** bent her head forward and down to give a sign
know better: be more sensible, reasonable (being more mature)

lake: probably lake Michigan □ **hill(s):** small mountain

empty: with nobody in them □ **wood(s)** (full of trees)
is all (that there was)

whambo!... boom: indicate a hard impact with a deep sound
line: (Am) queue □ (movie) **theater:** movie (Am), film
lugged: carried □ (soda) **pop** (bottles): sweet drink
earn (money, a living...) □ **show:** performance

screen: white surface on which films are projected
kept squinting: never stopped looking with almost closed eyes
ring: (object that has the shape of a circle) □ **yelling:** shouting: a yell, a shout or loud cry (as of excitement)
chased: ran after, pursued □ **across:** from one side to the other
back the other way: in the opposite direction
stomping: (Am) stamping, striking their feet forcibly, noisily

cartoon came on, and then a newsreel.

"Look, the atom bomb!" RT settled down for the first time.

The big gray cloud lifted on the screen, blew apart, battleships and cruisers burst open and rain fell.

RT held my arm tight, staring up at the burning whiteness. "Ain't that something, Doug, ain't it?" He jabbed my ribs.

"It's a whooperdoo, all right," I said, jabbing him back, giggling. "Wish I had an atom bomb! Blooie, there goes the school!"

"Bam! Goodbye Clara Holmquist!"

"Bam! There goes Officer O'Rourke!"

For supper there were Swedish meatballs, hot buns, Boston beans and green salad. Father looked very serious and strange and tried to bring up some important scientific facts he had read in a magazine, but Mom shook her head.

I watched Pop. "You feeling okay, Pop?"

"I'm going to cancel our paper subscription", said Mom. "You're worrying yourself right into ulcers. You hear me, Dad?"

"Boy," I said, "did I see a *film*! The atom bomb blew up a whole battleship down at the Elite."

Father dropped his fork and stared at me. "Sometimes, Douglas, you have the uncanny ability to say just the wrong thing at the wrong time."

I saw Mother squinting at me to catch my eye. "It's late," she said. "You'd better run on to the circus."

As I was getting my hat and coat I heard Father say in a low and thoughtful voice, "How would it be to sell the business? You know, we've always wanted to travel;

(Walt Disney) **cartoon** □ **newsreel:** short film of recent events
settled down: become calm

gray: (Am) grey □ **lifted:** went up □ **blew apart:** exploded
battleship(s), cruiser(s): warship □ **burst open:** broke open violently □ **tight:** firmly □ **staring:** looking fixedly □ **burning** (hot) □ **ain't** (isn't) **that something** (extraordinary)
jabbed: hit (with his elbow) □ **rib(s):** curved bone round upper part of body □ **a whooperdoo, all right:** sth really great
giggling: laughing uncontrollably □ **(I) wish** □ **blooie** (blow up), boom □ **there goes the school!:** no more school!
bam: boom! bang! □ **Clara...** (probably their school mistress)
officer: policeman
Swedish: from Sweden □ (round) **meat ball(s)** □ **bun(s):** small round sweet cake □ **bean(s):** green vegetable growing on tall climbing plant □ **bring up** (in the conversation), call attention by mentioning
shook her head: (in disapproval or disagreement) (≠ nodded)
pop: (Am, fam) dad(dy) □ (are) **you feeling okay?** (well)
cancel: stop □ **subscription;** subscribe to *Time*, pay regularly to receive it □ **worrying... ulcers:** becoming so anxious that you will no doubt get ulcers □ (do) **you hear?**
did I see a film!: what an extraordinary film I saw!
whole: entire □ **battleship:** big warship; fight a battle
fork (and spoon) □ **dropped:** let fall □ **stared** (fixedly)
Ray **Douglas** Bradbury □ **uncanny:** strange and hard to explain
wrong ≠ right; the right thing at the right place
squinting at: looking at me with half-closed eyes □ **catch my eye:** attract my attention

thoughtful: full of thought □ **how...:** what do you think of...
business: money-earning activity or place like a shop...

go to Mexico maybe. A small town. Settle down."

"You're talking like a child," whispered Mother. "I won't hear you carry on this way."

"I know it's foolish. Don't mind me. But you're right; better cancel the paper."

A wind was blowing the trees half over and the stars were all out and the circus lay in the country hills, in the meadow, like a big toadstool. Red Tongue and I had popcorn in one hand, taffy in the other, and cotton candy on our chins. "Lookit my beard!" Red Tongue shouted. Everybody was talking and pushing under the bright light bulbs and a man smacked a canvas with a bamboo cane and shouted about The Skeleton, The Blubber Lady, The Illustrated Man, The Seal Boy, while RT and I jostled through to the lady who torn our tickets in half.

We balanced our way up to sit on the slat seats just when the bass drums exploded and the jeweled elephants lumbered out, and from then on there were hot searchlights, men shooting from fiery howitzers, ladies hung by their white teeth imitating butterflies high up in the clouds of cigarette smoke while trapeze men rode back and forth among the ropes and poles, and lions trotted softly around the sawdust-floored cage while the trainer in white pants shot smoke and flame at them from a silver pistol. "Look!" RT and I cried, blinking here, gaping there, chuckling, ohing, ahing, amazed, incredulous, surprised, and entertained, out of breath, eyes wide, mouths open. Chariots roared around the track, clowns jumped from burning hotels, grew hair, changed from giants to midgets in a steam box. The

settle down: stop and stay there to live for some time
whispered: said softly, very quietly
won't: don't want to □ **carry on this way** (like this): behave in an excited and anxious manner □ **foolish:** stupid □ **don't mind me:** don't pay attention to me □ (we had) **better**

a wind... over: a wind made the trees bend; blow, blew, blown
lie, **lay**, lain (≠ lay, laid, laid); lay sth (flat) on..., put
meadow: area of grass, field □ **toadstool:** poisonous mushroom
taffy: (Am) toffee, sweet made of boiled sugar and butter
cotton candy: *barbe à papa* □ **chin(s):** part of the face below the mouth on which a man can have a **beard** (hair on chin)
60-watt **bulb(s)** □ **smacked:** hit □ **canvas** (for painting on...)
skeleton: all the bones supporting the human body
blubber: fat of whale *(baleine)* □ **seal:** *phoque...*
josteld through: made our way by pushing □ tear, tore, **torn;** tear in half; tear to pieces
balanced...: balance, equilibrium □ **slat:** wooden board
bass drums: *grosse caisse* □ **jewel(ed),** precious stone
lumbered: moved in a heavy, slow and noisy way
searchlight(s): powerful lamp □ **shooting... howitzer(s):** coming out of short heavy burning hot guns □ **butterflies:** insects with often beautifully-coloured wings; a butterfly □ **rode:** went
rope(s): strong thick cord □ **pole(s)** (to support tent...)
sawdust-floored: with floor covered with fine wood fragments
trainers train animals □ **pants:** (Am) trousers □ **shot:** sent
silver: white precious metal □ **blink**(ing): shut and open eyes quickly □ **gaping:** staring with open mouth □ **chuckling:** laughing quietly □ **ohing, ahing** in surprise, **amazed** □ **entertained:** amused □ **out of breath:** taking in air quickly □ **wide:** fully open □ **roared** (like lions) □ **track:** ring □ **grew hair** (suddenly) □ **giant(s)** ≠ **midget(s)** □ **steam:** vapour

band crashed and tooted and hooted and everywhere was color and warmth and sequins shining and the crowd thundering.

But along about the end of the show I looked up. And there, behind me, was a little hole in the canvas. And through that hole I could see the old meadowland, the wind blowing over it and the stars shining alone out there. The cold wind tugged at the tent very gently. And all of a sudden, turning back to the warm riot all around me, I was cold too. I heard Red Tongue laughing beside me and I half-saw some men riding a silver bike on a high, far-away, thin thread, the snare drum going tatatatatatatatatata, everyone quiet. And when that was over, there were two hundred clowns whacking each other's heads with bats and Red Tongue almost fell from his seat, screaming with it. I sat there and didn't move and at last Red Tongue turned and looked at me and said, "Hey, what's wrong, Doug?"

"Nothing," I said. I shook myself. I looked up at the red circus poles and the rope lines and the flaring lights. I looked at the zinc-oxide clowns and made myself laugh. "Lookit there, RT, that fat one over there!"

The band played "The Old Gray Mare She Ain't What She Used to Be."

"It's all over," said Red Tongue, breathlessly.

We sat while the thousands of stunned people walked away mumbling and laughing and pressing at each other. The tent was thick with cigar smoke and the musical instruments lay curled up and abandoned for a moment on the wooden dock where the band had shocked us with wave after wave of brass.

We didn't move because neither of us wanted it to be

(jazz...) **band** □ **crashed, hooted, tooted** (depending on the instruments) □ **warmth** ≠ coldness □ **sequin(s):** small round ornaments on clothes □ **crowd** (of people) □ **thundering:** applauding noisily □ **about the end:** towards the end
hole: opening through sth □ **canvas** (of which tent is made)

blow(ing), blew, blown □ **out there:** far away
tugged at: pulled hard with force □ **gently** ≠ noisily, violently
all of a sudden: suddenly □ **riot:** tumult, exuberance, excitement (of the circus people and the crowd)
beside: near □ **half:** (here) vaguely □ **riding** (bike, horse...)
thin ≠ thick □ **thread:** thin cord □ **snare drum:** *tambour à timbre* □ **quiet:** silent
over: finished
whacking: hitting hard □ (baseball, cricket) **bat(s)**
screaming: crying out loudly as in excitement, laughter...
at (long) **last:** in the end; after a long time
what's wrong (with) you?: have you got a problem?
shook myself (in order to forget about my anxiety)
flaring: burning with a bright light but uncertainly
made myself laugh: forced myself to laugh
lookit: look at it □ **fat** ≠ thin, slim
gray: (Am) grey □ **mare:** female horse □ **ain't:** isn't
used to be: was in the past and no longer will be
breathless (with emotion): out of breath (120.29)
stunned (with strong emotion), knocked senseless, amazed (120.28) □ **mumbling:** speaking indistinctly □ **pressing...:** pushing...
thick with: full of
curled up: as if bent double, forming twists or curls
wooden, golden...: made of wood... □ **dock:** platform
wave: movement as of the sea □ **brass** (instruments): wind instruments made of brass (bright yellow metal)

over.

"Guess we better go," said RT, not stirring.

"Let's wait," I said, tonelessly, not looking at anything. I felt the wood slat aching under my bottom after the long strange hours of music and color. Men were moving and slapping the collapsing chairs down into themselves to be toted away. The canvas strippings were being unhooked. Everywhere was the jingle and the snap and clatter of the circus falling apart.

The tent was empty.

We stood on the midway, the wind blowing dust in our eyes, leaves whipping off the trees. And the wind carried away all the dead leaves and all the restless people. The sideshow bulbs blinked off. We walked to the top of a nearby hill and stood there in the windy dark, our teeth chattering, watching the blue lights drift in the blackness, the white shapes of elephants floating, the sounds of men cursing and stakes being pried up. And then, like an immense sighing bellows, the main tent settling to earth.

An hour later the gravel road was amove with cars and trucks and golden cages. The pale meadow lay empty. The moon was rising and rime formed over every wet thing. RT and I walked slowly down across the meadow, smelling the sawdust. "That's all that's left," said Red Tongue. "Sawdust."

"Here's a stake hole," I said. I pointed. "There's another."

"You'd never know they were ever here," said RT. "It's like making it up in your mind." The wind blew across the empty meadow and we stood watching the black trees shake. There was not a light or a sound;

(I) guess (Am. think) **we** (had) **better** go □ **stirring:** moving
let's wait: let us wait □ **tonelessly:** (as if lifeless, without spirit)
aching: hurting □ **bottom:** behind (n)
color: (Am) colour
slapping: striking □ **collapsing** (so as to take up less space)
toted: (fam) carried □ **stripping(s):** long narrow piece
unhooked: taken off □ **jingle:** sound of metal objects striking together □ **snap, clatter:** sudden noises, shocks □ **falling apart:** falling to pieces, disintegrating
midway: (Am) centre of the site where the circus lay □ **dust:** small particles of earth □ **whipping off:** going quickly off
restless: excited ≠ calm
sideshow: separate small show at a circus □ **blinked off:** went quickly off □ **nearby** ≠ far □ **windy**; it's windy
chattering: trembling □ **drift:** be driven or carried away
shape(s): form
cursing: using bad language □ **stakes** (to hold ropes)... **pried up** (out of ground) □ **sighing:** letting out air □ **bellows** (to blow air into a fire) □ **main:** principal □ **settling...:** coming down
gravel: small stones □ **amove with:** full of, busy with □ **truck(s):** (Am) lorry
rising: coming up □ **rime:** white frost (on grass in cold early morning) □ **wet** ≠ dry
all that's left: all that remains
sawdust (on circus track) (120.25)
I pointed: I showed with my (index) finger

they were ever here (at all)
making it up: inventing, imagining it □ **mind:** intellect

shake (from side to side in the wind), shook, shaken

even all of the circus smell had finally blown away.

"Welp," said RT, scuffing his shoes. "We'll get the tar beat out of us if we ain't home *an hour ago*!" He smiled.

We walked back together down the lonely country road, the wind at our backs, our hands deep in our pockets, our heads down. We walked past the deep silent ravine and then we walked through the little streets of the town, past sleeping houses, where here and there a radio quietly played, and there was the sound of a last cricket and our heels thumping on the rough bricks in the middle of the long street, under the swaying, dim arc lamps at each corner.

I looked at all the houses and all the picket fences and all the slanting roofs and lighted windows and I looked at every tree and at all the bricks under my feet. I looked at my shoes and I looked over at RT trudging beside me, his teeth chattering. And I saw the courthouse clock a mile away, lifting up its moist white face in the moonlight, all the municipal buildings black and big. "G'night, Doug." I didn't answer as RT walked slowly on down the street between the houses at midnight and turned a far corner.

I crept upstairs and was in bed in a minute, looking out through my window at the town.

My brother Skip must have heard me crying for a long time before he put his hand over to feel my arm. "What's wrong, Doug?" he asked.

"Nothing," I sobbed quietly, eyes closed. "Just the circus."

Skip waited. The wind blew around the house. "What about it?" he asked.

"Nothing—except it won't come again."

even...: the smell itself □ **blown away**: gone, disappeared
welp: (fam) well □ **scuffing**: rubbing, scraping (2.13)
... tar...: be beaten up severely □ **ain't**: aren't
lonely: empty, deserted
... backs ≠ facing the wind □ **deep**: far down
our heads down (being sad) □ **past**: to and farther than
the ravine is often mentioned in R.B.'s stories (see *The Night*, interview and story p. 131 to p. 158)
quietly: softly (≠ loudly, noisily) □ **played**: was on
cricket: *grillon* □ **heel(s)**: back part of shoe □ **thumping**: hitting hard □ **rough**: of irregular surface □ **swaying** (from side to side) □ **dim** ≠ bright
picket fence(s) (dividing two areas of land)
slanting: in oblique position □ **roof(s)**: cover of house

trudging: walking laboriously, without spirit
chattering: knocking together (through cold or fear)
courthouse (justice) □ **lifting**: raising □ **moist**: wet
moonlight (in the night); sunlight (in the day)
g'night: good night
walked slowly (≠ quickly, fast) **on**: continued walking
midnight (12 o'clock at night) ≠ midday, noon; middle
crept (quietly, slowly so as not be noticed) □ **in a minute**: in no time
must have heard: had certainly heard □ **crying**, weeping ≠ laughing □ **put... over**: extended... □ **feel**: touch

sobbed: cried convulsively □ **closed**: shut

what about it?: so what?

except (that) **it won't come again**

"Sure it will," he said.

"No, it's gone. And it won't come back again. It's all gone where it was, nothing of it left."

"Try to get some sleep." Skip turned over.

I stopped crying. Somewhere, across town, a few windows were still glowing. Down at the rail station, an engine hooted and started and went rushing off between the hills.

I waited in the dark room, holding my breath, while one by silent one, the small, far-away windows of the little houses went dark.

sure: (Am) surely, certainly, no doubt
it's gone: it has disappeared or vanished (for ever here)

get some sleep: sleep (a little) □ **turn over** (the other side)
across: from one side to the other of
still (continuation) □ **glowing:** lighted □ **rail**(way) **engine:** locomotive □ **hooted:** whistled □ **rushing** (very fast)

holding my breath: not breathing (taking in air) for a short time
far-away: far, distant
went dark: became dark (the lights were switched off)

Grammaire au fil des nouvelles

Voici, dans l'ordre de leur apparition dans le texte, des phrases à compléter (ou non !) selon les indications données. Les numéros de pages renvoient à la Grammaire active de l'anglais *(Le Livre de Poche, 1989).*

"You ... not read the paper in the morning", Mom said (modal exprimant le conseil, p. 24).

You're *(old)* to know better (placez *enough* à l'endroit qui convient, p. 140).

"Indians?" "Not... *(Indians)* around here" (*much* ou *many*, p. 80).

You... run on to the circus (traduction de "tu ferais mieux de", p. 62).

As I was getting my hat and coat I heard Father ... *(say)*, "How would it be to sell the business?" (les verbes de perception, p. 60).

And when that was over there were two hundred clowns whacking ...'s heads with bats (pronoms réfléchis et réciproques, p. 124).

The Band played "The Old Mare She Ain't What She ... *(be)*" (passé révolu : pour opposer ce qui était vrai autrefois à ce qui ne l'est plus maintenant, p. 58).

The canvas stripping were ... *(unhook)* (le passif progressif, p. 52).

We walked back together down the lonely country roads, the wind at our ... *(back)*, our ... *(hand)* deep in our ... *(pocket)*, our ... *(head)* down (pluriel des noms ; problème des objets qui n'appartiennent pas en commun à différents possesseurs, p. 94).

My brother Skip ... *(hear)* me crying for a long time before he put his hand over to feel my arm (expression de la forte probabilité, de la quasi-certitude, p. 22, dans un contexte passé, p. 26).

I stopped ... *(cry)* (le gérondif ou nom verbal, p. 150).

Somewhere, across town, ... windows were still glowing (*a little* ou *a few ?*, p. 80).

THE NIGHT

Talking about the short story *The Night* (p. 137)

H. Y. Can you tell us about Green Town, Illinois?

R. B. Well, you know, I grew up in a small town, Waukegan, Illinois, thirty-five miles North of Chicago. When I was raised there, it had thirty thousand people. I lived on a street surrounded by a big deep ravine. On all sides was the wilderness: on the North, the East, the South and further West, so that I was within one or two blocks of the wilderness and I ran there to live. I'd walk through the ravine to school and I'd come back from seeing *"The Phantom of the Opera"* late at night through the ravine and my brother would run ahead...

H. Y. Skip, do you mean?

R. B. Yes. Skip would run ahead and hide and jump out to scare the hell out of me... It was the ideal town to live in until I was thirteen and left to stay in Los Angeles. Waukegan was a small town, a wilderness, it was nature. When I moved to Hollywood I moved into an environment of artificiality which I *also* loved. My life, then, was split in two halves: the wilderness half which went into my Green Town stories, *Dandelion Wine* and then Hollywood and Los Angeles which steered me into a technological age.

H. Y. What about the lake and the ravine? Very important in *The Lake*, I think.

R. B. Again we go back to the ravine, where I spent

Green Town: imaginary town often mentioned in R.B.'s stories
I grew up (as a child)
Waukegan: the real name of R.B.'s hometown □ **mile:** 1.609 m
raised: brought up (by parents) □ **people:** inhabitants
surrounded by a big deep (going far down) **ravine:** with a... ravine all around it □ **wilderness:** desert, uncultivated and uninhabited land □ **within... of:** not farther than... from **block(s):** buildings between streets □ **'d: would** indicates repeated action
The Phantom of the Opera: Lou Chaney's famous thriller
ahead: in front, in advance
skip: often mentioned in the stories
hide (so as to be invisible) □ **jump out:** come out suddenly
scare the hell (fam)...: make me terribly afraid
leave, **left,** left: went away □ **stay:** live, settle

moved to...: went to (Los Angeles) to live in a new home
loved: (talking about things) liked very much, was fond of
split in (or into): divided in (or into) □ **halves;** a half
Dandelion Wine (Grafton Books) is all about R.B.'s childhood
steered: took, led; steer, direct the course of (a ship...)
age: great period in history
The Lake (1942), written in an hour. "... I was in tears. I knew I had written the first really good story of my life."
spend (time), **spent,** spent

most of my young life. In fact I was rewarded three weeks ago, when I went back to my home town to visit the ravine. Today they have renamed it *Ray Bradbury Park*. So I was there for the re-dedication of the place that once terrified me. That was very gratifying and great fun for me. The ravine, of course, was important because every summer I would start in the middle of it and go all the way down to the lake one day and then the next day I would start in the other direction and follow it out into the country. So I had another adventure anytime I wanted to. It would take most of the day to get to the lake and most of the day to get to the country and along the way climbing trees and catching crayfish and watching the water striders. So the lake and the ravine were very important as places to hide out from my parents. My mother would come stand on the edge of the ravine at night and blow her whistle, really give it a big blast and we kids would all come tumbling up out of the ravine.

H. Y. Another terrible story is *The Night* too, isn't it?

R. B. Yes, that's a natural story, a real happening... It took place one summer night when I was about eight. My brother was playing baseball down the ravine somewhere. He came home late. When my mother called he wasn't there. Then all of a sudden the crickets got very quiet and I suddenly realized that any moment the dark could come up out of the ravine and get me and my mother, and nobody would know. That's a variety of death, a variety of nightmare and you have your first taste of real fright, at the age of seven or eight. So I put all that in my short story.

most of: the greater part of □ **rewarded:** given as reward (recompense) (in return for work, merit)
renamed: given the new name
re-dedication (ceremony)
once: at some time in the past □ **gratifying:** pleasing
fun: pleasure, enjoyment
start (walking) □ **middle:** centre
all the way down to...: as far as
next: following; follow, come after
follow: continue along □ **out** (of the ravine) **into...**
to (have another adventure) □ **most of...:** nearly all day
get to: arrive at, reach (after effort)
along the way: as I went along □ **climbing:** going up
crayfish: *écrevisse* □ **water strider(s)** (with long legs, on the surface of water) □ considered just **as**
hide, hid, hidden (22) □ **come** (and) **stand**
edge: limit □ **blow:** push air out producing sound
whistle (as of policemen directing traffic) □ **blast:** loud sound
come tumbling up (rolling, in confusion or disorder)

took place: happened □ **about:** approximately

came home: no preposition! □ **late** (at night) ≠ early
called (him to come home) □ **all of a sudden:** suddenly
got + adj: became □ **quiet:** silent
dark ≠ light □ **get me:** capture (and kill me)

nightmare: bad, frightening dream
taste of: experience of □ **fright:** fear □ put, **put,** put; put down (on paper), write; how shall I put it? (say it, express it)

THE NIGHT

I have written yarns about the night, in which only darkness and crickets and hidden ravine creeks and the sound of owls and late birds are the secret villains, each speaking of eternity and surprise murders.

(Preface by Ray Bradbury 1991.)

yarn(s): story, tale
darkness, dark ≠ light
cricket(s): *grillon*
hidden: invisible, secret; hide, hid, **hidden**
creek(s): (Am) small stream
owl(s): *hibou*
late: (here) flying late (≠ early) at night
murder: intentional killing of human being

You are a child in a small town. You are, to be exact, eight years old, and it is growing late at night. Late for you, accustomed to bedding in at nine or nine-thirty; once in a while perhaps begging Mom or Dad to let you stay up later to hear Sam and Henry on that strange radio that is popular in this year of 1927. But most of the time you are in bed and snug at this time of night.

It is a warm summer evening. You live in a small house on a small street in the outer part of town where there are few street lights. There is only one store open, about a block away: Mrs. Singer's. In the hot evening Mother has been ironing the Monday wash and you have been intermittently begging for ice cream and staring into the dark.

You and your mother are all alone at home in the warm darkness of summer. Finally, just before it is time for Mrs. Singer to close her store, Mother relents and tells you:

"Run get a pint of ice cream and be sure she packs it tight."

You ask if you can get a scoop of chocolate ice cream on top, because you don't like vanilla, and Mother agrees. You clutch the money and run barefooted over the warm evening cement sidewalk, under the apple trees and oak trees, toward the store. The town is so quiet and far off, you can only hear the crickets sounding in the spaces beyond the hot indigo trees that hold back the stars.

Your bare feet slap the pavement, you cross the street and find Mrs. Singer moving ponderously about her store, singing Yiddish melodies.

growing late: getting late; late ≠ early □ at night
accustomed to bedding in: used to going to bed
once in a week: occasionally □ **begging:** imploring
stay up: not to go to bed, stay awake
popular: that radio programme is popular with children
snug: warm and comfortable, cosy
summer (season): spring, summer, autumn (Am, fall), winter
in the outer part of town: far from the town centre (≠ inner)
street light(s): street lamp □ **store:** (Am) shop
block (of buildings between two streets) □ **Mrs. Singer's** (store)
ironing: smoothing the **wash** (clothes just washed) with a hot iron by pressing it against the "ironing board" (142.8)
staring: looking with wide open eyes for a long time
alone: with nobody else in the house

close ≠ open □ **relents:** gives way to compassion, yields

run (and) **get** □ **pint:** (Am) 47 cl □ **packs:** wraps (in paper...)
tight: firmly
scoop: what a scoop (instrument for serving ice cream) holds
on (the) **top** (of the pint): over, above; **top:** highest part
agrees: consents □ **clutch:** seize □ **barefooted:** without shoes
sidewalk (Am): pavement (to walk on) □ **apple(s),** pears: fruit
oak: *chêne* □ **toward(s):** in the direction of □ **quiet:** calm
far off: distant □ **cricket(s):** *grillon* □ making **sound(s)**
space(s): interval(s) □ **beyond:** farther than □ **hold back:** at a distance
bare: without clothing □ **slap:** strike quickly, hit
ponderously: slowly, labouriously □ **about:** here and there
singing: sing, sang, sung; a song

"Pint ice cream?" she says. "Chocolate on top? Yes!"

You watch her fumble the metal top off the ice-cream freezer and manipulate the scoop, packing the cardboard pint chock full with "chocolate on top, yes!" You give the money, receive the chill, icy pack, and rubbing it across your brow and cheek, laughing, you thump barefootedly homeward. Behind you, the lights of the lonely little store blink out and there is only a street light shimmering on the corner, and the whole city seems to be going to sleep...

Opening the screen door you find Mom still ironing. She looks hot and irritated, but she smiles just the same.

"When will Dad be home from lodge-meeting?" you ask.

"About eleven-thirty or twelve," Mother replies. She takes the ice cream to the kitchen, divides it. Giving you your special portion of chocolate, she dishes out some for herself and the rest is put away, "For Skipper and your father when they come."

Skipper is your brother. He is your older brother. He's twelve and healthy, red-faced, hawk-nosed, tawny-haired, broad-shouldered for his years, and always running. He is allowed to stay up later than you. Not much later, but enough to make him feel it is worthwhile having been born first. He is over on the other side of town this evening to a game of kick-the-can and will be home soon. He and the kids have been yelling, kicking, running for hours, having fun. Soon he will come clomping in, smelling of sweat and green grass

pint (of) **ice cream?:** Mrs. Singer's way of speaking shows how cheerful (joyful) she is, singing melodies...
fumble... top (cover) **off:** taking it off clumsily, maladroitly
cardboard: thick type of paper for making boxes, cards...
chock full: (fam) absolutely full
chill: cold □ **icy:** very cold □ **rubbing:** moving backwards and forwards □ **brow:** forehead □ **cheek:** side of face □ **thump homeward** (towards home) with feet striking heavily against pavement □ **lonely:** isolated □ **blink out** (like an eye that shuts)
shimmering: shining with a soft trembling light

screen door (to exclude insects, mosquitoes, outside the door)
smiles: has a happy expression on her face □ **just the same:** in spite of the heat and her irritation; all the same
lodge: fraternal organization such as the Freemasons...

(at) **about:** approximately □ **replies:** answers; a reply
kitchen: room used for cooking □ **divides** (it into portions)
dishes out: (fam) serves out
put away, ketp in the fridge for Skipper and the father

healthy ≠ ill □ **hawk:** bird of prey □ **tawny:** brownish yellow
broad-shouldered: with broad shoulders (joining arms to trunk)
he's allowed to stay up: he is given permission to stay up

worthwhile: useful, beneficial; it's worth(while) try<u>ing</u>
game: spell (short period) of play □ **kick** (a ball with foot)
can (Am): metal container to preserve food □ **kid(s):** child
yelling: shouting □ **having fun:** enjoying themselves
clomping, clumping: walking heavily □ **sweat:** perspiration

on his knees where he fell, and smelling very much in all ways like Skipper; which is natural.

You sit enjoying the ice cream. You are at the core of the deep quiet summer night. Your mother and yourself and the night all around this small house on this small street. You lick each spoon of ice cream thoroughly before digging for another, and Mom puts her ironing board away and the hot iron in its case, and she sits in the armchair by the phonograph, eating her dessert and saying, "My Lands, it was a hot day today. It's still hot. Earth soaks up all the heat and lets it out at night. It'll be soggy sleeping."

You both sit there listening to the summer silence. The dark is pressed down by every window and door, there is no sound because the radio needs a new battery, and you have played all the Knickerbocker Quartet records and Al Jolson and Two Black Crows records to exhaustion; so you just sit on the hardwood floor by the door and look out into the dark dark dark, pressing your nose against the screen until the flesh of its tip is molded into small dark squares.

"I wonder where your brother is?" Mother says after a while. Her spoon scrapes on the dish. "He should be home by now. It's almost nine-thirty."

"He'll be here," you say, knowing very well that he will be.

You follow Mom out to wash the dishes. Each sound, each rattle of spoon or dish is amplified in the baked evening. Silently, you go the living room, remove the couch cushions and, together, yank it open and extend it down into the double bed that it secretly is. Mother makes the bed, punching pillows neatly to plump them

knee(s): join between the upper and the lower leg
in all ways (manners): completely, absolutely
enjoying: finding pleasure in □ **core:** centre, heart
deep: (here) black, very dark; deep, profound

lick (with tongue) □ **spoon(s)** and forks □ **thoroughly:** completely □ **digging:** pushing your spoon into the ice cream to get another spoonful □ **case** in which the iron is put away (p. 140. 20) □ **armchair:** chair with supports for arms □ **by:** near
my Lands: my God, good gracious □ **hot** (adj); heat (n)
earth: soil □ **soaks up:** absorbs ≠ **let(s) out**
soggy: very wet and unpleasantly heavy (atmosphere)

the dark ≠ the light □ **pressed down:** sort of pushed
battery: a piece of apparatus for producing electricity
knickerbockers: trousers □ **quartet:** four musicians
crow(s): large black bird □ **record(s):** disc; play a record
to exhaustion: until you got tired of listening □ **hardwood floor:** *(parquet)* hardwood, strong heavy wood like oak (138.25)
flesh: soft substance of body □ **tip:** end (of nose...)
mo(u)lded into... squares: with square marks formed (molded) by the metal screen of the "screen door" (140.12)
a while: a time □ **scrapes:** takes away all that is left on the dish (not plate!) making a noise

follow: go after □ **wash the dishes:** do the washing-up
rattle: quick little noise □ **baked:** very hot; bread is baked in an oven; a baker('s shop) □ **remove:** take off or away
couch: sofa □ **cushion(s)** (to sit on) □ **yank it open:** open it by yanking (pulling suddenly) □ **double bed** ≠ single bed □ **punching** (striking) **pillows** *(oreillers)* **neatly** (nicely) □ **plump:** make big

up for your head. Then, as you are unbuttoning your shirt, she says:

"Wait awhile, Doug."

"Why?"

"Because. I say so."

"You look funny, Mom."

Mom sits down a moment, then stands up, goes to the door, and calls. You listen to her calling and calling Skipper, Skipper, Skiiiiiiiiperrrrrrrr over and over. Her calling goes out into the summer warm dark and never comes back. The echoes pay no attention.

Skipper. Skipper. Skipper.

Skipper!

And as you sit on the floor a coldness that is not ice cream and not winter, and not part of summer's heat, goes through you. You notice Mom's eyes sliding, blinking; the way she stands undecided and is nervous. All of these things.

She opens the screen door. Stepping out into the night she walks down the steps and down the front sidewalk under the lilac bush. You listen to her moving feet.

She calls again. Silence.

She calls twice more. You sit in the room. Any moment now Skipper will reply, from down the long long narrow street:

"All right, Mom! All right, Mother! Hey!"

But he doesn't answer. And for two minutes you sit looking at the made-up bed, the silent radio, the silent phonograph, at the chandelier with its crystal bobbins gleaming quietly, at the rug with the scarlet and purple curlicues on it. You stub your toe on the bed purposely to see if it hurts. It does.

unbuttoning: undoing the buttons (to take off clothes)
shirt: piece of clothing for the upper part of the body
awhile: for a short time

so: used to avoid repetition (of "wait awhile")
look: seem (by appearance) □ **funny:** strange, bizarre
sits down: sit, sat, sat □ **stands up:** stand, stood, stood

over and over: over and over again, again and again

pay no attention: do not take any notice (there is no answer from Skipper)

that is not...: that has nothing to do with ice cream... but with your anxiety
notice: observe □ **sliding:** moving slowly, continuously
blinking: shutting and opening quickly □ **way** (manner) (in which) she stands
stepping: walking, making a step or steps (to walk out)
step(s) (on which foot is placed to go up and down)
lilac bush: a number of lilac trees together (with white or purple flowers giving a sweet smell)
twice: two times; once, twice, three times...
any moment now: very soon
narrow ≠ broad (cf. broad-shouldered, 140.24), wide
hey!: a shout to call attention or express exultation

chandelier: hanging support for lights □ **bobbins** are round
gleaming: shining □ **rug:** carpet □ **scarlet:** bright red
curlicue(s): circle □ **stub** (hit) **toe** (digit of foot) **purposely** (intentionally) □ **hurts:** causes pain; hurt, hurt, hurt

Whining, the screen door opens, and Mother says:

"Come on, Shorts. We'll take a walk."

"Where to?"

"Just down the block. Come on. Better put your shoes on, though. You'll catch cold."

"No, I won't. I'll be all right."

You take her hand. Together you walk down St. James Street. You smell roses in blossom, fallen apples lying crushed and odorous in the deep grass. Underfoot, the concrete is still warm, and the crickets are sounding louder against the darkening dark. You reach a corner, turn, and walk toward the ravine.

Off somewhere, a car goes by, flashing its lights in the distance. There is such a complete lack of life, light, and activity. Here and there, back off from where you are walking toward the ravine, you see faint squares of light where people are still up. But most of the houses, darkened, are sleeping already, and there are a few lightless places where the occupants of a dwelling sit talking low dark talk on their front porches. You hear a porch swing squeaking as you walk near.

"I wish your father was home," says Mother. Her large hand tightens around your small one. "Just wait'll I get that boy. I'll spank him within an inch of his life."

A razor strop hangs in the kitchen for this. You think of it, remember when Dad has doubled and flourished it with muscled control over your frantic limbs. You doubt Mother will carry out her promise.

Now you have walked another block and are standing by the holy black silhouette of the German Baptist Church at the corner of Chapel Street and Glen Rock.

whining (plaintively, "crying" for absence of oil so to speak)
Shorts: pet name used affectionately (probably because Douglas is little)
block is a typically American word □ **better:** you had better
though: (used at the end of a clause) however, nevertheless

down St James Street: along
in blossom: at a high point of development; in full bloom
crushed (underfoot): pressed □ (green) **grass** (eaten by cows)
concrete: cement
darkening: growing dark(er) □ **reach:** arrive at, get to

off: at a distance □ **flashing...:** suddenly, briefly, showing...
lack of: absence of

faint: indistinct ≠ clear, sharp
are still up: are not in bed yet, cf. "stay up" (138.5)
darkened: darken, become dark (11)
lightless: without light □ **dwelling:** house... to live in
low: not loud; talk in a low voice ≠ talk in a loud voice
swing: seat held by chains (for children) □ **squeaking** (for lack of oil): making a short very high but not loud sound
large: big □ **tightens:** holds more firmly □ **'ll:** till
spank: strike with open hand □ **within an inch of...:** very hard (until the nearly dies)
strop: leather *(cuir)* band used to make razors cut well
doubled: made double □ **flourished:** brandished, waved about
frantic (with pain) ≠ calm □ **limb(s):** arm or leg
carry out...: put into practice (actually spanking him)

holy: sacred □ **silhouette:** contour, profile
church: building where people attend religious services

In the back of the church a hundred yards away, the ravine begins. You can smell it. It has a dark sewer, rotten foliage, thick green odor. It is a wide ravine that cuts and twists across the town, a jungle by day, a place to let alone at night, Mother has often declared.

You should feel encouraged by the nearness of the German Baptist Church, but you are not—because the building is not illumined, is cold and useless as a pile of ruins on the ravine edge.

You are only eight years old, you know little of death, fear, or dread. Death is the waxen effigy in the coffin when you were six and Grandfather passed away—looking like a great fallen vulture in his casket, silent, withdrawn, no more to tell you how to be a good boy, no more to comment succinctly on politics. Death is your little sister one morning when you awaken at the age of seven, look into her crib and see her staring up at you with a blind blue, fixed and frozen stare until the men come with a small wicker basket to take her away. Death is when you stand by her high chair four weeks later and suddenly realize she'll never be in it again, laughing and crying, and make you jealous of her because she was born. That is death.

But this is more than death. This summer night wading deep in time and stars and warm eternity. It is an essence of all the things you will ever feel or see or hear in your life again, being brought steadily home to you all at once.

Leaving the sidewalk, you walk along a trodden, pebbled, weed-fringed path to the ravine's edge. Crickets, in loud full drumming chorus now, are shouting to quiver the dead. You follow obediently

a hundred yards away: at a distance of a hundred yards
sewer: underground conduit for spent water ☐ **rotten:** having gone bad (eggs...) ☐ **foliage:** leaves ☐ **thick:** strong
twists: zigzags, goes in a zigzag
a place to let alone: a place to get away from
nearness: proximity, closeness

(as) **useless as...** (≠ useful)
edge: limit

fear: apprehension ☐ **dread:** terror ☐ **waxen:** pale ☐ **coffin:** box to hold a dead person ☐ **passed away:** died
vulture: bird of prey ☐ **casket:** (Am) coffin
withdrawn: uncommunicative, unsociable ☐ **good:** well-behaved
succintly: briefly and clearly ☐ **politics,** (adj) political
awaken: stop sleeping
crib: child's bed ☐ **staring up at:** looking up fixedly at
blind: unable to see ☐ **frozen:** cold, impassive
wicker basket: basket made of osier (with flexible branches)
by: near ☐ **high chair:** chair on high legs for a baby at table
realize: understand, are aware
laughing (when happy), **crying** (when unhappy)

wading: making its way with difficulty as if through water

brough home to you: made comprehensible ☐ **steadily:** constantly, inexorably ☐ **all at once:** suddenly
trodden: pressed with the feet; tread, trod, trodden, walk on
pebbled: paved with round stones ☐ **weed-fringed path:** way with weed (grass) on sides ☐ **in full drumming...:** sounding loudly ("**shouting**") ☐ **quiver:** shake ☐ **obediently** (obey sb)

behind brave, fine, tall Mother who is defender of all the universe. You feel braveness because she goes before, and you hang back a trifle for a moment, and then hurry on, too. Together, then you approach, reach, and pause at the very edge of civilization.

The ravine.

Here and now, down there in that pit of jungled blackness is suddenly all the evil you will ever know. Evil you will never understand. All of the nameless things are there. Later, when you have grown you'll be given names to label them with. Meaningless syllables to describe the waiting nothingness. Down there in the huddled shadow, among thick trees and trailed vines, lives the odor of decay. Here, at this spot, civilization ceases, reason ends, and a universal evil takes over.

You realize you are alone. You and your mother. Her hand trembles.

Her hand *trembles.*

Your belief in your private world is shattered. You feel Mother tremble. Why? Is she, too, doubtful? But she is bigger, stronger, more intelligent than yourself, isn't she? Does she, too, feel that intangible menace, that groping out of darkness, that crouching malignancy down below? Is there, then, no strength in growing up? no solace in being an adult? no sanctuary in life? no flesh citadel strong enough to withstand the scrabbling assault of midnights? Doubts flush you. Ice cream lives again in your throat, stomach, spine and limbs; you are instantly cold as a wind out of December-gone.

You realize that all men are like this. That each person is to himself one alone. One oneness, a unit in a society, but always afraid. Like here, standing. If you

brave: unafraid, fearless □ **fine:** wonderful
before: ahead (of you), first
hang back: walk slowly behind □ **a trifle:** a little
hurry on: walk or move quickly; hurry up, we're late!
pause: stop for a short time, make a pause

pit: natural hole in the ground (the ravine)
evil: anything that is bad, immoral; good and evil
nameless: without a name
when you have grown (become a grown-up, an adult)
label: give a label, classify □ **meaningless:** senseless
describe, description □ **nothingness:** emptiness
huddled shadow: dense darkness □ **trailed** (on ground) **vine(s)** (plant) □ **decay:** putrefaction □ **spot:** particular place
ceases, ends: stops □ **takes over:** begins and replaces civilisation and reason

belief (in God...) □ **private:** intimate □ **shattered:** broken to pieces, ruined □ **doubtful:** full of doubt, "fear", "dread"
stronger: strong ≠ weak; strength ≠ weakness
groping: grope, make one's way by feeling (like the blind)
crouching: bending close to ground □ **malignancy,** malignant, filled with desire to hurt
solace: comfort □ **flesh citadel:** (here) human being (adult)
withstand: resist □ **scrabbling** (with feet and hands to go over)
mid(dle of the) **night** □ **flush:** "empty" you of any courage
throat: passage in neck for food and air □ **spine:** backbone
December-gone: gone, past
each person: every one (of 2 or more) separately
oneness: unity, individuality (set apart from the others)

should scream now, il you should holler for help, would it matter?

You are so close to the ravine now that in the instant of your scream, in the interval between someone hearing it and running to find you, much could happen.

Blackness could come swiftly, swallowing; and in one titanically freezing moment all would be concluded. Long before dawn, long before police with flashlights might probe the disturbed pathway, long before men with trembling brains could rustle down the pebbles to your help. Even if they were within five hundred yards of you now, and help *certainly* is, in three seconds a dark tide could rise to take all eight years of life away from you and—

The essential impact of life's loneliness crushes your beginning-to-tremble body. Mother is alone, too. She cannot look to the sanctity of marriage, the protection of her family's love, she cannot look to the United States Constitution or the City Police, she cannot look anywhere, in this very instant, save into her heart, and there she'll find nothing but uncontrollable repugnance and a will to fear. In this instant it is an individual problem seeking an individual solution. You must accept being alone and work on from there.

You swallow hard, cling to her. Oh Lord, don't let her die, please, you think. Don't do anything to us. Father will be coming home from lodge-meeting in an hour and if the house is empty...?

Mother advances down the path into the primeval jungle. Your voice trembles. "Mom. Skip's all right. Skip's all right. He's all right. Skip's all right."

Mother's voice is strained, high. "He always comes

scream: cry out on a high note □ **holler:** (Am, fam): shout
would it matter?: would it be of any importance?
close to the ravine: very near the ravine

happen: (of events) take place, occur
swiftly: rapidly □ **swallow** (up): take in, cause to disappear
titanically: gigantically □ **freezing:** very cold (with fear)
dawn: first light of day □ **flashlight(s):** electric torch
probe: explore □ **disturbed:** (here) where sth wrong occurs
brain(s): intellect □ **rustle...:** move with little noise like leaves in the wind □ **within:** at a distance of less than

tide: current (like sea coming in) □ **rise:** come up (and "swallow" you, devour you)
loneliness: solitude □ **crushes...** (like an apple underfoot...): presses (146.9)
look to: be careful of or about □ **sanctity:** sacredness

in this very instant: (emphatic) right now □ **save:** except
nothing but...: nothing except...
will: power, force □ **to fear**, to dread: cf. nouns (148.11)
seeking: (here) asking for, calling for; seek, sought, sought, try to find □ **work:** act, do things
swallow (saliva, for fear) □ **cling** (close) **to** her □ **Lord** (Jesus Christ) □ **die:** stop living; be dead (result); death

primeval: very ancient, primitive
Mom: (Am) Mum, Mummy, Mother

strained: showing nervousness □ **high** (tone) ≠ low, deep...

through here. I tell him not to, but those darned kids, they come through here anyway. Some night he'll come through and never come out again—"

Never come out again. That could mean anything. Tramps. Criminals. Darkness. Accident. Most of all—death.

Alone in the universe.

There are a million small towns like this all over the world. Each as dark, as lonely, each as removed, as full of shuddering and wonder. The reedy playing or minor-key violins is the small towns' music, with no lights but many shadows. Oh the vast swelling loneliness of them. The secret damp ravines of them. Life is a horror lived in them at night, when at all sides sanity, marriage, children, happiness, are threatened by an ogre called Death.

Mother raises her voice into the dark.

"Skip! Skipper!" she calls. "Skip! Skipper!"

Suddenly, both of you realize there is something wrong. Something very wrong. You listen intently and realize what it is.

The crickets have stopped chirping.

Silence is complete.

Never in your life a silence like this one. One so utterly complete. Why should the crickets cease? Why? What reason? They have never stopped ever before. Not ever.

Unless. Unless—

Something is going to happen.

It is as if the whole ravine is tensing, bunching together its black fibers, drawing in power from all about sleeping countrysides, for miles and miles. From

not to (come) ☐ **darn(ed)** (!): damned (!) (malediction expressing anger) ☐ **anyway:** in any case, at any rate

tramp(s): vagabond, vagrant ☐ **most of all:** above all

all over the world: in the whole world, throughout the world
removed (from any other town): far, distant, lonely, remote
shuddering: trembling ☐ **wonder:** strangeness ☐ **reedy:** thin and high (sound) ☐ **minor-key:** sad set of notes
swelling: growing (like a river in prolonged heavy rain)
damp: rather wet, not thoroughly dry
at all sides: everywhere ☐ **sanity** ≠ madness; sane ≠ mad
threatened: menaced; a threat, a menace

raises her voice: speaks louder

intently: very attentively

chirping: making chirps (short sharp [high] sounds of some insects or of small birds); a chirp or a chirrup; to chirp

utterly: absolutely, completely
they have never stopped ever before: never ever: emphatic and informal form of "never"
unless: except if... ("something is going to happen")

tensing (up muscles) ☐ **bunching** together: gathering together
fiber(s): (Am), fibre(s) ☐ **drawing in:** taking in, getting
all about...: countrysides here and there, everywhere

dew-sodden forests and dells and rolling hills where dogs tilt heads to moons, from all around the great silence is sucked into one center, and you at the core of it. In ten seconds now, something will happen, something will happen. The crickets keep their truce, the stars are so low you can almost brush the tinsel. There are swarms of them, hot and sharp.

Growing, growing, the silence. Growing, growing, the tenseness. Oh it's so dark, so far away from everything. Oh God!

And then, way way off across the ravine:

"Okay, Mom! Coming, Mother!"

And again:

"Hi, Mom! Coming, Mom!"

And then the quick scuttering of tennis shoes padding down through the pit of the ravine as three kids come dashing, giggling. Your brother Skipper, Chuck Redman, and Augie Bartz. Running, giggling.

The stars suck up like the stung antennae of ten millions snails.

The crickets sing!

The darkness pulls back, startled, shocked, angry. Pulls back, losing its appetite at being so rudely interrupted as it prepared to feed. As the dark retreats like a wave on a shore, three kids pile out of it, laughing.

"Hi, Mom! Hi, Shorts! Hey!"

It smells like Skipper all right. Sweat and grass and his oiled leather baseball glove.

"Young man, you're going to get a licking," declares Mother. She puts away her fear instantly. You know she

dew: *rosée* □ **sodden:** very wet □ **dell(s):** valley □ **rolling hill(s):** small mountain rising and falling □ **tilt:** incline
sucked: drawn in □ **core:** centre

truce: temporary cessation of hostilities (of chirping here)
brush: touch □ **tinsel:** shining metallic ornament □ **swarms of:** a multitude of □ **sharp:** clearly visible against the sky
growing (in intensity), augmenting, increasing
tenseness: nervous anxiety

way: (Am) far □ **off:** away; 2 miles off □ **across...:** on the opposite side of □ **coming:** I'm coming

hi!: (Am) hello!
scuttering: running with short steps □ **padding down:** going softly down □ **pit:** natural hole in ground
dashing: rushing □ **giggling:** laughing continuously in an uncontrollable manner
suck up: draw in □ **stung:** hurt (as if by an insect), pricked
snail(s): small, soft animal with a shell on its back; at a snail's pace, very slowly
pulls back ≠ advances □ **startled:** jumping through surprise
rudely: rude, not at all polite
feed: eat; feed, fed, fed; food □ **retreats:** "pulls back"
wave: movement of the sea □ **shore:** land by the sea □ **pile out of it:** come out of it in a disorderly way; a pile, a heap

all right: (fam) no doubt, certainly
oiled: with oil on it □ **leather** (for making shoes...) □ **glove** (to protect hand) □ **lick(ing):** (fam) beat(ing), spank (146.24)
put(s) away: (here) forgets about □ **instantly:** immediately

will never tell anybody of it, ever. It will be in her heart though, for all time, as it is in your heart, for all time.

You walk home to bed in the late summer night. You are glad Skipper is alive. Very glad. For a moment there you thought—

Far off in the dim moonlit country, over a viaduct and down a valley, a train goes rushing along and it whistles like a lost metal thing, nameless and running. You go to bed, shivering, beside your brother, listening to that train whistle, and thinking of a cousin who lived way out in the country where that train is now; a cousin who died of pneumonia late at night years and years ago... You smell the sweat of Skip beside you. It is magic. You stop trembling. You hear footsteps outside the house on the sidewalk, as Mother is turning out the lights. A man clears his throat in a way you recognize.

Mom says, “That’s your father.”

It is.

it will be in her heart: she will never forget it

walk home: no preposition! (go home, return home...)
glad: happy, pleased □ **alive** ≠ dead
you thought: you thought... (he had died)
dim: not bright □ **moonlit,** sunlit, lit or lighted by the moon, by the sun
whistles: make a noise like a whistle; a policeman's whistle
shivering: trembling □ **beside:** near

way: (Am) far (in space and time); way back in the fifties

magic: mysterious charm □ **footstep(s):** sound made by foot walking □ **turning out:** stopping (a gas, oil or electric light...)
clears his throat (by coughing), clear obstructions from canal

Grammaire au fil des nouvelles

Voici, dans l'ordre de leur apparition dans le texte, des phrases à compléter (ou non !) selon les indications données. Les numéros de pages renvoient à la Grammaire active de l'anglais *(Le Livre de Poche, 1989).*

It ... *(grow)* late at night. Late for you, accustomed to bedding at nine or nine-thirty; once in a while perhaps begging Mom and Dad to let you... *(stay)* up later ... *(hear)* Sam and Henry on that strange radio (la forme progressive et la forme simple, p. 28 — *let* et *make* + ..., p. 62 — prépositions exprimant le but, p. 156).

He ... *(stay up)* later than you (substitut des auxiliaires modaux, p. 22).

The town is so quiet and far off, you ... only hear the crickets (auxiliaire modal souvent employé avec les verbes de perception, p. 60).

You are only eight years old, you know ... of ... death, ... fear or ... dread (*little* ou *few,* p. 80 — emploi ou non de l'article défini *the*, p. 70).

But she is ... *(big)*, ... *(strong)*, ... *(intelligent)* than yourself, ...? (comparatif de supériorité, p. 114 — question-tags, pp. 46-48).

Is there no flesh citadel *(strong)* to understand the scrabbling assault of midnights? (ajoutez *enough* à la place qui convient, p. 140).

You ... accept being alone and work from there (expression de l'obligation, p. 22).

He comes through here (ajoutez *always* à la place qui convient, p. 140).

The reedy playing of minor-key violins is the small towns ... *(music)* with no lights but ... shadows (génitif, p. 98 — *much* ou *many*, p. 80).

Something ... happen (futur proche, p. 44).

The crickets have stopped ... *(chirp)* (le gérondif, p. 150).

The stars suck up like the strong antennae of ten ... *(million)* snails (Les nombres cardinaux et ordinaux, p. 88).

THE THING
AT THE TOP OF THE STAIRS

TALKING ABOUT THE SHORT STORY *THE THING AT THE TOP OF THE STAIRS* (p. 165)

H. Y. What about *The Thing at the Top of the Stairs*?

R. B. Yes. That's an absolutely true story except for the ending. When I was four, five, six, seven, eight years old we lived in this little house in Waukegan, Illinois. The bathroom was upstairs. So, in the middle of the night, say at three o'clock, I had to go to the bathroom. I'd have to run half-way up the stairs and turn on the light in order to make it the rest of the way. Why my father turned the light off all night I don't know. He was saving money, I suppose, electricity. I understand that, when you are poor. But, it was a hell of a thing. I tried to get up the stairs with my eyes shut because I knew, if I looked up, the thing would be waiting for me at the top of the stairs. If I could get the light on first, it wouldn't be there. But, it was always a contest to see whether I would pee on the stairs first. Sometimes I'd go pee in the kitchen sink so I wouldn't have to go up those stairs at night... So, naturally, a day had to come when I write that short story. And when I go back to my hometown and go in the house and remember that staircase and the thing that used to be there, then I discover the old fear is still with me. I'm afraid to go up and see if it's waiting. And when I do, it's there, you know.

top ≠ bottom □ **stairs** (for walking up or down in a house)
true: real □ **except for:** with the exception of
ending, end ≠ beginning
Waukegan = "Green Town" in the stories □ **bathroom** with bath, washbasin, W.C. □ beginning, **middle,** end □ (let us) **say**
go to the bathroom (to urinate) □ **half** (1/2) **way**
turn on ≠ turn off □ **in order:** to □ **make it...:** succeed in going up to the end □ **why... I don't know:** notice the inversion
saving; save, economize
it was a hell of a thing: (fam) it was terribly frightening
with my eyes shut (closed)

get... on: turn on, switch on
contest: fight, struggle □ **whether:** if... or not □ **pee:** pass water (urine, 14) □ **go** (and) **pee** □ **sink** (for washing plates and dishes in) □ **naturally:** of course
had (inevitably) **to** come (it couldn't be helped)
my hometown (Waukegan, Illinois, where I was born and grew up) □ **staircase:** stairs □ **discover:** find out
old: dating back to my childhood □ **fear:** apprehension, fright □ **still** indicates continuation □ **waiting** (for me)

THE THING AT THE TOP OF THE STAIRS

I have put down my real fears of what I knew was waiting for me in the dark hall leading up to the attic shadows in my old home in Northern Illinois—the Thing that *is* still waiting there.

(Addition to the original Preface
by Ray Bradbury, August 1st, 1993.)

put down (on paper)
fear(s): apprehension
leading (a road leads to a town...)
attic: room at the top of a house just below the roof
shadow(s): dark shape (form)
Northern: of the North
still indicates continuation

He was between trains.

He had got off in Chicago only to find that there was a four-hour waitover.

He thought about heading for the museum; the Renoirs and Monets had always held his eyes and touched his mind. But he was restless. The taxicab line outside the station made him blink.

Why not? he thought, grab a cab and taxi thirty miles north, spend an hour in his old hometown, then bid it farewell for the second time in his life, and ease back south to train out for New York, happier and perhaps wiser?

Much money for a few hours' whim, but what the hell. He opened a cab door, slung his suitcase in, and said:

"Green Town and return!"

The driver broke into a splendid smile and flipped the meter-flag, even as Emil Cramer leaped into the back seat and slammed the door.

Green Town, he thought, and—

The Thing at the top of the stairs.

What?

My God, he thought, what made me remember *that* on a fine spring afternoon?

And they drove north, with clouds that followed, to stop on Green Town's Main Street at three o'clock. He got out, gave the taxi driver fifty dollars as security, told him to wait, and looked up.

The marquee on the old Genesee Theater, in blood red letters, said: TWO CHILLERS. MANIAC HOUSE. DOCTOR DEATH. COME IN. BUT DON'T TRY TO LEAVE.

No, no, thought Cramer. The Phantom was better.

between (two trains...) ≠ **among** (many other things)
got off (the train...) ≠ got into the train
... **waitover:** he had to wait four hours; wait for sth
heading for: (here) going to; head for: move towards
held his eyes: attracted him; hold, held, held
mind: intellect □ ... **restless:** ... had had little rest or sleep
blink: shut and open eyes quickly
grab: take (suddenly) □ **taxi:** go by taxi or **cab** (Am)
hometown (where he was born) □ **bid it farewell:** say goodbye to it □ **ease:** (here) go calmly
to train for...: go by train to... (to taxi, 8)
wiser: showing better judgement, more common sense; wise
whim: caprice
what the hell: (fam) no importance! □ **slung his suitcase** (to carry clothes...): threw with effort or roughly
and return: and back; a return ticket ≠ a single ticket
broke into...: smiled suddenly □ **flipped...** (to show the taxi was engaged) □ **even as:** just at the same moment as □ **leaped:** jumped □ **back** ≠ front □ **slammed:** shut violently
Greentown: see interview p. 30.27
top: highest part □ **stairs** (to go up or down in a house)

fine: nice, splendid □ **spring** (season), summer, autumn, winter
drove: went □ **cloud** (in sky, announcing rain) □ **follow:** come or go after □ **main:** most important, principal, chief
as security: in case he did not come back

marquee (over the entrance) □ **blood:** red liquid in the body
chiller(s): (fam) crime film □ **maniac house** (for mentally deranged people) □ **leave,** left, left: go (away, out)
the Phantom (of the Opera), Lon Chaney's famous movie (film)

When I was six, all he had to do was stiffen, whirl, gape, and point down into the camera with his ghastly face. *That* was terror!

I wonder, he thought, was it the Phantom then, plus the Hunchback, plus the Bat that made all of my childhood nights miserable?

And, walking through the town, he gave a quiet laugh of remembrance...

How his mother would give him a look over the morning cornflakes: What *happened* during the night? Did you *see* it? Was it *there*, up in the *dark*? How *tall*, what *color*? How did you manage not to scream *this* time, to wake your father: what, *what*?

While his father, from around the cliff of his newspaper, eyed them both, and glanced at the leather strop hung near the kitchen washstand, itching to be used.

And he, Emil Cramer, six years old, would sit there, remembering the stabbing pain in his small crayfish loins if he did not make it upstairs in time, past the Monster Beast lurking in the attic midnight of the house, shrieking at the last instant to fall back down like a panicked dog or scorched cat, to lie crushed and blind at the bottom of the stairs, wailing:

Why? Why is it there? Why am I being punished? What have I done?

And crawling, creeping away in the dark hall to fumble back to bed and lie in agonies of bursting fluid, praying for dawn, when the Thing might stop waiting for him and sift into the stained wallpaper or suck into the cracks under the attic door.

Once he had tried to hide a chamberpot under the

stiffen: become rigid □ **whirl:** move round very fast
gape: open his mouth wide □ **ghastly:** terrible, macabre

wonder: ask myself
hunchback: one with a deformed back □ **bat:** flying mouse-like animal that flies at night □ **miserable:** unhappy (not poor!)
quiet (with little noise) ≠ loud, noisy
of remembrance: remembering the time when he was a child
would: was in the habit of + v + ing

dark (n), darkness ≠ light □ **how tall** (was it?)
manage to: succeed in + v + ing □ **scream:** cry out loudly on a high note □ **wake:** cause to stop sleeping
cliff: high rock-face overhanging the sea (Dover, Etretat...)
eyed: watched carefully □ **glanced at the leather strop** (for sharpening razors): gave a quick look at... □ **washstand** with jug of water and basin on it (to wash face, hands) □ **itching:** waiting impatiently
stabbing: severe and sudden □ **crayfish** (used to emphasize the smallness): *écrevisse* □ **loins:** *reins* □ **make it...:** succeed in going upstairs □ **lurking:** wait secretly □ **attic:** room at the top of a house □ **shrieking:** screaming
scorched: burnt □ **crushed:** pressed, destroyed □ **blind:** unable to see □ **bottom** ≠ top □ **wailing:** crying with a loud, high voice

crawling, creeping (on hands and knees, slowly and quietly)
fumble (hesitantly) □ **in agonies:** tormented □ **bursting...:** urine coming out suddenly □ **praying** (asking God) **for dawn** (first light of day) □ **sift:** go through □ **stained:** dirty □ **suck:** be drawn into □ **crack(s):** narrow space or opening
once: on one occasion □ **hide,** hid, hidden

bed. Discovered, it was thrown and shattered. Once, he had run water in the kitchen sink, and tried to use it, but his father's radio ears, tuned, heard, and he rose in a shouting fury.

Yes, yes, he said, and he walked through the town on a day becoming storm colored. He reached the street on which he had once lived. The sun turned off. The sky was all winter dusk. He gasped.

For a single drop of cold rain struck his nose.

"Lord!" he laughed. "There it *is*. My house!"

And it was empty and a FOR SALE sign stood out by the sidewalk.

There was the white clapboard front, with a large porch to one side and a smaller one out front. There was the front door and, beyond, the parlor where he had lain on the foldout bed with his brother, sweating the night hours, as everyone else slept and dreamed. And to the right, the dining room and the door that led to the hall and the stairs that moved up into eternal night.

He moved up the walk toward the side porch door.

The Thing, now, what shape had it been, and color and size? Did it have a smoking face, and grotto teeth and hellfire-burning Baskerville eyes? Did it ever whisper or murmur or moan—?

He shook his head.

After all, the Thing had never really existed, *had* it?

Which was exactly why his father's teeth had splintered every time he stared at his gutless wonder of a son! Couldn't the child see that the hall was empty, *empty*!? Didn't the damned boy know that it was his own nightmare movie machine, locked in his head, that

shattered: broken into pieces
run: made flow □ **sink:** basin for washing plates and dishes
tuned: (here) ready to listen, alert □ **rose:** got up
shouting (out loud, crying) □ **fury:** rage, violent anger

storm: violent weather □ **reached:** got to, arrived at
once: in the past □ **turned off:** went off, disappeared
dusk: time just before night □ **gasped:** took in air suddenly
single: just one □ **struck:** hit; strike, struck, struck
Lord! (Jesus), my God!
empty ≠ full (of people) □ **for sale** (to be sold) □ **stood out:** was clearly visible □ **by:** near □ **sidewalk:** (Am) pavement
clapboard: (Am) covering to protect walls from rain
porch: (Am) veranda(h) □ **out front:** at the front (≠ back)
beyond: farther on □ **parlo(u)r:** sitting-room
foldout (sofa convertible into a bed) □ **sweating:** perspiring (with fear) □ **dreamed:** had dreams (visions during sleep)
right ≠ left □ lead, **led,** led; all roads lead to Rome
moved up: went up

walk (for walking in gardens) □ **toward(s):** in the direction of
shape: form; what shape is it?
size: dimensions □ **grotto:** natural cave (with sharp tooth-like rocks) □ **hell** ≠ paradise □ **burning:** be in flames □ *The Hound of the Baskervilles* by C. Doyle □ **whisper:** murmur □ **moan:** lament □ **shook his head** (in disapproval)

teeth: (sing) tooth
splintered: (fig.) broken to pieces □ **stared:** looked fixedly
gutless: without any courage □ **wonder(ful): marvel(lous)**
damned: (fam) wretched, confounded *(sacré, foutu, fichu)*
nightmare: bad dream □ **locked:** shut up

flashed those snowfalls of dread up through the night to melt on the terrible air?

Thump-*whack!* His father's knuckles cracked his brow to exorcise the ghost. Whack-*thump!*

Emil Cramer snapped his eyes wide, surprised to find he had shut them. He stepped up on the small porch.

He touched the doorknob.

My God! he thought.

For the door, unlocked, was drifting quietly open.

The house and the dark hall lay empty and waiting.

He pushed. The door drifted further in, with the merest sigh of its hinges.

The same night that had hung there like funeral-parlor curtains, still filled the coffin-narrow hall. It smelled with rains from other years, and was filled with twilights that had come to visit and never gone away...

He stepped in.

Instantly, outside, rain fell. The downpour shut off the world. The downpour drenched the porch floorboards and drowned his breathing.

He took another step into complete night.

No light burned at the far end of the hall, three steps up—

Yes! That had been the problem!

To save money, the damned bulb was *never* left burning!

In order to scare the Thing off, you had to run, leap up, grab the chain and yank the light *on*!

So, blind and battering walls, you jumped. But could *never find the chain!*

Don't look up! you thought. If you see *It*, and it sees *You*! No. No!

flashed: suddenly sent □ **dread:** fear, fright, terror
melt: (here) disappear (like snow in the sun), vanish
thump-wack!: bang! □ **knuckle(s):** finger joint □ **cracked:** hit, struck □ **brow:** forehead (part of face below hair)
snapped... wide (completely): suddenly opened his eyes wide
stepped up: walked up; a step (movement of foot in walking)
doorknob: round handle to open the door with

unlocked ≠ locked (shut with key) □ **drifting... open** (without having to be pushed open, of its own accord)
drifted further in: ... wider and wider (5)
merest: smallest □ **sigh:** sound □ **hinge(s)** (by which door is hung to frame) □ **... parlor** (for the dead before burial)
curtains: drapery □ **coffin-narrow:** as narrow (≠ wide, broad) as a coffin (box in which dead body is buried)
twilight(s): darkish light in sky when day is about to become night
downpour: heavy fall of rain □ **shut off:** isolated
drenched: made all wet □ **floorboards** (on which you walk)
drowned: (here) made inaudible □ **breathing:** sound he made when taking in air; to breathe
... burned: was on □ **far** (adj) ≠ near □ **step(s):** place for the foot to go up or down

save: economize □ **bulb:** glass part of an electric lamp
burning: burn, burnt or burned, burnt or burned
scare... off: make it go away by causing fear (fright)
yank: pull suddenly (the light chain to put on the light)
battering: hitting (against, because he was unable to see)

look up ≠ look down

But then your head jerked. You looked. You screamed!

For the dark Thing was lurching out on the air to slam flat down like a tomb lid on your scream!

"Anyone *home...?*" he called, softly.

A damp wind blew from above. A smell of cellar earths and attic dusts touched his cheeks.

"Ready or not," he whispered. "Here I *come.*"

Behind him, slowly, softly, the front door drifted, hushed, and slid itself *shut.*

He froze.

Then he forced himself to take another step and another.

And, Christ! it seemed he felt himself... shrinking. Melting an inch at a time, sinking into smallness, even as the flesh on his face diminished, and his suit and shoes became too large...

What am I *doing* here? he thought. What do I *need*?

Answers. Yes. That was it. Answers.

His right shoe touched...

The bottom of the stairs.

He gasped. His foot jerked back. Then, slowly, he forced it to touch the step again.

Easy. Just don't look up, he thought.

Fool! he thought, that's why you're here. The stairs. And the top of the stairs. That's *it!*

Now...

Very quietly, he lifted his head.

To stare at the dark light bulb sunk in its dead white socket, six feet above his head.

It was as far off as the moon.

His fingers twitched.

jerked: gave a jerk (a short quick movement)

for: because □ **lurching:** moving with sudden irregular movements □ **flat:** completely, directly □ **lid** (covering the tomb)
softly: in a soft (≠ loud) voice
damp: wet (≠ dry) □ **cellar:** underground room (for wine...)
earth(s): soil, ground □ **dust(s):** particles of earth □ **cheek(s):** part of face between nose and ears
front door: main entrance door (main: see 166.26)
hushed slid itself shut (shut slowly, softly [cf. drift 172.9,11])
froze (with fear): suddenly stopped and became completely still (without moving at all)

shrinking: becoming smaller, then **sinking into smallness**
an inch (2.54 cm) **at a time:** inch by inch
flesh: soft substance of body □ **suit:** jacket and trousers
large: big (wide, broad ≠ narrow)
he thought (to himself) □ **need:** want; be in need (n) of

jerked back: suddenly moved backwards (≠ forwards)

easy: take it easy, relax
fool!: you're a fool (a stupid man); (adj) foolish

now: now then
quietly: calmly □ **lifted:** raised
sunk(deep) in its socket □ **dead:** not functioning (176.9)
feet: (sing) foot = 30.48 cm □ **above** ≠ under, below
the moon shines at night in the sky
twitched: made little jerky uncontrollable movements

Somewhere in the walls of the house, his mother turned in her sleep, his brother lay strewn in pale winding sheets, his father stopped up his snores to—*listen.*

Quick! Before he *wakes.* Jump!

With a terrible grunt he flung himself up. His foot struck the third step. His hand seized out to yank the light-chain *there. Yank!* And there *again.*

Dead! Oh, Christ. No light. Dead! Like all the lost years.

The chain snaked from his fingers. His hand fell.

Night. Dark.

Outside, cold rain fell behind a shut mine-door.

He blinked his eyes open, shut, open, shut, as if the blink might yank the chain, pull the light *on*! His heart banged not only in his chest, but hammered under his arms and in his aching groin.

He swayed. He toppled.

No, he cried silently. Free yourself. Look! *See*!

And at last he turned his head to look up and up at darkness shelved on darkness.

"Thing...?" he whispered. "Are you there?"

The house shifted like an immense scale, under his weight.

High in the midnight air a black flag, a dark banner furled, unfurled its funeral skirts, its whispering crepe.

Outside, he thought, *remember*! it is a *spring* day.

Rain tapped the door behind him, quietly.

"Now" he whispered.

And balanced between the cold, sweating stairwell walls, he began to climb.

"I'm at the fourth step," he whispered.

the four **walls** of a house
strewn (all over or across the bed)
winding sheet(s) (to cover dead body); (white...) **sheets** on a bed
☐ **snore(s):** noisy way of breathing when asleep
quick! hurry up! ☐ **wakes:** stops sleeping
grunt (as of a pig) ☐ **flung... up:** moved himself up violently

lost: gone by (never to come back); lose, lost, lost

snaked: moved in a twisting way, like a snake (a serpent)

outside ≠ inside

blink is also a noun ☐ **pull the light on** ≠ pull... off
chest: upper front part of body ☐ **hammered:** struck, banged
aching: painful ☐ **groin:** part of body where legs meet
swayed (from side to side) ☐ **toppled:** fell down
free yourself (from that fear): free ≠ held up in prison
at (long) **last:** in the end, after a long time
darkness shelved on darkness; shelve: put (a book...) on a shelf

shifted: changed in position ☐ **scale(s)** for measuring your **weight** (in kilos...); I weigh (no t!) sixty-five kilos
midnight: 12 o'clock at night ☐ the French **flag** is blue, white and red ☐ **furled...:** rolled and unrolled ☐ **skirt(s):** (here) what flags and banners are made of (cloth)
tapped: struck lightly against

balanced: hardly stable ☐ **stairwell:** space where the stairs are
climb: go up

"Now I'm at the fifth..."

"Sixth! You *hear*, up there?"

Silence. Darkness.

Christ! he thought, run, jump, fall out in the rain, the light—!

No!

"Seventh! Eighth."

The heart throbbed under his arms, between his legs.

"Tenth—"

His voice trembled. He took a deep breath and—

Laughed! God, yes! *Laughed!*

It was like smashing glass. His fear shattered, fell away.

"Eleven!" he cried. "Twelve!" he shouted. "Thirteen!" he hooted. "Damn you! Hell, oh God, hell, yes, hell! And fourteen!"

Why hadn't he thought of this before, age six? Just leap up, shouting laughs, to kill that Thing forever!?

"Fifteen!" he snorted, and almost brayed with delight.

A final wondrous jump.

"Sixteen!"

He landed. He could not stop laughing.

He thrust his fist straight out in the solid dark cold air.

The laughter froze, his shout choked in his throat.

He sucked in winter night.

Why? a child's voice echoed from far off below in another time. Why am I being punished? What have I *done*?

His heart stopped, then let go.

His groin convulsed. A gunshot of scalding water burst forth to stream hot and shocking down his legs.

fifth: notice the change in spelling (five)
(do you) **hear?**

fall out...: get out (of the house) quick in the rain

throbbed: beat strongly and rapidly (with excitement)

took a deep breath: take a breath, breathe in (take in air)

smash(ing): break into pieces ☐ **shattered and fell away:** (fig.) broke suddenly and was gone (had disappeared all of a sudden)

hooted: laughed very much ☐ **damn you!:** go to hell!

thought of ☐ **age six:** when he was six (years old)
shouting laughs: hooting ☐ **kill:** put to death ☐ **forever:** eternally ☐ **snorted:** hooted ☐ **brayed** (like an ass) ☐ **delight:** intense pleasure and satisfaction ☐ **wondrous:** wonderful

landed: (here) arrived (at the top of the stairs)
thrust: pushed forward ☐ **fist:** hand with fingers closed
straight: directly ☐ **solid:** dense, compact
froze, choked: (here) was stopped ☐ **throat:** passage in the neck for air and food ☐ **sucked in** (as if trying to absorb it)
echoed: came back as an echo ☐ **far off:** far away
time: period in his life (his childhood)

let go: (here) started beating freely again
gunshot: sudden flow or stream ☐ **scalding:** as **hot** as boiling
burst forth: came out suddenly ☐ **to stream:** to flow

"No!" he shrieked.
For his fingers had touched something...
It was the Thing at the top of the stairs.
It was wondering where he had been.
It had been waiting all these long years...
For him to come home.

shrieked: cried out with a high sound; a shriek

waiting: wait for sb or sth; notice the construction: **waiting for him to** come (back) home

Grammaire au fil des nouvelles

Voici, dans l'ordre de leur apparition dans le texte, des phrases à compléter (ou non !) selon les indications données. Les numéros de pages renvoient à la Grammaire active de l'anglais *(Le Livre de Poche, 1989).*

The taxicab line outside the station made him ... *(blink)* (*make* et *let* + ..., p. 62).

No, no, thought Crammer. The Phantom was ... *(good)* (comparatif de supériorité, p. 114).

He gave a quick look of remembrance. How his mother ... give him a look over the morning cornflakes. And he, Emil Crammer, six years old, ... sit there (auxiliaire exprimant l'habitude, p. 56).

Once he had tried to hide a chamberpot under the bed. Discovered, it ... *(throw)* and ... *(shatter)* (passif au prétérit, p. 50).

After all the Thing had never really existed, ...? (question-tags, p. 46).

For the door, unlocked, ... *(drift)* quietly open (prétérit progressif, p. 30).

... save money, the damned bulb was never left burning./ ... scare the Thing off you had to run (prépositions exprimant le but, p. 156).

A damp wind blew ... above (prépositions indiquant la provenance, p. 152).

"I'm at the ... *(four)* step", he whispered. "Now I'm at the ... *(five)*" (les nombres ordinaux, p. 86).

He could not stop ... *(laugh)* (*stop* + ..., p. 150).

Why ... *(I, punish)*? What ...? *(I, do)* (le passif et la forme progressive, p. 52 — le present perfect, p. 32).

For his fingers ... *(touch)* something (pluperfect, p. 34).

TALKING ABOUT THE NUTS AND BOLTS
(Exclusive interview. July 16th 1990 — Summary)

The short story as a literary genre — How do you go about writing a short story? — "The theater of morning" — What is your definition of a short story? — Don't turn away from what is individually you — You learn writing by writing — Go find your own loves... — I was blinded by my own insecurities — My stories are my diary and my two murder mysteries are my autobiography — Do you write in the day, in the night, at any time or at regular hours? — Why do you write? — I have a cellarful of ideas — Ireland or a lesson in creativity — Let your imagination run... — Humor — Literary influences — Shakespeare, *Hamlet, The Sonnets* — The Dylan Thomas of America — Space travel and the immortality of the human race — My twelfth Christmas — Reading one's own short stories.

talking about the nuts *(écrous)* **and bolts** *(boulons)*, about (literary...) technique
go about: begin working at
blinded: made blind, unable to see
diary: journal in which you write about your experiences, feelings... every day
cellarful of: lots of; cellar: underground room where wine... is kept
Dylan Thomas (1914-1953): a great poet born in Swansea in Wales

H. Y. Now we're coming to a different subject altogether. What about the short story as a literary genre, as opposed to the novel, for instance?

R. B. I've always been a short story writer. When I was twenty-nine, my wife was pregnant, we had thirty dollars in the bank. So I went to New York and stayed at the Y.M.C.A. and met with various editors. They said: "Don't you have a novel?" and I said: "No, I'm a sprinter, I love the short story form because I can get out of bed in the morning, jump start an idea and by noon finish a story. It's great fun!" Novels are boring. If you are not careful you run down the hill. Suddenly you stop. You don't know what the hell to do next. But over the years I gradually learned more about character. So I began to write novellas like *Fahrenheit 451*. But the early part of my career was five hundred short stories! Thank God for that! Now I live off the royalties from all five hundred tales. Stories are superb because you get a seedling idea, work with it, complete it, and it's over and done! A novel is something else. It's hard to find the core of such a huge thing. You have to wait for it to leap on you unexpectedly. Now that I've learned how to write novels I'll do more of them.

H. Y. And how do you go about writing a short

a different subject altogether: a completely different subject

for instance: for example

pregnant: expecting a baby
stayed: stopped; stop at a hotel
Y.M.C.A. (hostel): Young Men's Christian Association

a sprinter runs very fast over short distances (here fig)
jump start an idea: suddenly get an idea going
by noon: before 12 □ **fun:** enjoyment □ **boring** ≠ interesting
careful: attentive □ **run... hill** (small mountain) [fig]
the hell (used for emphasis) □ **next:** afterwards □ **over:** in the course of □ **character:** people in books, their psychology
novella(s): short novel □ **early:** first in time (≠ late)

thank God for that: indicates great gratitude □ **live off** or on the money I receive as a writer **(royalties)** □ **tale(s):** story
seedling idea like a young plant grown from a seed *(graine) (See end of Preface, p. 13)* □ **... done:** finished □ **hard** ≠ easy
core: heart, centre □ **huge:** enormous, very big in size
leap: jump suddenly, **unexpectedly** (when you don't expect it to)
I've learned <u>how</u> **to...**
go about, set about + v + ing: begin working at

story?

R. B. You explode. You step out of bed in the morning and explode... I write blindly, out of blind need... In recent years I lie in bed at six a.m. and inside my head is what I call "the theater of morning". All these characters are trapped between my ears and they begin to talk to themselves. I'm not completely awake and I'm not asleep. I'm not dreaming and I am not *not* dreaming. I listen to the voices and when they reach a certain pitch I jump out of bed and run to trap them on paper before they escape. It's especially true if I'm working on a novel. Then the characters start talking all by themselves to solve problems. With short stories or poetry it'd be word-association. I would just type things out on paper, a series of nouns to see what I think of the nouns. I'll give you a good example of the way I behave. I was watching a television news programme several weeks ago when they told of an aviator who had died the previous week. Why were they telling his story? Because at the end of World War II he was shot down over France and his parachute saved him. Two years later, about to be married, his bride said: "Where is the parachute?" He brought her the parachute and she made the bridal gown out of the silk. Well, now, that's a fabulous woman, yes? A woman of metaphorical imagination. Instantly, I jumped from the TV set to the typewriter, wrote a poem about the bride, the parachute and the bridal gown. The final metaphor is when the aviator dies, you rip the bridal gown's seams and turn it into a winding sheet. A triple metaphor! This sort of thing happens to me all the time. Accidents. Surprises. Someone says something and I'm listening. But they're

explode (with energy...) □ **step out:** get out
blindly ≠ uncontrollably □ **out of:** driven by, urged by
six a.m. (ante meridiem): six in the morning □ **inside:** in
is: there is
characters: 184.22 □ **trapped:** caught (11) (as in a trap); a mouse trap □ **awake** ≠ sleeping
asleep: sleeping □ **dreaming;** dream, vision during sleep
the voices ("talking", speaking) □ **reach a... pitch** (degree): get loud enough □ **jump...:** get suddenly out... □ **trap:** catch
escape (from...) □ **true** ≠ false; speak the truth
start talking: begin to talk
by themselves (without me); by oneself, alone
it'd: it would (usually) □ **type** (with my typewriter, not write with my hand) □ "talk" is both a **noun** and a verb
example: a, not e!, instance □ **way** (in which) I...: manner
behave: act, do things □ **news:** report of recent events
told of: spoke about
the previous week: the week before; previous, preceding
war ≠ peace □ **shot down:** (plane) made to fall to the ground by hitting with a gun... □ **saved him** (from danger)
about to: on the point of + v + ing □ **bride:** woman about to be married or just married; bridal (of the bride)
bridal gown (dress) □ **out of:** from □ **silk:** smooth, soft, lustrous cloth □ **yes?:** isn't it? isn't that right?
instantly: at once □ **T.V. set,** radio set...
typewriter: 14; typewriting, typing; typist (secretary)

rip: tear, cut with quick motion □ **seam(s):** line of junction between two pieces of cloth □ **turn it into a winding sheet** (in which a dead body is wrapped): change it into...

not. They say things and don't hear what they're saying!... People give away their ideas...

H. Y. What is your own definition of a short story, if you have one?

R. B. An idea with a beginning, middle and end. That's over in ten or fifteen minutes when you read it. When you write it, it's over in two or three hours. If it doesn't finish itself quickly, then you may never finish it. I always try to do that but I'm not in charge. I don't control, my subconscious does all the work and when it's done I put it away and don't look at it for a couple of days. Then I come back when it's fresh. *Then* I can tell if the idea's good.

H. Y. Do you believe in creative writing?

R. B. In so far as you listen to your subconscious and not to anything outside... Somerset Maugham is my hero; I wrote him a love letter thirty-five years ago, praising his book *The Summing Up*, saying how important it was to me in my last year in high school. His wise, dry, wondrous way of looking at the world. He said: "Don't look to the left, to the right." Don't turn away from what is individually you. Look to your interior stuff. What do you *really* think about death or the universe or love. All the things that are really *you* must go into a story. If you follow the market-place you veer away from what is truly you. It never comes out, so you turn sour and die young. If you ignore yourself you will get old very very quickly.

H. Y. To come back to what we were saying before, what if a budding writer was to go to university?

R. B. That's disastrous. You can't learn writing at the university, you learn writing by writing, you learn

give away: reveal, divulge
own (and not another's), personal

middle; midday, the middle of the day or noon (184,19)
over: finished, ended; over and done with (for good)
write, wrote, written
doesn't finish itself: notice the reflexive pronoun
in charge (of): responsible (for) ("I don't control...")

done: finished (6) □ **put... away:** (here) forget it □ **a couple of:** (fam) a few □ **fresh** and new, other and different; make a fresh start (begin life again) □ **tell:** (here) know
believe (in God...) □ **creative writing** (classes in which one learns how to write stories...) □ **in so far as:** in as much as
outside: apart from that □ **S. Maugham:** an English writer (1874-1965); see his short stories in "Lire en..."
praising: complimenting □ *The Summing Up*, a comment on life, on S.M.'s own life's work (Penguin Books) □ **high school:** (Am) secondary school □ **wise:** reasonable □ **dry:** detached □
wondrous: (poetic) wonderful
turn away: refuse to look at
interior stuff (fam. thing): what is in you, not in others

follow... market-place: act according to what sells well
veer (change course like a boat) **away from** □ **truly:** really
turn sour (like milk after a time): become bad, bitter (fig)
get old (mentally): get + adj = become □ **quickly:** rapidly

what (would happen) **if** □ **budding:** just beginning
disastrous: catastrophic; a disaster, a catastrophe
by writing; you succeed by working

painting by painting. There are short cuts but you can get those short cuts from your fellow artists or fellow writers. The important thing is: painting a picture or a water-color every day of your life, doing a short story every single day or at least part of a short story, writing one poem a day for a thousand days!... You will improve that way. A teacher can't give you that. Teachers can only encourage you to keep up the work. At the university, they want you to take all these other subjects which prevent you from writing. So the very thing you went for, you don't do. So, what then? Write every day and go to the library every day! That's what education is, that's what college is. I wrote my stories every day for twenty years, and I went to the library every day! I wandered through all the rooms, I gave myself an education in the Renaissance, in music, in art history on every level I could. The history of the essay in every country of the world, all the great poetry, all the great plays: Molière, Camus, Anouilh!

H. Y. Shakespeare?

R. B. Shakespeare, Alexander Pope. You read all that yourself! You don't need a teacher for that. If you love it, it's ten times better because often teachers give you things you don't love, so you can't learn from that. Go find your *own* loves and *gradually* get curious about the other books on the shelf next to that love and then you build out from there by accretion. But it's *your* accretion, it's your love, it's your enthusiasm. Teachers can't guess at that...

H. Y. ...Can you tell us about the days when you sold newspapers on the streets of Los Angeles?

R. B. I suppose I was a very unusual newsboy... I

short cut(s): (fam) quicker, more direct way
fellow...: another of two or more people like yourself; a travelling fellow or fellow traveller, my fellow men...
water-colo(u)r: painting (colours mixed with water, not oil)
every single day (for emphasis) □ **at least:** not less than
one poem a day: ... every day, per day; 70 miles an hour
you will improve that way: that's how you'll become better
keep up: continue

subject(s): maths, Latin... □ **prevent:** stop □ **very:** used for giving force; I went to the very top □ **you went for:** you expected to do □ **library** ≠ bookshop (where you buy books)
education: teaching, training of mind □ **college** comes after high school in the U.S.A.
wandered: went from room to room without anything special in view
level: particular stage or standard; reach a high level
great: wonderful, marvellous
play(s): *Hamlet* is probably R.B.'s favourite play (202,31)

Alexander Pope: an English poet and essayist (1688-1744)

times: indicates multiplication; 5 times 10 is 50
you can't learn from that: notice the preposition "from"
go (and) **find** (Am) □ **gradually:** little by little
(book) **shelf** (to put away books) □ **next to:** just near
build out...: (fig) learn more and more □ **accretion:** gradual addition, accumulation
guess at: sense, feel, suppose
the days when...: the time when...
newspaper(s), paper(s) like *The New York Herald Tribune*...
unusual: uncommon □ **a newsboy** (Am) sells or delivers papers

couldn't see myself. I didn't know how excellent I was in various fields. I was blinded by my own insecurities. My fears prevented me from seeing myself. When I graduated from high school I'd done a lot of stage acting. I wrote the senior talent show but I didn't really believe in myself. I had a blind need to write but I never saw myself as a fairly interesting person. Over the years people would invite me to parties and seat me at the head of the table, O.K.? I was the entertainer, the jokester, the fool alright! And they all looked at me and I'd make funny remarks, but I didn't realize that I *was* O.K., but fearful... I was fearful of women until I was in my twenties. I had no experience. I think that's true for many men. They won't admit that they're frightened of the whole experience. Finally when I was thirty I met Aldous Huxley and Christopher Isherwood and Gerald Heard, the English philosopher, and each of them told me what I was: I was O.K., I was good, I was excellent. Aldous Huxley at tea one day leaned forward and said: "Do you know what you are?" and I said: "No. What?" He said: "You are a poet, a poet!" I said: "My God, *am I?*" But I didn't know it, I didn't know that I was good until these peers or super-peers told me that I was all right. And then I met Bertrand Russell when I was thirty-three years old, a couple of years later, and Bertrand Russell told me I was O.K... How wonderful!... This helps you calm down and accept yourself...

H. Y. Bernard Berenson, the great art historian, sent you a letter from Italy too, didn't he?

R. B. Yes. He wrote me and said: "This is the first fan letter I've written in eighty-nine years." Well, I mean, that's the sort of thing that counts; building a structure

field(s): domain □ **blinded:** made blind (unable to see)
fear(s): apprehension, terror, fright; fearful
graduated from...: (Am) pass exam on leaving... □ **stage acting** (as an amateur actor) □ **senior:** (Am) student in last year at school (or university) □ **... believe...:** I had no self-confidence
fairly: rather, moderately □ **over:** in the course of
seat me: make me sit
head: most important end □ **entertainer** (who entertains people by telling funny (amusing) things or jokes), **jokester, fool** (who behaves stupidly to make people laugh) □ **alright:** no doubt
fearful: full of fear (3) □ **fearful of:** afraid of
in my twenties: from 20 to 29 □ **... true for:** the case of
admit: confess □ **frightened:** filled with fright, fear

Huxley('s *Brave New World*) □ **Isherwood:** American writer

OK or okay, all right (24), alright □ **good;** good at sth
leaned forward(s): bent forward(s) (towards me)

am I: the italics emphasize the idea of surprise or difficulty in believing what Aldous Huxley had told him
peer(s): with the same activity □ **super-peers:** extraordinary people □ **B. Russel** (1872-1970), English philosopher and mathematician □ **a couple of:** (fam) a few

calm down: become calm or less upset, cool down
B. Berenson (1865-1959), American art critic; his letter to R.B. is to be found in the introduction to *The Stories of Ray Bradbury*, Alfred A. Knopf, New York 1986 (containing 100 stories) □ **I mean:** I want to say: mean, meant, meant
counts: is of considerable importance, matters

under your false sense of disaster, until finally you calm down. You don't want to overreact and say: "Boy, oh boy! I'm super great from here on." No, but you finally say: "My God, now at least I know who I am." I *didn't*. It was all in my work but I didn't see it as an outside person looking in...

H. Y. ... Do you keep a diary?

R. B. No, but my stories are my diary and my two murder mysteries are my autobiography. There's so much of me in there with my friends. Still I'm sorry I haven't kept a diary, especially with people like Bertrand Russell, Bernard Berenson..., John Huston or Sir Carol Reed when I lived in London thirty years ago and wrote a screenplay for him. I remember much of what they said. My memory is there, quite vivid. Yet I regret not having been a diary-keeper.

H. Y. Do you write in the day, in the night, at any time, or at regular hours?

R. B. In the morning. Yes, the morning's the best time when you have all of your energy. It happens in the middle of the night too. When you are working on a novel, any time your subconscious wants to write, you get up and do it...

H. Y. A trite question: why do you write?

R. B. Because you get an idea that's so irresistible that if you let it die, you would slowly die too. If you get a concept and don't express it, have fun with it, then each day you die a little bit... I get at least one good idea a day, sometimes two or three and I write them down. I have a cellarful of ideas, things that haven't been written, thousands and thousands of notes and at least five hundred short stories that I haven't published yet,

false, because it existed only in his imagination (≠ real)
overreact: react more than is reasonable □ **boy, oh boy!:** indicates great excitement □ **from here** (now) **on**
at least: as a minimum
an outside person: sb from the outside (≠ inside)

keep a diary (in which you write about your experiences, feelings... regularly)
murder (crime) **mysteries:** *Something Wicked This Way Comes, Death is a Lonely Business*, two novels (Grafton Books) □ **still:** yet, however, nevertheless
John Huston('s *Moby Dick*), **Carol Reed,** famous film directors; R.B. wrote the screenplay for *Moby Dick* after Melville's novel

memory: sth that is remembered □ **vivid:** clear and detailed
diary-keeper or diarist

the best: good, better, the best ≠ bad, worse, the worst

middle; midnight (12 o'clock at night); midday or noon

get up: step out of bed, rise from bed
trite: banal, unoriginal
idea: in his Preface, R.B. call himself "a keeper of ideas", "an idea beast" (animal) whose ideas leap (jump) at him
have fun: enjoy yourself; fun, pleasure, enjoyment
a little bit: (fam) a little □ **at least:** not less than ≠ at the most
write down: note down (on a piece of paper)
a cellarful of: lots of; cellar, underground room; wine cellar

I haven't published yet: up to now

maybe never will. They're not good enough.

H. Y. How do you know?

R. B. ...Well, I look through my files and then I'll find a story where maybe just the idea is good. Then I throw out the original story and do a new one...

H. Y. ...And what about Ireland? Quite a few stories are set in Ireland. I'm thinking of *McGillahee's Brat* and *Getting Through Sunday Somehow*.

R. B. ...Again this is a lesson in creativity. All the things you take in, you don't know you take in, until you test them. I try to teach people just to go to the typewriter, stick your platen down your throat, throw up, then clean up at noon. You don't know what's in there! People wrote to me in Ireland and asked: "Will you write stories about Dublin?" I said: "I don't know. I don't have time to see anything. I'm busy writing *Moby Dick*. But, secretly, every hour at night, I'd walk in Dublin's rain. I'd be driven back and forth from Kilcock to Dublin where I lived at the hotel. I was observing things. When I'd been home from Ireland a year, this voice spoke in my head one night and said: "Ray darling" and I said: "Who is it?" It said: "Oh, God, you know, it's Nick your cab-driver who drove you every night, you remember, from Kilcock to Maynooth, to Dublin. Do you remember all those night-rides?" I said: "Yes." He said: "Would you mind putting it down?" So I began to put down one by one these little incidents. Next thing I knew, an oilwell of Irish memories erupted. Now I have six hundred pages of short stories, plays and poetry about Ireland. I'll give you a good example of this sort of thing. On Sunday, nothing happens in Dublin. You must buy your cinema

never will (publish)

look through: examine ☐ **files:** papers (put away in a file)
just: only ☐ **throw out** ≠ keep
a new one: notice the use of "one" to avoid repetition
quite a few: a good number of
... set in Ireland: the action takes place in Ireland ☐ **brat:** (pejorative) (bad-mannered) child ☐ **getting through Sunday somehow:** spend the (monotonous) Sunday in one way or another ☐ **take in:** notice, absorb (mentally)
stick: (fam) put ☐ **platen:** *rouleau* ☐ **throat:** passage in the neck for food and air ☐ **throw up:** vomit
clean up: make perfectly clean (≠ dirty) and tidy (in order)
in there: in your heart and brain (mind, intellect)

R.B. spent 7 months in Ireland when he was asked by John Huston to write *Moby Dick*, the screenplay after Melville's novel
driven (in a taxi) **back and forth:** to and fro

home: back in the U.S.A.
one night, one day (not "a"!)

cab-driver, taxi-driver; cab (Am) taxi

ride(s): journey in a vehicle, on an animal...
mind: object to ☐ **putting it down** (on paper): write

next thing I knew: before I had time to realize ☐ **an oilwell... erupted:** (fig) lots of memories suddenly came out ☐ **I have six hundred pages about Ireland:** see *Green Shadows, White Whale*, a novel set in Ireland (Alfred A. Knopf, New York, 1992 (*La Baleine de Dublin*, Denoël, 1993. *Le Monde* review, 10-9-1993)

tickets ahead of time or you can't get in. All the stage shows are sold out. The pubs are closed until, God knows, 4.30 in the afternoon, so you can't drink. And so, in the middle of Sunday I'm sitting, at 4 o'clock in the afternoon, in the salon of the Royal Hibernian Hotel waiting for the pub to open with my wife and children and nurse and there's this dreadful silence and the rain coming down, the mist, the fog. The sun has already gone down. It's the middle of winter. The doom is surrounding you. I was sitting there with nobody saying anything. You can hear the porcelain cups rattling against the false teeth, as the people pour the tea in. Finally, in the middle of all this, in the far corner of the room, the door opens and this old man — eighty years old — shuffles in, looks around at everyone and says: "Getting through Sunday, *somehow*?" Then he turns and goes back out, and the door shuts. Well, you never forget *that*, do you? I don't know who that old man was but I wrote a poem about him entitled *Getting Through Sunday Somehow*. So you just let your imagination run, finally, and the stories write themselves...

H. Y. ... And what about the sense of humor? What is your definition of humor?

R. B. Oh, my definition is me, as you've seen...!

H. Y. Can you extend this?

R. B. I don't take myself seriously. I have a good sense of humor about myself. I've been forced into it. I've had to survive, with people who doubted me. Therefore I had to learn to joke and not take their insults seriously and to make fun of them and myself at the same time... I call myself the Martian Pumpkin, you know. I'm sort of orangish in color and my background

ahead of time: in advance □ **stage:** on which actors play
sold out: all sold; sell, sold, sold □ **closed:** shut
4.30 in the afternoon □ **so:** therefore, in consequence

waiting for the pub to open: notice the infinitive clause
dreadful: terrible, awful; dread, great fear
mist is less dense than **fog;** it's misty; it's foggy
gone down, set ≠ risen □ **doom** (and gloom): desolation
is surrounding you: is all about you
rattling against: hitting and making quick little noises

in the far (≠ near) **corner** (at the other end of the room)
the door opens: no reflexive pronoun!
shuffles: walks by dragging his feet slowly along
getting through: spending □ **somehow:** God knows how!
the door shuts: no reflexive pronoun!

entitled...: whose title is...

the stories write themselves, "I'm not in charge. I don't control" (188.9,10)
humo(u)r; have a sense of humour

extend this: say more about this

I have been forced into it: be forced into doing sth
doubted me: had doubts about me (as to my capacities)
therefore: consequently □ **to joke:** tell jokes (to cause laughter)
make fun of: laugh at
Pumpkin (associated with Halloween): large round fruit
sort of: rather □ **background:** environment, surroundings

is Mars and when I call people I say: "This is the Martian calling"... Being able to turn things inside out to surprise yourself and to surprise others... Well, I'll give you a good example of perfect humor, an example of the way my humor works. I was in Paris eleven, twelve years ago for the Jules Verne anniversary of his birth — and I was asked to be on the Champs-Élysées on Bastille Day to review the troops with the President of France in the same grandstand, O.K.? And the next day I was interviewed by a reporter from a left radical newspaper. He said: "Monsieur Bradbury, are you a pacifist?" I said: "I think I am, yes. I've proven it time and again." And he said: "Well, then, how is it that a pacifist is on the Champs-Élysées on Bastille Day reviewing the troops with the President of France?" I said: "My dear young man, I've been going to dog shows all my life and going home and raising cats." So, that's a perfect answer. They used it as the headline on the story. But that all came suddenly, you see, I didn't think of it, it popped off my tongue. And that's what you hope for with the sense of humor, to say something frivolous but which is not true. It's better than being serious, isn't it?...

H. Y. Which writers would you say have influenced you?

R. B. Oh, there are so many. Fairy tales, to begin with. I still have all of my children's books from when I was four and five years old, the legend of *The Beauty and the Beast, Snow White*, all those things that are so beautiful, all the Grimms' *Fairy Tales*, Andersen's *Fairy Tales* and so I grew into mythology, Greek mythology, Roman mythology... I loved all those stories, the Norse myths... It's all great stuff, stories of life and death and

call (on the phone); a phone call □ **this is... calling** or this is... speaking (to introduce yourself) □ **turn things inside out** (with the usual inside parts [of socks...] on the outside); (fig) introduce things in an unexpected way (manner)
the way (in which) □ **works:** functions, operates

birth; birthday □ **I was asked:** notice the construction
Bastille Day: July 14 □ **to review;** a review
grandstand: principal stand (set of seats covered by a roof)
left ≠ right □ **radical:** in favour of great, rapid changes

proven: prove, proved, proved or proven (not often used)
time and again: often □ **how is it?:** why is it? How comes?

dog show(s): where dogs are shown □ **raising:** bringing up

headline (printed in large letters at top of article)
story: newspaper article □ **suddenly:** all of a sudden
popped off my tongue: went away suddenly (out of my mouth)
hope for: notice the preposition; hopeful ≠ hopeless
true; truth ≠ lie; speak the truth ≠ tell lies; a liar

fairy tale(s) like Grimm's, Andersen's... □ **to begin with**
all of (without any exception) □ **from** (the time) **when...**

the Grimms, the Martins, the Wilsons
grew into: became acquainted with, discovered
Norse: relating to ancient Scandinavia
great stuff (fam): wonderful things

love. And then there is Buck Rogers in comic strip form, Tarzan in the Sunday paper, the Tarzan books, Edgar R. Burroughs' John Carter's adventures on Mars. I could never have written *The Martian Chronicles* if it hadn't been for Mr. Burroughs and his Martians. And then over the years Jules Verne who still holds up very well. I've read him a lot the last twenty years again, and he's still wonderful. There is also H. G. Wells, of course, the wonderful *Invisible Man* and *The Time Machine* which are still running very well indeed... I fell in love with Shakespeare when I was fifteen and with the great poets one by one over a period of time, Gerard Manley Hopkins, Dylan Thomas..., Alexander Pope in the last twenty-five years or so, and then Charles Dickens. A lot of English writers since I was in my late teens and early twenties, people like John Collier who is one of the finest writers in the last sixty years in England; he came over to America later on to write for the Hitchcock TV series. Roald Dahl is another one I read thirty-five years ago..., Evelyn Waugh, Molière, a lot of the great French playwrights and English playwrights. Sean O'Casey... So I've learned from a multitude of people, people like John Steinbeck, Ernest Hemingway, Udora Welty, Katherine Ann Porter, Edith Wharton, Willa Carther, a lot of women writers... Female writers have so much to teach us, to make us complete human beings.

H. Y. Is it true that you carry about the works of Shakespeare with you wherever you are?

R. B. Yes. Shakespeare and Alexander Pope and books on Shakespeare. I try to learn more. It's a never-ending process, isn't it? And I find *Hamlet* is just a fountain to bathe in. It's quite an incredible piece of

comic strip: series of drawings or cartoons that tell a story

Burrough's *Under The Moon of Mars* (1912), reprinted as *The Princess of Mars* in 1917, *Tarzan of Apes* (1917); John Carter, the earth man, is the hero of *Under the Moon of Mars* □ **over:** in the course of □ **holds up** (successfully even now)
the last twenty years: notice the position of last (recent)
H.G. Wells (1866-1946), an English novelist

run(ning): continue to be read, "hold up very well" (6)

Hopkins (1844-1889), an English poet □ **Dylan Thomas** (1914-1953), a Welsh poet born in Swansea (204. 10 to 20) □ **or so:** approximately □ **in my late** (≠ early) **teens:** eighteen, nineteen years old; (in my) **early twenties:** twenty-one, twenty-two years old □ **finest**; fine (of high quality)

Roald Dahl (1916-1990) whose stories are edited in "Lire en..."
E. Waugh (1903-1966), an English writer
playwright(s): a writer of plays □ **O'Casey**, an Irish playwright or dramatist (1880-1964) □ **learned from...**
Eudora Welty (born in 1909), an American short story writer
Porter, Wharton, Carter: American women writers

carry about (here and there) □ **works**; the complete works of **Shakespeare** (1564-1616)

never-ending: that never stops □ **process:** series of developments or actions
bathe in (as in water for pleasure) □ **incredible:** unbelievable

work. I read Shakespeare's Sonnets constantly, learning his fresh insights which are still fresh four hundred years later, and then I carry Emily Dickinson. Right now I'm re-reading here in Paris F. Scott Fitzgerald's *Tender Is The Night* because he wrote about Paris, I think, better than any other American writer, certainly better than Hemingway. Hemingway missed a lot of things but Fitzgerald caught them. So, there are certain writers I go back to again and again, a lot of essayists like Aldous Huxley over the years.

H. Y. I once called you "The Dylan Thomas of America". How do you react to this?

R. B. Oh, that's fine because he loved words! He munched them. He ate them. He blew them out of his ears. He was a volcano. We were supposed to meet back in 1952 in Los Angeles and somehow it just never happened. Then quite suddenly in November of 1953 he was dead. It was so very frustrating to have him leave the earth so soon because so much of him was so glorious.

H. Y. We've talked about childhood... What other themes would you consider as the themes in your work?

R. B. I don't usually think about it, you know. These things just happen... Space travel, immortality..., which is what space travel offers to us if we land for the moon again, if we land for Mars, if we colonize along the way, if we build the starships, which some day we will build. I don't know how soon, five hundred years, a thousand years, that's a small period of time, though. Eventually we'll build them and when we do, we guarantee the immortality of the human race. If we care about it, if we

a piece of work (news, information, advice, furniture...)
fresh: original ≠ banal □ **insight(s):** mental penetration
E. Dickinson (1830-1886): American poet □ **right:** precisely, exactly
re-reading: reading again □ **Fitzgerald** (1896-1940), American novelist and short story writer: *The Great Gatsby* (Penguin Books)... *Pat Hobby and Orson Welles*, stories ("Lire en...")
missed: did not see or notice, fail to see or notice
caught ≠ missed
I go back to: to whom I go back □ **Aldous Huxley** (1894-1963), English novelist and critic (192.19)
once: one day, on one occasion

fine: okay
munched: ate with enjoyment □ **blew... out** (as if exploding)
back (in the past)
somehow: for one reason or another

it was so very frustrating: notice the emphasis □ **leave** (left, left)
the earth (the world): die
glorious: wonderful, marvellous, splendid
childhood: time and condition of being a child; adulthood...
consider as: look upon as

usually: as a rule
just happen: happen, that's all □ **space travel;** spaceship
land for: go there and land on
along the way: on the way, at the same time
starship, spaceship... □ **build,** built, built (houses...)

though: however □ **eventually:** in the end (as a result)

care: feel concerned or interested

care about it, and I think we do, at least I do. So, I am dedicated to space travel... I hate it when people like Sir Edmund Hillary when he was asked why he climbed Everest, he said because it was there. Well, that is the dumbest reason for doing anything I've ever heard. That's no reason to go. You have got to have a real reason and the real reason is the proliferation of life, the excitement of living, the fact that we are alive, the fact that the eye was invented several billion years ago. If the eye had not been invented by creation, by the life force, by God, by whatever you want to call it, we wouldn't have space travel because you don't reach for something you can't see. So, because the eye was invented several billion years ago, we see the stars and we want to go back to them because that's where we came from. So, that's a huge theme again and again in my essays, in my poetry, in my short stories, in my novels, that, because we have been given the gift, we have to give back. We owe, we owe the universe. As far as we know, in this part of the universe, we're the only creatures, so far, that are cognizant of their position, that realize what they are and who they are and what their destiny can be, I mean... to evolve into peace, to evolve into space, to do better than we've done... It's a miracle we've survived to this time. We are dangerous people one to another. Nevertheless, with all those failures and all the morbidities, all the murders, all the wars, over and above all of that, is the beauty of life itself, the fact that we have managed to survive and that we dream survival and want us to live for the next million years. Well, space travel gives us the chance to do that...

H. Y. I look upon you as a poet more than

at least: in any case, at any rate
dedicated to: very interested in □ **hate** ≠ love
when he was asked: notice the construction

dumb(est): stupid □ ... **reason for** + v + ing

excitement: strong feeling of happiness □ **alive:** living
several billion years: no "s"! billion (Am) *milliard*, (British, English) *million*
whatever: anything at all that □ **call:** name; a name
reach for: try to get or to get hold of

go back to: return to
huge: (here) extremely important; very big, immense □ **again and again**, time and time again: very often, repeatedly
we have been given the gift (present) (3) □ **give back** (in return)
owe: are in debt (fig); owe money □ **as far as...:** in as much as we know □ **so far:** up to now
cognizant ≠ ignorant □ **realize:** know, understand

I mean (to say), I want to say □ **peace** ≠ war

to this time: till now □ **dangerous one to another**
nevertheless: in spite of this □ **failures:** "morbidities, murders (crimes), wars" (faults, mistakes) □ **over and above all of that** (there) **is...**
managed to: succeeded in + v + ing □ **dream survival** (impossible though it seems to be) □ **next:** to come (in the future), to follow □ **chance:** opportunity, occasion
look upon you as...: consider you as...

anything else.

R. B. Oh! Well! *(laughter)*... On my twelfth Christmas, my parents bought me a toy-dial-typewriter, which is one of those small toy devices where you have a disc that you must turn to press down and print one letter at a time. It takes about two hours to write one page but I was *writing*! I started doing a lot of my writing during the time when I was thirteen, fourteen and fifteen. I would get magazines and tear beautiful photographs out of them by Stieglitz, people like that, and great photographers of the early part of the century. And then I would take the photographs and I would write poems to go with the photographs. So it was a way of learning metaphors. I was doing miniature haïku in a way except I didn't know what haïku were, and it taught the eye, it taught the mind to look for beauty and to try to describe it.

H. Y. How do you feel when reading your short stories on tape?

R. B. Well, it's a challenge because you want to try to achieve emotionally, in your delivery, whatever is in the story and if you're lucky, along the way you get caught up in it like in *The Small Assassin*, which has much to do with my own life. Or the story called *The Wish*, which is about my father... I wish for my father to come back from the dead, you know. I want to see him for five more minutes and tell him I love him and say goodbye to him forever... I suddenly realize he has returned and then I run out to the graveyard for an encounter with him. It's a very emotional thing and when I read it I wind up again in tears as I do with the other story *Bless Me, Father, for I Have Sinned.*

twelfth: 12th; twelve (notice the change in spelling)
toy-dial-typewriter: to play with, to type (not to write) (with a circular plate with letters) □ **device(s):** apparatus
print: (here) type □ **one letter at a time:** one letter, not two, each time □ **it takes...;** how long does it take to do it?
started doing: I began to do

tear... out: pull out
Stieglitz (1864-1946), an American photographer
the early (≠ late) **part of the century:** the beginning of the century; this is the 20th century; century = 100 years
way: manner, method, means
haïku: (pl. haïku) Japanese verse (poem) formed of three lines

look for: try to discover

on tape; tape recording; tape (on which sound can be recorded)
challenge: sth stimulating
achieve: accomplish □ **delivery:** reading □ **whatever is:** all that is □ **lucky:** fortunate □ **along the way... caught up:** as you read you get involved □ **has much to do with:** is largely inspired by or is closely connected with
I wish for my father to come: notice the infinitive clause
the dead ≠ the living
for five more minutes or for another five minutes
forever: for all time
graveyard, churchyard or cemetery in a bigger town
encounter: meeting; encounter sb, meet (with) sb
I wind up in tears: I end up crying (as was indeed the case when R.B. read *Bless Me Father...* for us on tape)

Vocabulary

The following are about 2.500 words found in the stories followed by their meaning in their context.

— A —

ability habileté, capacité, don
able to (be) pouvoir (faire), être capable de (faire)
about à peu près, environ ; au sujet de, à propos de
above all par-dessus tout, surtout
absolutely absolument, parfaitement
accept accepter
accretion accroissement, accumulation
accustomed to habitué à
ache faire mal, être douloureux
achieve atteindre ; accomplir
aching douloureux
across d'un côté à l'autre de, de l'autre côté de
act jouer (cinéma, théâtre)
actual fact (in) réel, véritable
actually en fait
additional supplémentaire
adjust ajuster, arranger ; **adjust (to)** s'adapter (à)
adopt adopter
adult adulte
advance avancer
advertising publicité
advice conseils ; **a piece of advice** un conseil
afraid of (be) avoir peur de
after all après tout
again encore, à nouveau
against contre
agonies (suffer) souffrir le martyre
agony douleur extrême ; angoisse
agree être d'accord
ah faire "ah"
ahead devant, en avant, à l'avant
ahead of time en avance, à l'avance

aisle allée (entre deux rangs)
alive en vie, vivant
all right (pour) sûr, pas de doute ; très bien
allow (sb to do) permettre (à qqn de faire)
almost presque
alone seul
along le long de
already déjà
alright nul doute, certainement ; bel et bien
altogether complètement, tout à fait
always toujours (répétition)
amaze stupéfier, ébahir
amazement stupéfaction, stupeur
among parmi, entre (plusieurs)
amove with animé par, plein de
amplify amplifier
ancient très vieux, antique
angel ange
anger colère ; mettre en colère
angry with sb, at sth en colère contre qqn, qqch.
anniversary anniversaire (d'un événement)
annoying agaçant, énervant
another un autre
answer réponse ; répondre
antenna *(plur)*, **antennae** antenne
anyway de toute façon
apart en pièces, en morceaux ; **blow apart** exploser
appetite appétit
applaud applaudir
apple pomme
approach (s')approcher (de)
arc lamp lampe à arc
aria aria
arise, arose, arisen se lever
arm bras
armchair fauteuil
around à peu près, environ ; dans les parages, autour (de)
around (be) être par là, présent
around here par ici, dans les parages
artwork œuvre d'art
as en tant que, comme ; tandis que, alors que
as a matter of fact en fait
as for quant à
as long as du moment que, tant que, pourvu que
ashamed (be, feel) avoir honte
ask for sth demander qqch.
asleep endormi
assault attaque violente et brusque
at least au moins
at long last enfin
at times parfois
atom bomb bombe atomique
attic grenier
aunt tante
awake, awoke ou **awaked, awoken** ou **awaked** (se) réveiller
awake éveillé, réveillé
awaken (se) réveiller
away (au) loin ; **away from** loin de
awe crainte mêlée de respect ou d'admiration

awful affreux, terrible
awhile un instant, un peu

— B —

back dos ; arrière ; à nouveau ; (pour évoquer le temps écoulé) ; **two years back,** il y a deux ans
back (be) être de retour
back East... là-bas (au loin) dans l'Est...
back (go) retourner
back and forth (go) aller et venir
background milieu (familial, social...)
back seat siège arrière
bake cuire au four
balance équilibre ; mettre ou tenir en équilibre
bald chauve
bamboo bambou
band orchestre (autre que classique, **orchestra**)
band (brass) fanfare
bang battre (à coups répétés) ; claquer ; détoner
banner bannière, étendard
Baptist, baptiste
bare nu
barefooted pieds nus
base on baser, fonder (sur)
basement sous-sol
basket panier
bass drum grosse caisse
bat chauve-souris ; batte (baseball)
bathe se baigner
bathroom salle de bain
batter frapper, battre
battery pile (de poste de radio...)
battleship cuirassé
be allowed to être autorisé à
be to do with concerner
be up être debout (non encore couché)
bean haricot
beard barbe
beast bête, animal
beat, beat, beaten battre
beat up tabasser, battre, frapper
beauty beauté
beckon faire signe
become, became, become devenir
bed in aller se coucher
bedside chevet
beg solliciter, quémander ; mendier ; supplier
begin, began, begun commencer
beginning début
behave se conduire, se comporter
behavior *(Am),* **behaviour** comportement, conduite
behind derrière
being (human) être humain
belief croyance
believe croire
bellows soufflet
belong appartenir ; être originaire, natif de

below sous, en dessous (de); plus bas
belowstairs en bas
bench banc
bend (bent, bent) down se pencher
beneath sous
bereave, bereft, bereft priver, déposséder
bereft endeuillé
beside à côté de
bet, bet ou **betted, bet** ou **betted** parier
between entre (deux)
beyond au-delà (de)
bid (bade ou **bid, bidden** ou **bid) sb farewell** dire au revoir à qqn
bike vélo ; **motorbike** moto
billion *(Am)* milliard
bird oiseau
birth certificate acte, extrait de naissance
birthday anniversaire
bit (a little) un petit peu
bite, bit, bitten mordre
bits (for two) pour deux sous, pour trois fois rien
black noir
blackboard tableau noir
blackness ténèbres
blade brin (d'herbe)
blast coup strident, sonnerie ; explosion ; exploser ; faire sauter
blazes (why in) pourquoi diable ?
bless bénir
blessing bénédiction, grâce, faveur (divine)
blind aveugler ; aveugle
blindly aveuglément, comme un aveugle
blink clignotement ; cligner des yeux ; vaciller (lumière)
blink off s'éteindre
block *(Am)* pâté de maisons entre deux rues
blood sang ; **blood red** rouge sang
bloom out s'épanouir
blossom (in) en fleur(s)
blossom s'épanouir, fleurir
blot out masquer, effacer
blow, blew, blown souffler
blow away s'envoler, disparaître
blow over renverser, abattre (arbre...)
blow up faire sauter, faire exploser
blubber blanc de baleine
blueprint bleu (d'architecte)
blunder faute, grosse erreur
board planche
board (on) à bord
bob pendiller, être suspendu (en se balançant)
bobbin (crystal) pendeloque (de cristal)
boisterous exubérant, bruyant, turbulent
bone os
bookstore *(Am)* librairie
bored (get) se lasser, s'ennuyer
boring ennuyeux

born (be) naître
borrow emprunter
both les deux, l'un et l'autre
bother ennuyer, embêter, tracasser, gêner
bottom bas (des escaliers...) ; fond (du jardin...) ; derrière, postérieur
bound bondir
box boîte
boxcar wagon (de marchandises) couvert
boy! bigre ! wouah !
brain cerveau
brass band fanfare
brass cuivre ; **the brass** les cuivres (musique)
brat gosse
brave brave, courageux
braveness bravoure
bray braiement ; braire ; éclater, résonner
break through enfoncer, percer
break accroc
break, broke, broken casser, rompre, interrompre
breakfast petit déjeuner
breath respiration, souffle
breath (out of) à bout de souffle
breath (under one's) à mi-voix
breathing respiration, souffle
breathless hors d'haleine, haletant
breathlessly (en) haletant
breeze brise
brick brique
bridal de mariée ; **bridal gown** robe de mariée
bride (future) mariée
bright éclatant, lumineux, vif, clair
bring back ramener
bring out faire ressortir
bring up mentionner
broad-shouldered aux épaules larges
brother frère
brow front
bruise bleu, meurtrissure
brush frôler, effleurer ; brosser
budding en herbe, naissant
build, built, built construire
building bâtiment
bulb ampoule
bullet balle
bully (petite) brute, tyran (dans les écoles)
bun petit pain au lait
bunch bouquet ; groupe, bande
bunch together rassembler, grouper
bureau *(Am)* commode (souvent à miroir)
burn, burnt, burnt brûler
burning brûlant
burst, burst, burst éclater
burst forth sortir précipitamment, surgir
burst into tears fondre en larmes
burst open s'éventrer, éclater
bury enterrer
bush buisson
business commerce, affaire ; les affaires
busy occupé

but mais ; sauf, excepté
butterfly papillon
buy, bought, bought acheter
by près (de) ; **come by** passer (par là)
by that time à ce moment-là
by the time lorsque, avant que
by the way au fait, à propos

— C —

cab *(Am)*, **taxi** taxi
cabdriver chauffeur de taxi
cage cage
calendar calendrier
call appeler, nommer
calm down se calmer, s'apaiser
camera appareil photo, **cine camera** caméra
can *(Am)* boîte de conserve
cancel annuler
candy *(Am)* bonbon(s)
cane canne
cantata cantate
canvas toile ; tableau
car voiture; *(Am)* wagon de chemin de fer
card carte (jeu)
cardboard carton
care about se soucier (de), s'intéresser (à)
care for aimer, apprécier
career carrière
careful consciencieux, soigneux; **careful (be)** faire attention
carefully avec précaution
carnival *(Am)* fête foraine; **carnival man** forain
carry (trans)porter
carry away emporter
carry on continuer
carry out tenir (une promesse) ; exécuter
cartoon dessin animé, dessin humoristique
cartoonist dessinateur, caricaturiste
case boîte, étui
casket *(Am)* cercueil
cat chat
catch cold prendre froid
catch sb's eye attirer l'attention de qqn
catch, caught, caught attraper
caught up in sth (get) être pris dans qqch.
cease cesser
ceiling plafond
cellar cave
cellarful réserve
cement ciment
century siècle
certainly certainement
chain chaîne; **light chain** cordon (à tirer pour allumer et éteindre)
chair chaise
chalkdust poussière de craie
challenge défi
chamberpot pot de chambre
chance occasion, risque
chandelier lustre

change (se) transformer, (se) changer
channel filière, chaîne ; canal
chapel église, temple (non conformiste)
character personnage (roman)
charge foncer, se précipiter
charge (be in) être responsable
chariot char
chase chasser, poursuivre
chatter claquer (dents)
check vérifier; *(Am)* chèque
cheek joue
chest poitrine
chew mâcher
chicken poulet
child, *(plur)* **children** enfant
childhood (be in one's second) (retomber en) enfance
childish puéril, enfantin
childlike innocent, pur (comme un enfant)
chill *(n)* froid
chill sb's blood glacer le sang de qqn
chiller film d'horreur
chin menton
chirp chanter (grillon, petit oiseau)
chock-full plein à ras bord
choke étouffer
choose, chose, chosen choisir
chorus (in) en chœur
Christian chrétien
Christmas Eve la veille de Noël
Christmas-shop faire les achats de Noël
chuckle rire, glousser
church église
chute glissière (à charbon)
circumcise circoncire
circus cirque
citadel citadelle
city ville
clapboard bardeau
clarity clarté
clatter vacarme, fracas
clean propre ; entièrement, complètement
clean up tout nettoyer
clear one's throat s'éclaircir la voix
cliff falaise
climb up grimper, monter
cling, clung, clung to s'accrocher à
clock horloge, pendule
clomp marcher lourdement
close fermer
close to au bord de, sur le point de ; tout près de
clothes vêtements, habits
clothing-dummy mannequin de couturière
cloud nuage
clutch serrer fort
coal charbon
coat manteau
coffin cercueil
cognizant of ayant connaissance de
coil enrouler
cold froid
collapse se plier (chaise...)
collect collectionner, rassembler

colo(u)red coloré
come, came, come venir
come again revenir
come along arriver
come back revenir
come home rentrer chez soi
come on allez ! allons ! viens ! voyons !
come out paraître, sortir, être publié ; se manifester, apparaître
comfortable agréable, rassurant, réconfortant ; confortable
comic strip bande dessinée
comment (on) faire des commentaires (sur)

commit commettre
complete complet, total
conclude conclure, achever, terminer
concrete béton
confess confesser ; admettre
confessional confessionnal
conjure up évoquer
conquer conquérir, vaincre
consider envisager
considering étant donné (les circonstances...)
constantly constamment, sans cesse
contest lutte, combat
continue continuer
control maîtriser, contrôler ; contrôle, maîtrise
convince convaincre
cool frais ; calme, décontracté ; froid (inamical) ; effronté
copy exemplaire
core centre, cœur
corner coin
cotton candy *(Am)* barbe à papa
couch canapé
count compter
counter comptoir
countless innombrable
country pays ; campagne
countryside campagne, paysage de campagne
coupla (couple of) quelques
couple of (a), deux ; *(fam)* quelques
course (of) bien sûr
courthouse palais de justice
cousin cousin
cover with couvrir de
crack fente, fissure ; fêler
crash fracas ; faire un grand bruit
crawl ramper, se traîner
crayfish écrevisse
creative writing création littéraire
creature être vivant, créature
creek crique ; anse *(Am)* ruisseau, petit cours d'eau
creep, crept, crept aller à pas de loup, se glisser ; ramper
crêpe crêpe
crib berceau
cricket grillon
criminal criminel
cross traverser
crouch s'accroupir

crow corneille
crowd foule, multitude
cruiser croiseur
crush écraser, presser
cry cri ; crier ; pleurer
cry out crier pour appeler qqn ; pousser un cri
cubicle box, cabine
cup one's hands mettre ses mains en coupe
cup tasse
curb *(Am)*, **kerb** bord du trottoir
curl up enrouler ; **curl oneself up** se pelotonner
curlicue fioriture (en forme de cercle)
curse jurer ; maudire
curtain rideau
curve tournant, courbe
cushion coussin
cut, cut, cut couper
cut oneself from se couper (d'un groupe)

— D —

dad papa
daffodil jonquille
dammit nom de nom ! zut !
damn satané
damn (give a) s'en ficher
damned maudit, sacré, fichu
damnfool bougre d'idiot
damp humide
dance danse ; danser
dandelion pissenlit
dare, dared ou **durst, dared** oser
dark noir, sombre ; obscurité, noir
darken (s')assombrir
darkness obscurité, ténèbres
darling chéri
darn (damn, damned) sacré, fichu
darned *(fam)* vachement (très), sacrément, rudement
dash s'élancer, se précipiter
daughter fille
dawn aube, point du jour
day (a) par jour
days (in those) en ce temps-là
dead mort ; hors d'usage
dead (the) les morts
dear cher
death mort *(n)*
deathbed lit de mort
decay décomposition, pourrissement
decent convenable
declare déclarer
dedicate dédicacer ; **dedicate oneself to** se consacrer
deep haute (herbe) ; profond
defend défendre
defender défenseur
delight joie, plaisir
deliver remettre, rendre ; livrer, distribuer
delivery livraison ; élocution, débit
dell vallon
deny nier, refuser d'admettre ; refuser

depress déprimer, attrister
describe décrire
deserted désert *(adj)*
deserve mériter
despair (in) au désespoir, désespéré
dessert dessert
destroy détruire
device appareil
dew-sodden gorgé de rosée
dial cadran
diamond terrain (de baseball)
diaper *(Am)* couche (bébé)
diary journal (intime) ; **keep a diary** tenir un journal
die mourir
dig, dug, dug creuser, piocher
dig up déterrer
dignify donner de la dignité à
dim faible, pâle
dime pièce de dix *cents (Am)*
diminish diminuer
dirty sale
disappear disparaître
disappearance disparition
disaster désastre
discover découvrir
dish out *(fam)* servir
dish plat
dishes (the) la vaisselle
disintegrate désintégrer, désagréger
distance (in the) au loin
distant loin ; éloigné
disturb troubler, déranger
dive plonger ; plongeon
divide diviser, partager
do, did, done faire
dock estrade
dog show exposition canine
doll poupée
done over *(fig)* massacré
doom destin (funeste), catastrophe
door porte
doorknob poignée, bouton de porte
double bed lit à deux places
double plier en deux, replier, doubler
doubt douter de, avoir des doutes sur ; doute
doubtful peu convaincu, incertain, indécis, qui a des doutes
down below en bas, plus bas
downpour pluie torrentielle, déluge
downtown *(Am)* au centre-ville
dozen douzaine
drain (down the) fichu, perdu
drama drame, pièce de théâtre
draw, drew, drawn tirer ; dessiner
dread terreur
dreadful épouvantable, affreux
dreadfully terriblement, horriblement
dream rêve ; **dream, dreamt** ou **dreamed, dreamt** ou **dreamed** rêver
drench tremper
dress (s')habiller
drift traînée, nuage ; dériver ; être poussé ou emporté (par le vent)
drift away s'en aller (d'une

allure nonchalante) ; aller à la dérive ; être emporté (par le vent)
drift open s'ouvrir d'elle-même (porte)
drinking fountain fontaine d'eau potable
drive dynamisme, énergie ; **drive, drove, driven** conduire, aller en voiture
drive out faire sortir ; chasser
drop laisser tomber, lâcher ; goutte
drown noyer ; étouffer (son)
drowning noyade
drum tambouriner ; tambour
dry caustique, mordant ; sec
dumb bête, idiot
dusk crépuscule
dust poussière
dwelling demeure

— E —

each chaque, chacun
eager désireux, avide
eagerness désir, avidité
ear oreille
early tôt, de bonne heure ; **in the early morning** de bon matin, au début de la matinée
earn gagner (de l'argent, sa vie) ; mériter
earn one's living, earn a living gagner sa vie
earnestly avec conviction, avec sérieux
earth terre
ease calmer, tranquilliser, soulager
easily facilement
east est
easy facile ; du calme !
eat, ate, eaten manger
echo (*plur* **echoes**) écho
echo retentir, résonner, se répercuter
edge bord
effigy effigie
elegiac élégiaque
elm orme
else (sb, sth) qqn, qqch d'autre
embarrassed gêné, embarrassé
embody exprimer, concrétiser ; incarner
embrace étreindre, embrasser
emotionally avec émotion
empty vide
encounter rencontre ; rencontrer
encourage encourager, rassurer
end finir, cesser, s'arrêter ; fin
ending fin
engine locomotive ; moteur, machine
enjoy apprécier, aimer
enough assez
enrolment effectif *(n)*
entertain amuser, divertir
entertainer celui qui amuse la galerie
entertainment amusement, divertissement, distraction

entire entier, complet
entitle intituler
entry entrée
environment milieu, cadre
envy envie ; envier
erase effacer
eraser éponge (tableau) ; gomme
errands (run) faire des commissions ; **errand** commission, course
erupt apparaître, faire irruption
especially particulièrement
essay essai
essence essence, essentiel, fond
essential essentiel *(adj)*
establish établir
eve veille
even même
even as au moment même où, alors même que
even if même si
even more encore plus
even though même si
evening soir
eventually finalement, à la longue
ever jamais, toujours ; jamais (dans une interrogation)
ever since depuis (que)
every other day tous les deux jours
everywhere partout
evil mauvais, malveillant ; le mal
evolve évoluer, se développer
except sauf, excepté, hormis
excite exciter, agiter
excitement excitation, exaltation
exhaustion épuisement
exhilaration joie, allégresse
exist exister
exorcise exorciser
expect attendre, prévoir
experience expérience ; vivre (une expérience...)
explode exploser, éclater
express exprimer
expressly expressément
extend étendre ; développer, prolonger
extra (personne...) supplémentaire
eye regarder, observer ; œil
eyelid paupière

— F —

face visage ; cadran ; faire face à
faced with confronté à
fact fait
fade s'effacer, passer
fail décevoir, laisser tomber, manquer à ses engagements envers ; échouer
failure manquement ; échec
faint vague, peu précis, flou
fairly assez, plutôt
fairy tale conte de fées
faithful fidèle
fall, fell, fallen tomber
fall apart s'écrouler, tomber en morceaux

fall away se dissiper
fall in love (with) tomber amoureux (de)
fall silent se taire
false faux
familiar familier
family famille
fan admirateur
fancy imagination, fantaisie ; caprice
fantasy imagination, fantaisie
far away au loin
far end l'autre bout
far off au loin, dans le lointain
farewell adieu
fashion mode
fashion (out of) démodé
fast rapide ; rapidement, vite
fat gros, gras ; graisse, gras
favorite *(Am)*, **favourite** préféré
fear crainte, appréhension ; craindre
fearful peureux, craintif
feed, fed, fed nourrir, donner à manger à
feed on se nourrir de
feel, felt, felt sentir, se sentir, ressentir ; tâter, toucher
feel (how does it?) quelle impression cela fait-il (de...) ?
fellow compagnon ; homme, type
fever fièvre
few (a) quelques
fiber fibre (musculaire...)
fickle inconstant, volage
field domaine
fiery ardent, brûlant
fight, fought, fought combattre, lutter contre ; dispute
figure silhouette
figure (out) compter, calculer
file classeur, dossier
fill remplir
finally finalement
find, found, found trouver, constater, découvrir
find out trouver, découvrir
fine bien, très bien, en forme ; beau, merveilleux
finger doigt
fire feu
fire-engine voiture de pompiers
fireworks feu d'artifice
first premier ; en premier, d'abord
fist poing
fit convenir à
fixed fixe
flag drapeau ; **the (meter) flag is down** le taxi est pris
flame flamme
flaring éclatant (lumière)
flash (faire) briller (brièvement) ; étinceler ; jeter (éclairs)
flash on s'allumer en un éclair
flashlight torche électrique
flat plat ; carrément, nettement, pile, en plein
flesh chair
flick donner une chiquenaude
fling, flung, flung jeter, lancer
flip donner un petit coup à, donner une chiquenaude

float (faire) flotter ; arroser (bien)
floor plancher, sol
floorboard latte de plancher
flourish brandir
flower fleur
flush inonder ; nettoyer à grande eau
flutter voltiger, s'agiter
fly, flew, flown voler ; prendre l'avion ; faire voler ; passer vite, filer (le temps)
fog brouillard
foldout, foldaway pliant (lit)
foliage feuillage
folk(s) gens ; famille, parents
follow suivre
fool *(n)* imbécile, idiot
foolish stupide, idiot
foot *(plur* **feet**) pied (30, 48 cm)
footstep bruit de pas
for pour ; car ; parce que
force force ; forcer, contraindre
forehead front
forest forêt
forever pour toujours, à jamais
forget, forgot, forgotten oublier
forgive, forgave, forgiven pardonner
forgiveness pardon
fork fourchette
forward en avant, vers l'avant
fountain fontaine
foursome (partie à) quatre joueurs (golf...)
frantic frénétique
freak monstre
free gratuitement, bénévolement ; gratuit ; libre ; libérer
freedom liberté
freeze, froze, frozen rester figé sur place ; geler
freezer congélateur
freezing glacial
fresh nouvellement, fraîchement (arrivé...) ; frais
freshness fraîcheur, spontanéité
friendship amitié
fright effroi, peur
frighten effrayer, faire peur à
frivolous frivole
from then on dès lors, à partir de ce moment-là
front devant ; façade ; de devant
front door porte d'entrée
front of (in) en face de
frost givre
frown froncer les sourcils
frozen glacé, gelé
frustrating frustrant
fry frire
fulfill accomplir, réaliser
full (of) plein (de) ; complet ; entier
full-stop point final ; **come to a full-stop** s'arrêter complètement
full-time (à) plein temps
fumble tâtonner ; aller à tâtons ; manier maladroitement
fun (be) être amusant
fun (have) s'amuser
fun of (make) se moquer de
funeral parlor dépôt mortuaire, salle de pompes funèbres

furiously furieusement, avec acharnement
furl rouler (drapeau, parapluie...)
furniture meubles, mobilier
furniture (a piece of) meuble (un)
further plus loin
fury fureur, furie

— G —

galley épreuve (édition)
game partie (sport, jeu) ; jeu
gape rester bouche bée ; ouvrir la bouche toute grande
gape at regarder bouche bée
gasp haleter, suffoquer ; avoir le souffle coupé (d'étonnement...)
gather se réunir, se rassembler
gaze at contempler
gentle doux
gently doucement
germ warfare guerre bactériologique
German allemand
gesture faire des gestes, mimer ; geste
get, got, got obtenir ; avoir ; aller chercher
get + *adj* devenir
get in entrer
get late se faire tard
get off descendre (d'un train, d'une voiture...)
get over se remettre de
get through achever, aller jusqu'au bout
get to do arriver à faire (après des efforts, des difficultés) ; atteindre
get up se mettre debout ; se lever (le matin)
get used to s'habituer à
ghastly horrible, effrayant
ghost fantôme
giant géant
gift présent, cadeau
giggle pouffer de rire ; glousser
girlfriend petite amie
give, gave, given donner ; émettre (un son...)
give away révéler
glad heureux, content, joyeux
glance regard, coup d'œil ; **glance at** ou **glance upon** jeter un coup d'œil à, sur
glass verre
gleam luire, briller
glen vallée
glint reflet
glove gant
glow luire, rougeoyer
go, went, gone aller
go + *adj* devenir
go about s'y prendre (pour faire qqch)
go back revenir, remonter
go by passer, s'écouler (temps)
go down se coucher, descendre (soleil)
go off partir, s'en aller, quitter
go on continuer

go through traverser
God (my) mon Dieu !
goddam sacré, fichu
golden doré ; en or
gone disparu
gone (be) disparaître ; être mort
good bon ; bien
gosh! ça alors !
gown robe longue
grab saisir
grab hold of empoigner, saisir
gradually petit à petit, peu à peu
graduate obtenir un diplôme
graduation *(Am)* remise des diplômes
grammar grammaire
grandma mémé, mamie
grandmother grand-mère
grandstand tribune
grape raisin
grass herbe
gratifying agréable, satisfaisant
gravel gravier, gravillon
graveyard cimetière
gravity pesanteur
gray *(Am)*, **grey** gris
great grand ; merveilleux
great-grandfather arrière-grand-père
Greek grec
green vert
grief chagrin, peine
groin aine
grope tâtonner
grotto grotte
grow, grew, grown grandir, croître ; (faire) pousser
grow + *adj* devenir
grow up grandir, devenir adulte
grownup adulte
grunt grogner, grommeler
guarantee garantie
guess deviner ; *(Am)* croire, penser
guilty coupable
gunshot coup de feu
gutless lâche, qui n'a rien dans le ventre

— H —

hail salut (bonjour)
hair cheveux
half *(plur)* **halves** moitié
half-way mi-chemin
hall entrée, vestibule, couloir
hammer marteler
hand tendre, passer
hand back rendre, repasser
handy accessible, sous la main
hang, hung, hung suspendre ; être suspendu
hang back rester en arrière
happen arriver (événement), se passer
happening événement
happiness bonheur
happy heureux
hard difficile, dur
hardly à peine
hardwood bois de feuillus

harsh dur, cruel
hat chapeau
hate haine, détester
haunt hanter
have to... avoir à, devoir (faire qqch)
have to do with concerner
hawk-nosed au nez de faucon
head (at the head of) au bout de (la table...)
head down tête basse ; tête baissée
head for se diriger vers
headfirst la tête la première
headline titre (journal)
head-on de plein fouet
healthy en bonne santé, sain, vigoureux
hear, heard, heard entendre
heart cœur
heat chaleur
heel talon
hell! (what the) et alors ! on s'en fout ! peu importe !
hell ! merde ! nom de Dieu !
hell, no! oh, que non !
hellfire feu de l'enfer
help aide, secours ; aider
help (cannot) + *v* + *ing* ne pouvoir s'empêcher de faire
here on (from) à partir de maintenant
hero héros
hi *(Am)* salut ! bonjour !
hide, hid, hidden (se) cacher
hide out se cacher, rester caché
high chair chaise haute (pour petits enfants)
high school *(Am)* lycée
high up en haut, là-bas
hill pente, colline
hinge gond
history histoire
hit, hit, hit frapper ; coup
hit for aller vers, partir pour
hoarse enroué, rauque
hobby passe-temps favori
hoist hisser, soulever (qqch de lourd)
hold, held, held tenir, retenir
hold back retenir, tenir à distance
hold on to se cramponner à, s'accrocher à
hold up tenir, résister
hole trou
holler se plaindre, récriminer ; brailler, hurler
holy saint, sacré
hometown ville natale
homeward en direction de la maison
honesty honnêteté
hoot siffler, mugir ; **hoot (with laughter)** s'esclaffer, rire aux éclats
horror horreur
horse cheval
host foule
hot (très) chaud
hour heure
house maison
how is it...? comment se fait-il que... ?
howitzer obusier (canon court)

huddle entasser, serrer (les uns contre les autres) ; se blottir
hug serrer dans ses bras, étreindre
huge énorme, vaste, immense
hum vrombir, ronfler
humming bourdonnement
hunchback bossu
hundred cent
hundreds of des centaines de
hurl jeter, lancer (avec violence)
hurry on se dépêcher, continuer à la hâte
hurt, hurt, hurt blesser, faire mal (physiquement et moralement)
husband mari, époux
hush calme, silence ; faire taire
hydrogen bomb bombe à hydrogène

— I —

ice cream glace
icicle glaçon (aux toits...)
icy glacial
idiotic idiot, stupide
illumine éclairer
imitate imiter
impact impact
impeach mettre en accusation, attaquer
improve progresser ; (s')améliorer
in order to pour, afin de
in so far as dans la mesure où
in time à temps
inability incapacité, impuissance
inarticulate incapable de s'exprimer
incense encens
inch pouce (2,54 cm)
income revenu(s)
incredible incroyable
incredibly incroyablement
incredulous incrédule
indeed vraiment, en effet
inner interne, intérieur, intime
inquire demander, s'informer
insert ajouter, introduire, insérer
inside à l'intérieur (de)
inside out à l'envers
insight pénétration, perspicacité
instance (for) par exemple
instantly sur-le-champ, immédiatement
instead of au lieu de
intangible intangible
intently avec une vive attention
interesting intéressant
intermission *(Am)* entracte
intermittently par intermittence
interrupt couper la parole ; interrompre
invader envahisseur
invent inventer
iron fer ; repasser
iron-smelling à l'odeur de fer
ironing board planche à repasser
irritated irrité

itch démangeaison ; éprouver des démangeaisons ; avoir une envie qui vous démange

— J —

jab enfoncer ou planter dans
jacket jaquette (livre)
Japanese Japonais
jaw mâchoire ; **his jaw dropped** il en est restée bouche bée
jealous jaloux
jeer huer, railler, se moquer
jerk secouer (par saccades) ; se mouvoir par saccades ; saccade, sursaut, secousse
jewelled orné ou paré de bijoux ou de pierreries
jig about, around sautiller, gigoter (**jigger** qqn qui...)
jingle tintement, cliquetis ; tinter, cliqueter
job emploi, poste, place
joke plaisanter, blaguer
jokester plaisantin, humoriste
jolt tressauter, cahoter
jostle through se frayer un chemin, se bousculer
joy joie
joyful joyeux
jug pot, pichet
July juillet
jump sauter
June juin
jungle jungle
jungled enchevêtré (comme la jungle)
just seulement, uniquement, rien de plus que

— K —

keep, kept, kept garder
keep + *v* + *ing* continuer à
keep oneself busy s'occuper
keep up continuer
keep warm se réchauffer
keeper gardien
kick donner un coup de pied
kid *(fam)* enfant, gamin, gosse
kill tuer
kind genre, sorte
kiss embrasser
kitchen cuisine
knead pétrir
knee genou
knock coup ; donner un coup
knock down renverser
know, knew, known savoir, connaître
know better comprendre
knuckle articulation ou jointure du doigt

— L —

label étiquette ; cataloguer
lace dentelle
lack of manque de

lake lac
lamp (street) réverbère
land terre, pays ; atterrir
landing atterrissage
Lands! (my) mon Dieu !
lapse into silence se taire, s'enfermer dans le mutisme
large grand
last dernier
last (at) enfin, à la fin
late tard, avancé, tardif
lately récemment
later (on) plus tard
lattice treillage, claire-voix ; **lattice window** fenêtre treillissée
laugh rire
laugh at se moquer de
laughter *(n)* rire
launch se lancer
laundry blanchisserie ; linge
lawn gazon
lay (laid, laid) claim to revendiquer
lead, led, led (to) mener (à), conduire (à)
lead back ramener
leaf (*plur* **leaves**) feuille
lean, leant ou **leaned, leant** ou **leaned** se pencher
leap, leapt ou **leaped, leapt** ou **leaped** bondir, sauter
leather cuir
leave, left, left laisser, quitter, s'en aller
leave off s'arrêter, cesser
leave-taking adieux, départ
lecture donner une conférence
left gauche
left (be) rester ; **I have no money left** il ne me reste pas d'argent
leg jambe
leisurely fait sans se presser, calmement
let, let, let laisser ; permettre
let alone ignorer, ne pas s'occuper de, ne pas fréquenter
let go lâcher
let in laisser entrer
let out (re)lâcher, libérer
let out laisser sortir, lâcher
level niveau
library bibliothèque
lick lécher
licking *(fam)* raclée, rossée
lid couvercle
lie mensonge ; mentir
lie, lay, lain être allongé, être couché, se trouver là
lie down s'allonger, se coucher
life vie
lifetime (a) toute une vie
lift ascenseur ; lever, soulever ; s'élever, se soulever
lift up (sou)lever, relever
light lumière ; phare ; **light, lit** ou **lighted, lit** ou **lighted** éclairer, allumer ; tomber (sur), atterrir (sur)
lighten éclairer ; éclaircir
lightless éteint, sans lumière
like comme
like (be) ressembler
likewise pareillement, de même
lilac lilas
limb membre

line ligne ; *(Am)* queue ; ligne de chemin de fer
lip lèvre
listen to écouter
live habiter, vivre
live off vivre de
living room salon
load fardeau, charge, poids
lock serrure ; fermer à clef, verrouiller ; bloquer (mécanisme...)
lodge loge (des francs-maçons)
loin reins
loneliness solitude
lonely isolé, solitaire
loner *(n.)* solitaire
long longtemps ; long
long last (at) à la longue, à la fin des fins
look + *adj* paraître, sembler
look down upon regarder de haut, mépriser
look like ressembler à
look out regarder dehors
look over jeter un coup d'œil à
look to veiller à
look up lever les yeux
look upon considérer
Lord (Jesus) Seigneur (Jésus)
lose (lost, lost) sight of sb, sth perdre qqn ou qqch de vue
loser *(n.)* perdant
lost perdu
lot of (a) beaucoup de
loud bruyant ; fort (son)
loudness force (de la voix, du bruit)
lousy moche
love amour ; aimer (qqn) ; adorer, aimer beaucoup (qqch)
loving affectueux, tendre
low bas (voix)
lower baisser
luck chance
luckily par bonheur, heureusement
lucky (be) avoir de la chance
lug traîner, tirer
luggage bagages
lumber out sortir d'un pas lourd
lunch déjeuner
lung poumon
lurch out... sortir... en titubant
lurk se cacher, se tapir
lyric paroles (chanson...)

— M —

mad fou
made-up monté, fait (lit)
madly à la folie, follement
mail *(Am)* courrier
main principal (le plus grand, le plus important) ; **main street** grand-rue
mainly principalement, essentiellement
make, made, made faire, fabriquer
make + *adj* rendre
make a stop s'arrêter (bus, train)

make it parvenir à faire qqch, arriver, réussir
make up maquillage ; inventer (de toutes pièces), imaginer
malignancy méchanceté, malveillance
man homme
manacle menotte
manage to réussir à, parvenir à, arriver à
maniac *(n, adj)* fou, maniaque, dément
map carte (géogr.)
march marcher, défiler
mare jument
market-place place du marché
marquee grande tente ; chapiteau
marry sb épouser qqn, se marier avec qqn
Martian Martien
mass multitude
masterpiece chef-d'œuvre
matter sujet, question ; **mean to** + *v* avoir de l'importance
matter (no) peu importe
maybe peut-être
meadow pré, prairie
mean, meant, meant signifier, vouloir dire ; avoir l'intention de
mean méchant, mesquin
meaningless dépourvu de sens **(meaning)**
meanness méchanceté, mesquinerie
meatball boulette de viande
meet (with) rencontrer
meeting réunion
melt fondre
memorial monument funéraire
memory souvenir ; mémoire
menace menace ; menacer
mere pur, simple (rien que) ; **the merest...** le moindre
meter compteur
middle (in the) au milieu
midget nain
midnight minuit
midway *(Am)* centre de la fête foraine
mile mile (1,609 km)
milk lait
mill around grouiller, fourmiller (autour)
mind esprit (intellect) ; faire ou prêter attention à, voir une objection à
mine mine
minister pasteur
minor-key ton mineur
Mint (hôtel de la) Monnaie
miserable malheureux, triste
miss manquer ; regretter l'absence de ; **I miss you** vous me manquez
miss out on laisser passer, ne pas profiter de
missus *(slang)* madame
mist brume
mistress maîtresse
mix (se) mélanger ; se mêler (aux autres)
moan gémir
moist humide
mold mouler, modeler

mom maman
Monday lundi
monster monstre
month mois
moon lune
moonlight clair de lune
moonlit éclairé par la lune
morbidity morbidité
morning matin
most le plus ; très, bien ; **most of** la plupart de
mostly principalement
mother mère
mother-in-law belle-mère
mound monticule
mourn se lamenter, pleurer
mouth bouche
move remuer, bouger
move away déménager ; s'éloigner
move up monter
moved ému
movie *(Am)* film
moving en mouvement ; émouvant
mow, mowed, mowed ou **mown** tondre
mumble marmonner
munch croquer, dévorer à belles dents
murder meurtre
murmur murmure ; murmurer
mirror miroir, glace
muscled musclé
museum musée
mushroom champignon
mutilate mutiler, estropier
mutter marmonnement ; marmonner, marmotter
mystery mystère

— N —

naked nu ; dénudé, dépouillé
name nom
nameless sans nom
narrow étroit
near près de ; proche
nearby près, tout près, à proximité
nearness proximité
neat propre, net
neatly impeccablement
neck cou ; **back of the neck** nuque
need besoin ; avoir besoin de
neglect négliger, délaisser
neither of us ni l'un ni l'autre d'entre nous
nervous nerveux, agité
never ne... jamais
never-ending sans fin
nevertheless néanmoins, toutefois
new nouveau ; neuf
New Year's Day jour ou premier de l'an
news informations, actualités
newsboy vendeur de journaux
newspaper journal
newsreel actualités (filmées)
next prochain, suivant ; ensuite, après

nice agréable
night nuit
nightmare cauchemar
nightride promenade en voiture de nuit
nod incliner la tête ; faire un signe de tête affirmatif
none aucun
nonsense non-sens, absurdité
noon (at) (à) midi
norse nordique
north nord
nose nez
nothingness néant
notice remarquer
noun nom (grammaire)
novel roman
novelist romancier
novella court roman
now maintenant ; or, alors
nowhere nulle part
nurse bonne d'enfants, nurse ; soigner

— O —

oak-tree chêne
obediently avec obéissance
occasion (on) à l'occasion
odo(u)r odeur
odorous odorant, parfumé
office cabinet (docteur) ; bureau
official officiel
often souvent
ogre ogre
oh faire "oh"
oil huiler
oilwell puits de pétrole
ointment onguent, pommade
old vieux
once (all at) tout à coup, tout d'un coup
once in a while une fois de temps en temps
once autrefois ; une fois, un jour ; une fois que
one by one un à un, un par un
oneness unité
only seulement
open (s')ouvrir ; ouvert
open-mindedness ouverture d'esprit
opposite opposé, d'en face
orangish orangeâtre
order to (in) pour, afin de
orphan orphelin
other than autre que
otherwise autrement
out of à cause de, par, grâce à ; en dehors de, hors de ; sur **(12 out of 20)**
out of here hors d'ici
out of nothing à partir de rien
out of sight hors de vue
outer extérieur
outer space cosmos
outlet exutoire
outside devant, (au) dehors (de)
over sur, au-dessus (de) ; plus de ; fini, terminé ; au cours de (années...)
over and over à maintes reprises

over and over again encore et encore
over there là-bas
overreact réagir avec excès ou excessivement
owe être redevable envers ; devoir
owl hibou
own propre (personnel)

— P —

pack paquet ; emballer, empaqueter ; faire sa valise
pad aller à pas feutrés
pain douleur, souffrance
painfully douloureusement
paint peindre ; peinture
painter peintre
painting peinture ; tableau
pale pâle
palm paume
palpitate palpiter
palpitor soulève-assiette
pancake crêpe
pandemonium tohu-bohu
panel panneau
paneling *(Am)*, **panelling** panneaux, lambris, boiseries
panic paniquer ; panique
pantry office
paper journal
parenthood, condition de parents
parlo(u)r petit salon
part partie
particular particulier, spécial
party fête, réception
pass passer
pass away mourir
passenger passager, voyageur
past *(n)* passé ; devant ; **go past a house** passer devant une maison
past (that long) il y a si longtemps
path chemin
pathway sentier, chemin étroit
pattern patron, modèle ; **pattern of living** mode de vie
pause pause, arrêt, silence ; faire une pause
pavement trottoir
pavestone dalle ; pavé
paving pavage, dallage
pay paye, salaire
pay, paid, paid payer
pay attention to faire ou prêter attention à
payment paiement, règlement
peace paix
pebble galet, caillou
peculiar bizarre, étrange
pee faire pipi
peer pair, égal ; regarder d'un air interrogateur, scruter
people gens
perfect parfait
perform exécuter (numéro), donner une représentation
perhaps peut-être
personally personnellement
phantom fantôme
phonograph *(Am)* électrophone

photo(graph) photo(graphie)
picket piquet, pieu
picture photo(graphie)
pie tourte
piece morceau, bout
pile tas, pile
pile out sortir pêle-mêle
pillow oreiller
pint pinte (U.S. = 0,47 litre ; G.B. = 0,57 litre)
pistol pistolet
pit fossé, trou
pitch hauteur, ton (voix), degré ; rebondir
pity dommage
place endroit, lieu
place (in) à la place (de), au lieu (de)
plan projeter, prévoir à l'avance
platen rouleau (machine à écrire)
platform quai (de gare)
play pièce de théâtre ; passer (un disque)
playground cour de récréation ; terrain de jeu
playwright dramaturge
pleasantly aimablement, agréablement, plaisamment
please faire plaisir à
pleasure plaisir
plump up tapoter, faire bouffer (oreiller...)
plus plus
pocket poche
poetry poésie
point moment ; montrer, désigner, indiquer du doigt
pole perche, mât, poteau
polish astiquer, faire briller
politics politique
pomegranate grenade
ponderously lourdement
pool bassin, piscine
poor pauvre
pop boisson gazeuse
pop off sortir, partir brusquement
popular en vogue, à la mode, populaire
porch *(Am)* véranda
porter *(Am)* employé dans les wagons-lits ; porteur
portion part, portion
possibly (who could) mais qui donc pourrait...?
pour down couler à flots, ruisseler
pour in verser, servir
poverty pauvreté
powder keg poudrière
power puissance, pouvoir
praise louer, faire l'éloge de
pray prière ; prier
preach prêcher
pregnant enceinte
première première
press presser, écraser ; donner un coup de fer
press at each other se serrer, se presser (les uns contre les autres), se bousculer
press down appuyer
pretty passablement, plutôt, assez
prevent from empêcher de

previous précédent
pride fierté, orgueil
priest prêtre
primeval des premiers âges du monde, primitif
print imprimer, publier
private privé, intime
probe explorer, sonder
process méthode, processus
promise promesse
prompt sb to do sth pousser, inciter qqn à faire qqch
properly comme il faut
prove, proved, proved ou **proven** prouver
pry up arracher
publish publier
pull tirer
pull back reculer
pull in faire entrer, tirer qqn à l'intérieur
pull off reculer, se retirer
pull up arracher
pulverize to dust réduire en poussière, pulvériser
pumpkin citrouille ; potiron
punch donner un coup de poing à
punish punir
purple violet
purposely à dessein, exprès
push pousser
push out pousser à sortir
put, put, put mettre
put away mettre de côté, ranger
put down mettre par écrit, noter, inscrire
put in inscrire (son nom), s'inscrire
put it dire, exprimer
put on mettre (chaussures, vêtements)
put out éteindre ; avancer (la main...)
put up dresser, monter

— Q —

quick rapide
quickness rapidité, vitesse
quiet calme
quiet (be) taisez-vous !
quietly doucement ; calmement
quit, quit ou **quitted, quit** ou **quitted** cesser, arrêter
quite vraiment, tout à fait, complètement
quite a few un assez grand nombre de...
quiver trembler
quote citation ; citer

— R —

rabbi rabbin
race espèce, race ; courir à toute allure
rail rail
railroad station *(Am)*, **railway station** gare de chemin de fer
rain pluie

raise (sou)lever ; élever (enfants)
rattle cliquetis ; s'entrechoquer
ravine ravin
razor rasoir
reach atteindre
reach out étendre le bras, la main pour atteindre
react réagir
read, read, read lire
reading lecture
ready prêt
real vrai, réel
realize se rendre compte
really vraiment, réellement
reason raison
rebuild reconstruire
recall rappel (d'un souvenir) ; rappeler
receive recevoir
recently ces derniers temps, récemment
recognize reconnaître
record archive, document, registre ; disque
red rouge
red-faced rougeaud, rubicond
red-hot *(Am)* bonbon rouge à la cannelle
reedy nasillard, aigu
refer to faire allusion à, se référer à
reflect refléter, réfléchir
reflection reflet
refugee réfugié
regular régulier, *(n)* habitué
reject refuser, rejeter
relationship rapport, lien, relation
relative parent, membre de la famille
relax se détendre
relent céder, se laisser fléchir
reluctant peu disposé, peu enthousiaste
remain rester
remember se rappeler, se souvenir de
remembrance souvenir ; mémoire
remind sb of sth rappeler qqch à qqn
remove enlever
removed lointain, éloigné
rename rebaptiser
repeat répéter
reply réponse ; répondre
reporter journaliste
repugnance répugnance
restless agité
retort répliquer, rétorquer
retreat reculer, se replier
return revenir, réapparaître
review passer en revue
reward récompense
rib côte (corps humain)
ribbon ruban
ricochet ricocher
ride tour (de manège...) ; **ride, rode, ridden (a bicycle, a horse** faire de la bicyclette, du cheval)
right droit ≠ gauche **(left)** ; vrai, juste, exact
right (be) avoir raison

right here ici même
right now en ce moment, à l'instant même
rime givre
ring anneau ; cercle
riot débauche (de couleurs...), profusion
rip déchirer
rise, rose, risen se lever
rite rite, rituel
road chemin, voie, route ; rue
roar hurlement, grondement ; rugir
rock roche(r)
rocking chair fauteuil à bascule
roll rouler
rolling ondulant, ondulé
Roman romain
romance histoire d'amour ; poésie ; merveilleux
roof toit
room chambre ; pièce
root racine
rope corde
rose rose
rotten pourri ; mauvais, moche
rough rugueux, rêche ; inégal, accidenté (terrain)
rough and tumble mêlée, bagarre
row rang, file
royalties droits d'auteur
rub frotter
rudely grossièrement, brutalement
rug petit tapis
ruin ruine ; ruiner, gâter, gâcher
run, ran, run courir ; couler ; être répandu (bruit) ; continuer à marcher (roman, pièce de théâtre...)
run away se sauver, s'enfuir en courant
run by passer en courant
run down descendre en courant
run off se sauver, s'enfuir (en courant)
run out tirer à sa fin (période de temps) ; sortir en courant
runaway fugueur
rush se précipiter
rush in (faire) rentrer précipitamment, en toute hâte
rustle bruissement
rustling bruissement

— S —

sail voyager en bateau ; glisser
sale (for) en vente
salesman vendeur ; représentant de commerce
same (as) même (que)
same (just the) cependant, néanmoins
same (the) la même chose
sanctity caractère sacré
sanctuary sanctuaire
sand sable
sanity bon sens, jugement sain
sarsaparilla salsepareille
save économiser ; sauf, excepté
sawdust-floored au sol recouvert de sciure (de bois)

say, said, said dire
say disons
scalding brûlant
scale, (pair of) scales balance
scare faire peur à, effrayer; **scare sb off** faire partir qqn en lui faisant peur
scarlet écarlate
scatter s'éparpiller
scent odeur
schoolboy écolier, élève
scientific scientifique
scoop cuiller à glace; boule de glace; prendre de la glace (à la cuiller)
scorch brûler légèrement
scrabble grimper (à l'aide des pieds et des mains)
scrape gratter, racler
scratch gratter
scream crier, pousser des cris perçants
screen paravent; rideau; écran
screen door porte grillagée
screenplay scénario
scuff frotter ses chaussures contre le sol, d'avant en arrière
scutter filer, déguerpir
seal phoque
seam couture
search rechercher
search for sth... chercher qqch
searchlight projecteur
season saison
seat siège, banquette; faire asseoir
seat oneself s'asseoir
second seconde
security garantie, caution
see, saw, seen voir
seed graine
seedbed couche, semis
seedling semis, jeune plant
seek, sought, sought chercher
seem sembler, paraître
seize saisir, attraper
self (the) le moi
self-conscious timide, gêné
sell, sold, sold vendre
send, sent, sent envoyer
send out envoyer (à l'étranger)
senior *(Am)* terminale (lycée)
sense sens; sentir, se rendre compte de; pressentir
separate séparé, distinct
sequin paillette
series (a) série, collection
set poste (télévision, radio); **set, set, set** poser, placer
set back ramener en arrière
set (be) se passer, se dérouler (action d'un roman)
settle down s'installer; se calmer
settle (in) s'installer
settle to earth se poser à terre
sewer égout
shadow ombre; recouvrir d'une ombre; assombrir; jeter une ombre sur
shake, shook, shaken secouer
shalt *(archaïque),* **shall**
shame honte
shame (it is a) c'est dommage
shame (what a) quel dommage!

shape état ; forme
share partager
share in partager, prendre part à
sharp distinct, net ; perçant, pénétrant, nettement découpé, aux arêtes vives
shatter (se) fracasser, se briser
shave, shaved, shaved ou **shaven** raser
shawl châle
sheet drap
shelf (*plur* **shelves**) étagère, rayon
shelve mettre (des livres...) sur un rayon
shift bouger, changer de position, osciller
shimmer miroiter, chatoyer
shine, shone ou **shined, shone** ou **shined** briller ; faire briller, astiquer (chaussures...)
ship bateau
shirt chemise
shiver trembler, frissonner
shock bouleverser ; frapper d'horreur, d'indignation
shoe chaussure, soulier
shoelace lacet de chaussure
shoot, shot, shot tirer (canon, fusil...)
shoot down abattre, descendre (aviation...)
shop magasin
shore rivage, côte
short cut raccourci
shortness petite taille ; petitesse
short of à court de ; **short of breath** hors d'haleine
short story nouvelle
shoulder épaule
shout crier
show spectacle ; **show, showed, shown** montrer ; se remarquer, se voir, être visible
shriek cri perçant ; crier, pousser des cris perçants
shrink, shrank, shrunk (se) rétrécir, (se) réduire
shudder trembler
shuffle in entrer d'un pas traînant, en traînant les pieds
shut, shut, shut fermer
shut off isoler, couper (de)
side côté ; camp, équipe (sport)
side + *nom* latéral, de côté
sides (at all) de toutes parts
sideshow(s) attraction(s)
sidewalk *(Am)* trottoir
sift passer (comme à travers un tamis, **sieve**)
sigh soupir ; soupirer
sign panneau
silent silencieux
silently silencieusement
silhouette silhouette (sur horizon)
silk soie
silver argent
sin péché ; pécher
since depuis (que) ; étant donné que, puisque
sing, sang, sung chanter
single unique, seul

single (every single day...) tous les jours... sans exception
sink évier ; **sink, sank, sunk** s'enfoncer, sombrer
sinner pécheur
sister sœur
sit, sat, sat être assis
sit down s'asseoir
sit up se redresser, s'asseoir bien droit
sixty soixante
size taille, dimension
skeleton squelette
sketch croquis, ébauche
skin peau
skirt jupe ; **skirts** basques
sky ciel
slam (faire) claquer (porte...), fermer violemment
slant pencher, être incliné
slap claque, giffle ; grande tape ; donner une tape à
slap down rabattre brusquement
slat latte
sleep sommeil ; **sleep, slept, slept** dormir
sleet neige fondue
slender élancé, mince
slice couper, trancher
slide, slid, slid glisser
slide oneself shut (se) (re)fermer en glissant
sling, slung, slung lancer, jeter
slowly lentement
slush neige fondante ou fondue ; gadoue
smack frapper, donner une tape à
small petit
smallness petite taille, petitesse
smash briser, casser
smell odeur ; **smell, smelt** ou **smelled, smelt** ou **smelled** sentir
smile sourire *(n. et v.)*
smile at sb sourire à qqn
smoke fumée ; fumer
smoking fumant
smudge (légère) tache, traînée
snail escargot
snake serpent ; serpenter
snap claquement ; claquer
snap open... ouvrir... brusquement
snare drum tambour à timbre
sneak, sneaked ou **snuck** *(Am)*, **sneaked** ou **snuck** *(Am)* entrer furtivement
snore ronflement ; ronfler
snort grognement ; grogner
snort dire en s'étranglant de rire
snow neige
snowfall chute de neige
snowy neigeux
snug douillet, confortable
so si, tant, tellement ; donc
so far jusqu'ici ; jusqu'à présent
so long à bientôt
so on (and) et ainsi de suite
so that si bien que
soak up absorber
sob sanglot ; sangloter
society société
socket douille (d'ampoule...)

soda-pop *(Am)* soda (boisson gazeuse)
soft doux
softly doucement
soggy lourd (chaleur, atmosphère)
solace consolation
sold out épuisé, vendu
solve résoudre
somehow d'une façon ou d'une autre
sometime un jour ou l'autre, un de ces jours
sometimes parfois
somewhere quelque part
son fils
soon tôt
sorry désolé
soul âme
sound son, bruit ; résonner, retentir
sound like ressembler à (à entendre)
sour (turn) devenir aigre ; *(fig.)* s'aigrir
south sud
space espace
space travel voyages dans l'espace
spank donner une fessée à
speak, spoke, spoken parler
speak the truth dire la vérité
speak up parler plus fort et distinctement ; parler franchement
spend, spent, spent passer (du temps) ; dépenser (de l'argent)
spin, spun ou **span, spun** tournoyer
spine épine dorsale, colonne vertébrale
spirit away faire disparaître comme par enchantement, subtiliser
spirits (in good) de bonne humeur
splinter (se) fendre ou (se) briser en éclats
split, split, split fendre, déchirer ; diviser ; partager
spoil, spoilt ou **spoiled, spoilt** ou **spoiled** gâcher, gâter
spoon cuiller
spot endroit, coin
spring printemps
sprinter sprinteur
square place, square ; carré
squeak grincer
squint loucher
squint at lorgner
stabbing pain douleur lancinante
stage scène (théâtre)
stain tacher, souiller
stair marche (escalier)
staircase escalier
stairs escalier
stairwell cage d'escalier
stake piquet
stand, stood, stood se tenir debout ; se trouver là ; supporter, tolérer
stand by se tenir près de
stand up se tenir debout, se lever

star étoile
stare at regarder fixement
start commencer ; démarrer
start + *v* + *ing* commencer à faire
start out partir, se mettre en route
startle faire sursauter, faire tressaillir
state état
station gare
stay rester, séjourner
stay up rester debout, ne pas se coucher
steadily régulièrement, fermement, sans s'arrêter
steam buée, vapeur ; fumer (liquide, vêtements mouillés...)
steer conduire, diriger
step marche (d'escalier...) ; pas ; faire un ou des pas
step down descendre
step into entrer
step out sortir
stick, stuck, stuck enfoncer, planter ; coller
stick with rester avec
stiffen se raidir
still encore, toujours (continuation) ; néanmoins, cependant ; calme ; **hold still** se tenir immobile
sting, stung, stung piquer (insecte...)
stir agitation, mouvement ; remuer, bouger
stomach estomac, ventre
stomp marcher d'un pas lourd
stop arrêt ; s'arrêter
store *(Am)* magasin, boutique ; entreposer ; conserver
storm tempête
stove cuisinière (fourneau)
straight droit ; tout droit, directement
strain tendre fortement
strange étrange, bizarre
strangely curieusement, étrangement
stranger *(n)* inconnu, étranger
strangle étrangler, étouffer
stream courant, flot ; ruisseau
street rue
street light lampadaire
strength force
strew, strewed, strewn répandre, éparpiller, joncher
stricken affligé, blessé (âme)
strider *(Am)* araignée d'eau
strike, struck, struck frapper, taper ; sonner (heure)
string, strung, strung enfiler (perles...)
strip(ping) longue pièce ou bande (de toile...)
strong fort, puissant
strop (ou **strap**) cuir à rasoir
stub écraser
student élève, étudiant
stuff chose, truc
stun stupéfier, abasourdir
subject sujet
subscription abonnement (à un journal...)
succeed réussir

succinctly succinctement, en peu de mots
such a... un tel...
suck aspirer, absorber, engloutir
suckle allaiter
sudden (all of a) soudain, soudainement
suddenly soudainement
suit costume
suitcase valise
sum up résumer
sum-total résultat, total
summer été
sun soleil
sunlight (lumière du) soleil
supper dîner
sure *(Am)*, **surely** sûrement, assurément
surprise surprendre
surround entourer
survival survie
survive survivre
suspect soupçonner, suspecter
swallow avaler, engloutir
swarm foule, multitude
sway osciller, vaciller
sweat sueur, transpiration ; suer, transpirer
Swedish suédois
swell *(Am)* sensationnel, formidable ; **swell, swole, swollen** (se) gonfler, grossir
swift rapide
swiftly rapidement
swim, swam, swum nager
swimming-pool piscine
swing balançoire ; **swing, swung, swung** se balancer
swing wide (s')ouvrir en grand (en faisant osciller)
syrup sirop

— T —

taffy *(Am)* bonbon au caramel
take, took, taken prendre ; supporter, accepter ; mettre (du temps)
take a walk faire une promenade
take chances prendre des risques
take in recueillir (orphelin...) ; saisir, comprendre
take it out on se défouler sur
take oneself seriously se prendre au sérieux
take over prendre la relève
take place avoir lieu
take sb to... emmener qqn à...
tale conte
talk parler
talking bavardage
tall grand
tank char
tap robinet ; taper légèrement, tapoter
tape bande magnétique, cassette
tapestry tapisserie (ouvrage en tissu)
tar goudron ; **beat the tar out of**

sb battre qqn comme plâtre (avec violence)
taste goût ; aperçu, échantillon
tawny-haired aux cheveux couleur fauve
taxi taxi ; aller en taxi
teacher professeur
tear, tore, torn déchirer
tear larme
tear off arracher
teens (be in one's) être adolescent
teeth (*sing* **tooth)** dents
tell, told, told dire, raconter
tend soigner
tense (oneself) (se) tendre
tenseness état de tension, degré de tension
tent tente, chapiteau
tenure (have no) n'avoir aucune sécurité d'emploi
terrific formidable
terrifying terrifiant, épouvantable
test essayer
test for faire des essais pour découvrir
thank remercier
theater *(Am)*, **theatre** théâtre ; **movie theater** *(Am)* cinéma
theme thème, sujet
then puis, alors, ensuite
therefore par conséquent
thick fort (odeur) ; épais
thick with rempli, bourré de ; **thick with smoke** enfumé (pièce)
thin fin, mince
thine *(archaïque)* ton, ta, tes
thing chose
think (thought, thought) of penser à
thoroughly complètement
thou *(archaïque)* tu
though cependant ; bien que
thought pensée
thoughtful sérieux, réfléchi
thousand mille
thousands of des milliers de
thread fil
threaten menacer
throat gorge
throat (clear one's) s'éclaircir la voix
throb palpiter
through à travers ; grâce à
throw, threw, thrown jeter, lancer
throw up vomir
thrust, thrust, thrust fourrer, enfoncer, planter
thumbprint marquer l'empreinte du pouce ; empreinte d'un pouce
thump taper sur, cogner ; battre fort (cœur)
thump-whack! et tap !
thunder tonnerre d'applaudissements ; applaudir à tout rompre
ticket billet (de train....)
tide marée
tiger tigre
tight solidement, fermement, serré
tighten (se) resserrer

till jusqu'à (ce que)
tilt incliner, pencher
time temps, moment ; fois, occasion
time (at a) à la fois
time (on) à l'heure
time machine machine à remonter le temps
tinsel paillettes, cheveux d'ange (décorations de Noël)
tip bout, extrémité
tired fatigué
tired of (be) en avoir assez de
tiredness fatigue, lassitude
titanically de manière titanesque, gigantesque
toadstool champignon vénéneux
today aujourd'hui
toe doigt de pied, orteil
together ensemble
tomb tombe
tone ton, tonalité
tonelessly d'une voix blanche
tongue langue
tonight ce soir
too aussi, également ; trop
toot siffler
top sommet, dessus ; toupie
top (at the) (en) haut, (au) sommet
topple perdre l'équilibre, basculer, culbuter
torment tourmenter
toss lancer, projeter en l'air
tote trimballer
tote away emporter, ranger
touch toucher
tour périple, voyage
toward(s) vers, en direction de
towering très haut, imposant
town ville
toy jouet
track piste
trail traîner, pendre à terre
train train ; aller en train ; **train yard** *(Am)*, **foods yard** dépôt, cour des marchandises
trainer dompteur
tramp vagabond
transit passage, transit
trap prendre au piège, coincer, bloquer ; piège
trapeze man trapéziste
travel voyage ; voyager
tread, trod, trodden marcher sur, fouler
tree arbre
tremble trembler
trial procès
trick tour (de prestidigitation), farce, blague ; **trick shop** magasin de farces et attrapes
trifle (a) un peu
trite banal
trodden foulé, battu (sentier)
trolley car *(Am)* tram, tramway
troop troupe (militaire)
trot trotter
trouble difficulté, problème, peine
truce trêve, relâche
truck *(Am)*, **lorry** camion
trudge se traîner, marcher en traînant les pieds
true vrai

truly vraiment, réellement
trunk malle
try essayer
tuck in rentrer
tug at tirer sur
tumble dégringoler ; gambader
tune in se mettre à l'écoute
tuned in to (be) être à l'écoute de
turn tourner
turn + *adj* devenir
turn about se retourner ; faire volte-face
turn away se détourner, refuser
turn grey devenir grisonnant, grisonner
turn into changer en, transformer en
turn off (s')éteindre ; détourner
turn on allumer
turn out éteindre
twelfth douzième
twice deux fois
twilight crépuscule
twist tordre, entortiller, serpenter
twitch se contracter (convulsivement)
type out taper à la machine
typewriter machine à écrire

— U —

ulcer ulcère
unaccountably inexplicablement
unbutton déboutonner
uncanny étrange
uncle oncle
uncontrollable incontrôlable
undecided indécis
under sous
underfoot sous les pieds
understand, understood, understood comprendre
unexpectedly subitement, alors qu'on ne s'y attend pas
unfulfilled inaccompli, non réalisé
unfurl déployer, dérouler
unguent onguent, baume
unhook décrocher
unit unité
unite unir
universal universel
universe univers
unless à moins que
unlocked non fermé à clef (porte)
unpredictable imprévisible
unsightly disgracieux, laid
until jusqu'à (ce que)
unusual étrange, bizarre
up en l'air, en haut
up to a point jusqu'à un certain point, dans une certaine mesure
uprising soulèvement, révolte
upstairs en haut
upward vers le haut
urge forte envie
use usage ; utiliser, se servir de
use (it's no) ça ne sert à rien
use (no) + *v* + *ing* inutile (de faire)

useless inutile
usual habituel
usually habituellement, d'habitude
utterly complètement, tout à fait

— V —

vacation *(Am)* vacances
valley vallée
value valeur
vanilla vanille
vanish disparaître
various divers
veer away from s'éloigner de
veld(t) veld(t), plateau herbeux en Afrique du Sud
very (at that ... instant) à cet instant même
viaduct viaduc
villain traître, scélérat
vine plante rampante, grimpante, vigne
violin violon
vivid vif, net, précis
voice voix
volcano volcan
vow (take a) faire vœu
vulture vautour

— W —

wade avancer (dans l'eau, dans l'herbe haute...)
wail gémir, pousser des gémissements
wait for attendre
waitover attente (entre deux trains...)
wake, woke ou **waked, woken** ou **waked** se réveiller, s'éveiller
walk allée ; promenade ; marcher
walk away partir, s'en aller
walk back revenir, rentrer
walk down descendre (à pied)
walk off partir
wall mur
wallpaper papier peint
wander errer, flâner
want vouloir, désirer
war guerre
warm chaud, tiède
warmth chaleur
wash linge, lessive ; laver
wash the dishes faire la vaisselle
washing lessive, lavage
washstand console, table de toilette, lavabo
watch regarder, observer
water eau ; arroser ; **make or pass water** uriner
water-colour aquarelle
wave vague ; faire signe de la main
waxen cireux (teint), de cire **(wax)**
way façon, manière, moyen ;

sens ; très loin (dans l'espace ou dans le temps)
ways (both) à l'aller et au retour
weak faible
wear, wore, worn porter (vêtements, chaussures...)
weather temps (qu'il fait)
weather cock girouette
weave, wove, woven tisser
weed-fringed bordé de mauvaise herbe **(weed)**
week semaine
weep, wept, wept pleurer
weight poids
weird surnaturel, mystérieux
well well bon, enfin, bref
wet humide, mouillé
whack donner un (ou des) grand(s) coup(s)
whatever quoi que ce soit ; quel que soit
whatever (none...) pas le moindre
wheeze respiration bruyante ou sifflante (d'asthmatique)
wherever où que + *subj.*, partout où
whether... or si... ou si
while moment ; pendant que
whim caprice, fantaisie
whine gémissement prolongé ; gémir
whip off (s')enlever brusquement
whirl tournoyer, tourbillonner ; se retourner brusquement
whisper murmure, chuchotement ; murmurer, chuchoter
whistle sifflet ; siffler
white blanc
whiteness blancheur
whizz aller à toute vitesse en sifflant
whole entier, complet
why eh bien, tiens, tenez
wicked mauvais, méchant
wicker osier
wide large ; écarquillé, grand ouvert (yeux...) ; en grand (porte ouverte...)
wife femme, épouse
wilderness étendue déserte, région sauvage
wildly furieusement, avec frénésie
will volonté, force
willing (to) (be) être disposé (à faire)
wind vent
wind, wound, wound serpenter, faire des zigzags ; **wind up in tears** finir en larmes
winding sheet linceul
window fenêtre
windy exposé au vent, venteux
wine vin
wing aile
winter hiver
wintry d'hiver ; glacial
wipe essuyer
wipe out... off the map rayer de la carte, anéantir, raser
wise sage, avisé
wish souhait ; souhaiter ; désirer
withdrawn renfermé (personne)

within à moins de (tant de mètres, etc.)
without sans
withstand, withstood, withstood résister à
wonder chose étonnante, prodige, merveille ; se demander ; s'émerveiller
wonderful merveilleux
wondrous merveilleux
wood bois
wooden de bois, en bois
word mot, parole
work travail ; œuvre ; fonctionner ; marcher (plan, projet...)
work (piece of) travail (un)
work out réussir, marcher
world monde
World War II Seconde Guerre mondiale
worn usé
worried (be) être inquiet, s'inquiéter
worry s'inquiéter
worse pire
worthwhile qui vaut la peine
wrap emballer, empaqueter, envelopper
wrinkle ride ; (se) rider
write, wrote, written écrire
write down écrire, noter, mettre par écrit
writer écrivain
wrong qui ne va pas, mal choisi, inopportun, mauvais...

— Y —

yank tirer d'un coup sec ; **yank a door open** ouvrir brusquement une porte
yard cour ; dépôt (de gare...) ; yard (91,44 cm)
yarn (longue) histoire
year année, an
yell hurler
yep *(fam)* ouais
yet pourtant, cependant
yet (not) ne pas... encore
Y.M.C.A. abréviation de **Young Men's Christian Association** sorte d'auberge de jeunesse
young jeune.

Composition réalisée par COMPOFAC - PARIS

IMPRIMÉ EN FRANCE PAR BRODARD ET TAUPIN
Usine de La Flèche (Sarthe).
LIBRAIRIE GÉNÉRALE FRANÇAISE - 6, rue Pierre-Sarrazin - 75006 Paris.
ISBN : 2 - 253 - 05740 - 1

30/8649/3